Dracula
Unbound

Dracula
Unbound

BRIAN W. ALDISS

GraftonBooks
A Division of HarperCollins*Publishers*

FOR FRANK

who was sitting at our dining table
when the spectre arose

05141770

GraftonBooks
A Division of HarperCollins*Publishers*
77–85 Fulham Palace Road,
Hammersmith, London W6 8JB

Published by GraftonBooks 1991

Copyright © Brian W. Aldiss 1991

A CIP catalogue record for this book is
available from the British Library

ISBN 0–246–13773–8

Phototypeset by Input Typesetting Ltd, London
Printed in Great Britain by
HarperCollinsManufacturing Glasgow

Nicht sein kann, was nicht sein darf.

Gondwana Ranch

Texas 75042

USA

18 August 1999

Dearest Mina,

Soon we'll be living in a new century. Perhaps there we shall discover ill-defined states of mind, at present unknown. You, who have returned from the dead, will be better able to face them than I.

For my own part, I am better prepared than I was to acknowledge that many people spend periods of their lives in more unusual mental states – not neurotic or psychotic – than science is at present inclined to allow. I also know those nameless psychic states valued by many rebels of society. They are not for me. In the account that follows – in which we both feature – there's terror, horror, wonder, and something that has no name. A kind of nostalgia for what has never been experienced.

Did all this happen? Was I mad? Did you pass through those dreadful gates at the end of life? I still see, with shut eyes but acute mental vision, those unhallowed things that appeared. And I believe that I would rather be mad than that they should run loose on the world.

Have patience and hope. We still have a long way to go together, dearest.

Your loving Joe

1

A sale of books was held in the auction rooms of Christie, Manson & Woods, Park Avenue, New York, on 23rd May 1996.

A first edition of Bram Stoker's novel *Dracula* was sold for £21,700 to an anonymous buyer. The volume was published in Cr. 8vo. by Constable & Co. of Westminster, in May 1897, bound in yellow boards blocked in red. This copy was in remarkably fine condition.

On the flyleaf was written, in faded Stephens' ink:

To Joseph Bodenland,
Who gave the mammals their big chance –
And me a title –

Affectionately

This perplexing message was dated Chelsea, May 1897, and signed with a flourish by the author, Bram Stoker.

In the region of the planet enduring permanent twilight stood the Bastion.

All the territory about the Bastion was wrinkled and withered as aged skin. Low ground-hugging plants grew there, some with rudimentary intelligence, capable – like the creatures inhabiting the Bastion – of drinking human blood.

Six men were walking in single file through this dangerous area, progressing towards the dark flanks of the Bastion. The men were shackled to each other by a metal chain clamped to their upper arms. In the heat of the perpetual evening, they were scantily clad. They went barefoot.

They made no haste as they progressed forward, walking with heads and shoulders drooping, their dull gaze fixed on the ground. The stiffness of their movements owed less to the weight of their chains than to a prevailing despair, to which every limb of their bodies testified.

Low above them flew the guardian of this human line. The flier exhibited a degree of majesty as his great wings beat their way slowly through the viscous air. He was as much a creature of custom as the six men below him, his duty being merely to see that they returned to the warrens of the Bastion.

Before their fighting spirit was eroded, these six had often in the past plotted escape. It was rumoured that somewhere ruinous cities still stood, inhabited by tribes of men and women who had managed to hold out against the Fleet Ones as the centuries declined:

that somewhere those virtues by which humans had once set great store were still preserved, against the onslaught of night.

But no one incarcerated in the Bastion knew how to reach the legendary cities. Few had stamina enough to endure long journeys overland.

All the six desired at present was to return to their prison. Their shift as cleaners in the Mechanism was over for the day. Soup and rest awaited them. The horror of their situation had long since dulled their senses. In the underground stabling, where humans and animals were indifferently herded together, the myrmidons of the Fleet Ones would bring round their rations. Then they could sleep.

As for the weekly levy of blood to be paid while they slept . . . even that nightmare had become mere routine.

So they negotiated the path through the bloodthirst-plants and came with some relief to the stoma gaping at the base of the Bastion, waiting to swallow them. The guardian alighted, tucked away his wings, and directed them through the aperture. Hot and foetid air came up to meet them like a diseased breath.

The concretion into which they disappeared rose high into the saffron-tinted atmosphere, dominating the landscape in which it stood. It resembled a huge anthill. No conceptions of symmetry or elegance of any kind had entered the limited minds of its architects. It had reared itself upwards on a random basis. Its highest central point resembled a rounded tower, reinforcing the impression that the whole structure was a kind of brute phallus which had thrust its way through the body of the planet.

Here and there on the flanks of the Bastion, side features obtruded. Some resembled malformed limbs. Some twisted upwards, or sideways. Some turned down and burrowed again into the ravaged soil, serving as buttresses to the main structure.

The main portions of the Bastion lay below ground, in its unending warrens, stables, and crypts. The structure above ground was blind. Not a window showed. The Fleet Ones were no friends of light.

Yet on higher levels orifices showed, crudely shaped. Much coming and going was in evidence at these vents. Here the Fleet

Ones could conveniently launch themselves into flight: as they had done at the beginning of time, so now at its end.

Only the orifice at the top of the pile, larger than all the others, was free of sinister traffic. It was reserved for the Prince of Darkness himself, Lord Dracula. This was his castle. He would launch himself from this great height whenever he was about to go on a mission into the world – as even now he was preparing to do.

As the shift of six began its winding descent into underground levels, to rest in the joyless inanition of slaves, four other men of different calibre were preparing to leave the Mechanism.

These four, in luckier days, had been scientists. Captive, they remained free of shackles, so that they could move without impediment in the building. The genetically non-scientific species who held them in captivity had abducted them from various epochs of past history. They were guarded. But because they were necessary for the maintenance of the Mechanism, their well-being within the Bastion was assured. They merely had to work until they died.

The leader of the quartet came down from the observatory, checking the time on his watch.

This leader, elected by common consent, was a tall man in his late thirties. The Fleet Ones had captured him from the Obsidianal Century. His brilliant mind and indomitable spirit were such that others took courage from him. Someone once claimed that his brain represented the flowering of the sapient Homo sapiens. The plan about to be transformed from theory to action was a product of his thought.

'We have two minutes to go, friends,' he said now, as they were closing down their instruments.

The Mechanism – ignorantly so called by the Fleet Ones – was a combined solar observatory and power house. All space observatories had long been destroyed by the deteriorating sun.

It was the power function which was all important. From the platforms of the Mechanism, shelving out like giant fungi, the solar satellites were controlled which drained the energies of the sun. These energies were redirected to meet the needs of the Fleet Ones. And in particular the needs of the Fleet Ones' single innovatory form of transportation.

7

The scientists were forced to work for their hated enemies. They ran everything as inefficiently as possible. Because the Mechanism was lighted brilliantly to allow the humans to work, the Fleet Ones would not enter. They posted their guardians outside, continually circling the immense structure.

'Delay here,' said the leader, sharply. The four of them were in the foyer, preparing to go off shift and be returned to the Bastion. He glanced again at his watch.

'According to our predictions, there's now a minute to go.'

Beyond the glass doors, they could see the familiar tarnished landscape like a furrowed brow. In the distance, failed hills, shattered river beds, all lost in an origami of light and shade. Nearer at hand, the prodigious thrust of the Bastion, circled by leathery fliers. As a sudden stormy wind buffeted them, the fliers resembled dead leaves blowing at autumn's call. Shunning the light, they had no knowledge of the phenomenon approaching from space.

Just outside the doors, fluttering like a bat, the lead guardian on duty came down to an unsteady landing. He braced himself against the wind.

Lifting a hand to shield his brow, he stared in at the scientists, his red eyes set amid the dark skin and fur of the sharp-fanged visage. He beckoned to them.

They made some pretence of moving towards the doors, heading instead for a metal reception counter.

Thirty seconds to go.

The lower western sky was filled with a sun like an enormous blossom. It was the flower which had already destroyed all the flowers of Earth. Imperfectly round, its crimson heart crackled with stamens of lightning. The solar wind blew its malevolent pollens about the planets. Round it orbited the four solar stations which were leaching it of its energies, sucking them down into the subterranean storehouses of the Mechanism. On the face of this great helium-burner moved vortices which could swallow worlds. They showed like rashes of a disease, as if they worked at the débridement of an immense bloated organ.

In the midst of this solar turmoil – as those in the observatory had discovered – a magnesium-white eruption flowered.

'Now,' cried the leader. The thirty seconds were up.

They flung themselves down on the floor behind the metal barrier, burying their heads in their arms, closing their eyes.

Precisely on the time they had estimated, the shell flash ejected from the sun. It illuminated the world with floods of light and fury. Screaming wind followed it in a shock wave, travelling along down the throat of the system until, many hours later, it punched itself out beyond the heliopause and far into outer space. As it radiated outwards, it licked with its scorching tongue much of the atmosphere from the vulnerable worlds in its path.

Only the four scientists were prepared for the event.

They lay behind their shelter while the world smouldered outside. Their guardian had fallen like a cinder.

They rose cautiously at last. They stood. They stared at each other, stared at the blackened landscape outside, where the Bastion remained intact. Then, according to plan, they headed for the stairs leading to the upper floors.

Their hair sparkled and sang as they moved. Electrostatic action in the tormented air rendered the elevators inoperative.

Oxygen was scarce. Yet they forced themselves on, knowing they must act now, while the Fleet Ones were stunned.

Through waves of heat they climbed, dragging the vitiated air into their lungs. On one landing they collected a wing from a store cupboard, on another landing another wing. Sections of body structure, improvised from dismantled parts of the Mechanism, were also gathered as they climbed. By the time they reached the observatory on the highest level, they needed merely to secure the various parts together and they had a glider large enough to carry a man.

The landscape they surveyed was covered in fast-moving smoke. The pall washed against the two edifices of Bastion and Mechanism like a spring tide.

One detail they did observe. The bloodthirst-plants were cautiously poking their muzzles from the ground again. They were intelligent enough, yet part of nature enough, to sense when the shell flash was coming, and to retreat underground from it. But the men wasted little time in observing the phenomenon.

'Is the air calm enough for flight?' a small bearded man asked the leader. 'Suppose all the cities containing men have just been destroyed by fire?'

'We've no alternative but to try,' said the leader. 'This is our one chance. The next shell flash is many lifetimes away.' Yet he paused before climbing into the glider, as if to hear what his friends had to say at this solemn moment.

The bearded man perhaps regretted his hesitations in the face of the other's courage.

'Yes, of course you must go,' he said. 'Somehow we have to get word of what is happening here back to the far past. Stoker has to be informed.'

The scientist standing next to him said, in sorrowful disagreement, 'Yet all the old legends say that Dracula destroyed Stoker.'

The leader answered firmly, addressing them all, with the sense of parting heavy upon them. 'We have argued the situation through sufficiently. Those old legends may be wrong, for we well understand how history can be changed. Our given three-dimensional space is only one dimension within the universe's four-dimensional space. Time is a flexible element within it. No particle has a definite path, as the uncertainty principle states. We have been enslaved here at the end of the world in order to help generate the colossal voltages the Fleet Ones require to regiment those paths. I shall seek out the other end of their trail – and there I believe the legendary Stoker is to be found. It is Stoker after all who is one of Earth's heroes, the stoker – as his name implies – who brought fire with which to burn out a great chance for all mankind.'

'So he did,' agreed the others, almost in chorus. And one of them, the youngest, added, 'After all, this horrendous present, according to the laws of chaos, is a probability only, not an actuality. History can be changed.'

The leader made to step into the glider. Again the bearded man detained him.

'Just wait till these winds have died. The glider will have a better chance then.'

'And then the Fleet Ones will be back on the attack. It's necessary that I go now.'

He looked searchingly into their faces. 'I know you will suffer for this. My regret is that we were unable to fashion a plane large enough to carry all four of us. Always remember – I shall succeed or die in the attempt.'

'There are states far worse than death where the Fleet Ones are concerned,' said the bearded man, mustering a smile. He made to shake the leader's hand, changed his mind, and embraced him warmly instead.

'Farewell, Alwyn. God's grace guide you.'

The leader stepped into the machine.

The others, as prearranged, pushed it to the edge of the drop – and over. The glider fell until its wings bit into the air. It steadied. It began to fly. It circled, it even gained height. It began heading towards the east.

The scientists left behind stood watching until the glider was faint in the murk.

Their voices too went with the wind.

'Farewell, Alwyn!'

CHAPTER I

State Route 18 runs north from St George, through the Iron Mountains, to the Escalante Desert. One day in 1999, it also ran into a past so distant nobody had ever dared visualize it.

Bernard Clift had worked in this part of Utah before, often assisted by students from Dixie College with a leaning towards palaeontology. This summer, Clift's instincts had led him to dig on the faulty stretch of rock the students called Old John, after the lumber-built jakes near the site, set up by a forgotten nineteenth-century prospector.

Clift was a thin, spare man, deeply tanned, medium height, his sharp features and penetrating grey eyes famous well beyond the limits of his own profession. There was a tenseness about him today, as if he knew that under his hand lay a discovery that was to bring him even greater fame, and to release on the world new perspectives and new terror.

Over the dig, a spread of blue canvas, of a deeper blue than the Utah sky, had been erected, to shade Clift and his fellow-workers from the sun. Clustered below the brow of rock where they worked were a dozen miscellaneous vehicles – Clift's trailer, a trailer from Enterprise which served food and drink all day, and the automobiles and campers belonging to students and helpers.

A dirt road led from this encampment into the desert. All was solitude and stillness, apart from the activity centred on Old John. There Clift knelt in his dusty jeans, brushing soil and crumbs of rock from the fossilized wooden lid they had uncovered.

Scattered bones of a dinosaur of the aurischian order had been

extracted from the rock, labelled, temporarily identified as belonging to a large theropod, and packed into crates. Now, in a stratum
below the dinosaur grave, the new find was revealed.

Several people crowded round the freshly excavated hole in
which Clift worked with one assistant. Cautious digging had
revealed fossil wood, which slowly emerged in the shape of a coffin.
On the lid of the coffin, a sign had been carved:

Overhead, a vulture wheeled, settling on a pinnacle of rock near
the dig. It waited.

Clift levered at the ancient lid. Suddenly, it split along the middle
and broke. The palaeontologist lifted the shard away. A smell, too
ancient to be called the scent of death, drifted out into the hot dry
air.

A girl student with the Dixie College insignia on her T-shirt
yelped and ran from the group as she saw what lay in the coffin.

Using his brush, Clift swept away a layer of red ochre. His
assistant collected fragile remains of dead blossom, placing them
reverently in a plastic bag. A skeleton in human form was revealed,
lying on its side. Tenderly, Clift uncovered the upper plates of the
skull. It was twisted round so that it appeared to stare upwards at
the world of light with round ochred eyes.

The head offices and laboratories of the thriving Bodenland Corporation were encompassed in bronzed-glass curtain walls, shaped
in neo-cubist form and disposed so that they dominated one road
approach into Dallas, Texas.

At this hour of the morning the facade reflected the sun into the
eyes of anyone approaching the corporation from the airport – as
was the case with the imposing lady now disembarking from a
government craft in which she had flown from Washington. She

was sheathed in a fabric which reflected back something of the lustre from the corporation.

Her name was Elsa Schatzman, three times divorced daughter of Eliah Schatzman. She was First Secretary at the Washington Department of the Environment. She looked as if she wielded power, and did.

Joe Bodenland knew that Elsa Schatzman was in the offing. At present, however, he had little thought for her, being involved in an argument with his life's companion, Mina Legrand. While they talked, Bodenland's secretary continued discreetly to work at her desk.

'First things first, Birdie,' said Bodenland, with a patience that was calculated to vex Mina.

Mina Legrand was another powerful lady, although the genial lines of her face did not proclaim that fact. She was tall and still graceful, and currently having weight problems, despite an active life. Friends said of her, affectionately, that she put up with a lot of hassle from Joe; still closer friends observed that of late he was putting up with plenty from Mina.

'Joe, your priorities are all screwed up. You must make time for your family,' she said.

'I'll make time, but first things first,' he repeated.

'The first thing is it's your son's wedding day,' Mina said. 'I warn you, Joe, I'm going to fly down to Gondwana without you. One of these days, I'll leave you for good, I swear I will.'

Joe played a tune on his desk top with the fingers of his left hand. They were long blunt fingers with wide spade-like nails, ridged and hard. Bodenland himself resembled his fingers. He too was long and blunt, with an element of hardness in him that had enabled him to lead an adventurous life as well as succeeding in the competitive international world of selling scientific research. He set his head towards his right shoulder with a characteristic gesture, as he asked: 'How long has Larry been engaged to Kylie? Under a year. How long have we been pursuing the idea of inertial disposal? Over five years. Millions of dollars hang on today's favourable reception of our demonstration by Washington. I just have to be here, Birdie, and that's that.'

'Larry will never forgive you. Nor will I.'

15

'You will, Mina. So will Larry. Because you two are human. Washington ain't.'

'All right, Joe – you have the last word as usual. But you're in deep trouble as of now.' With that, Mina turned and marched from the office. The door closed silently behind her; its suction arm prevented it from slamming.

'I'll be down there just as soon as I can,' Bodenland called, having a last-minute twinge of anxiety.

He turned to his secretary, Rose Gladwin, who had sat silently at her desk, eyes down, while this heated conversation was going on.

'Birth, death, the great spirit of scientific enquiry – which of those is most important to a human being, Rose?'

She looked up with a slight smile.

'The great spirit of scientific enquiry, Joe,' she said.

'You always have the right answer.'

'I'm just informed that Miss Schatzman is en route from the airport right now.'

'Let me know as soon as she arrives. I'll be with Waldgrave.'

He glanced at his watch as he went out, and walked briskly down the corridor, cursing Washington and himself. It annoyed him to think that Larry was getting married at all. Marriage was so old-fashioned, yet now, on the turn of the century, it was coming back into fashion.

Bodenland and his senior research scientist, Waldgrave, were in reception to welcome Miss Schatzman when she arrived with her entourage. She was paraded through the technical floor, where everyone had been instructed to continue working as usual, to the laboratory with the notice in gilt on its glass door, INERTIAL RESEARCH.

Bodenland's judicious answers in response to her questions indicated that Schatzman had been properly briefed. He liked that, and her slightly plump forties-ish figure in a tailored suit which signalled to him that human nature survived under the official exterior.

Various important figures were gathered in the lab for the demonstration, including a backer from the Bull-Brunswick Bank. Bodenland introduced Schatzman to some of them while technicians made everything finally ready. As she was shaking hands with the Bank, one of Bodenland's aides came up and spoke softly in Bodenland's ear.

'There's an urgent call for you from Utah, Joe. Bernard Clift, the archaeologist. Says he has an important discovery.'

'Okay, Mike. Tell Bernard I'll call him back when possible.'

In the centre of the lab stood a glass cabinet much resembling a shower enclosure. Cables ran into it from computers and other machines, where two assistants stood by a switchboard. The hum of power filled the air, lending extra tension to the meeting.

'You have all the technical specifications of the inertial disposal principle in our press and video pack, Miss Schatzman,' Bodenland said. 'If you have no questions there, we'll move straight into the demonstration.'

As he spoke, he gave a sign and an assistant in a lab coat dragged forward a black plastic bag large enough to contain a man.

Waldgrave explained, 'The bag is full of sand, nothing more. It represents a consignment of nuclear or toxic waste.'

The bag was shut in the cabinet, remaining in full view through the glass as computers briefly chattered their calculations.

'Energy-consumption rates are high at present. This is just a prototype, you appreciate. We hope to lower tolerances in the next part of the programme, when we have the okay from your department,' Bodenland said. 'Obviously energy-input is related to mass of substance being disposed of.'

'And I see you're using solar energy in part,' Schatzman said.

'The corporation has its own satellite, which beams down the energy to our dishes here in Dallas.'

Waldgrave got the nod from his boss. He signalled to the controls technician, who pressed the Transmit pad.

The interior of the cabinet began to glow with a blue-mauve light.

Two large analogue-type clocks with sweep-hands were visible, one inside the cabinet, one on a jury-rig outside, facing the first one. The sweep hand of the clock in the cabinet stopped at 10.16. At the same time, the clock itself began to disappear. So did the black plastic bag. In a moment it was gone. The cabinet appeared to be empty.

17

A brief burst of applause filled the room. Bodenland appeared noticeably less grim.

The party went to have drinks in a nearby boardroom, all tan leather upholstery and *dracaena* plants in bronze pots. There was a jubilation in the air which even the formality of the occasion did not kill.

As she sipped a glass of Perrier, Schatzman said, 'Well, Mr Bodenland, you appear to have invented the long-awaited time machine, no less.'

He looked down into his vodka. So the woman was a fool after all. He had hoped for better. This woman was going to have to present his case before her committee in Washington; if she could reach such a basic misunderstanding after studying all the documentation already sent to her over the computer line, the chances for government approval of his invention were poor.

'Not a time machine, Ms Schatzman. As we've made clear, our new process merely halts time-decay – much as refrigeration, let's say, slows or halts bacterial action. We found a sink in real time. The bag in the cabinet disappeared because it became suddenly stationary with regard to universal time-decay. It remained – it remains at 10.16 this morning. We are the ones who are travelling forward in time, at the rate of twenty-four hours a day. The bag remains forever where we put it, at 10.16. We can reach back and retrieve it if necessary, though the expenditure of energy increases geometrically as we progress further from entry point.

'The inertial disposal process is far from being a time-machine. It is almost the reverse.'

Ms Schatzman did not greatly enjoy being talked down to. Perhaps her remark had been intended humorously. 'The department will need to enquire into what happens to substances isolated in 10.16, or any other time. It would be irresponsible simply to isolate considerable amounts of toxic waste in time with no clear picture of possible consequences.'

'How long do you estimate such an enquiry might take?'

'We're talking about something unprecedented, a disturbance in the natural order.'

'Er – not if you have an understanding of the science of Chaos.'

18

She understood she had been snubbed. 'An enquiry will of course occupy some weeks.'

Bodenland took a generous swig of his vodka and inclined his head in her direction.

'The disposal of toxic waste represents one of the world's most pressing problems, Ms Schatzman. No one wants the stuff. Only a decade ago the cost of disposal of nuclear waste as prescribed by US law was $2,500 per tonne. It's twenty times higher now, and rising. Only last week the death of a whole village through the dumping of an illegally manufactured pesticide, Lindane, was reported in Bulgaria.

'That's where we come in. Bodenland Industries have developed a foolproof way of ridding the world of such evils. All we need is your department's clearance. You must persuade your committee not to stand in the way of progress.'

She pronounced the last word at the same moment as he did. 'Progress,' echoing it ironically. ' "Progress" cannot be achieved at the expense of safety. You're familiar with that concept. It's what we call the Frankenstein Syndrome.' She attempted lightness of tone. 'You know the Department will do what it can, Mr Bodenland. You also know how thoroughly this new advance will have to be investigated. We have our responsibilities – there are security aspects, too. May I suggest that meanwhile you turn your inventive mind to other matters?'

'Sure,' he said, setting his glass down and rising. 'I'm going to turn my inventive mind to being a late guest at my son's wedding.'

A jazz band was playing an arrangement of 'Who's Sorry Now?' when Joe Bodenland entered the main reception rooms of the Gondwana Ranch, the home in which he and Mina had lived for a decade. At present it was full of flowers and guests.

Some of the wedding guests were dancing, some drinking, and some no doubt otherwise engaged. The caterers hired for the occasion were bearing savoury and sweet dishes to and fro, while the popping of champagne corks could be heard above the noise of the band.

Bodenland exchanged compliments and good wishes with a

number of family friends as he made his way to where Larry Boden-land stood with his bride, receiving congratulations.

Kylie greeting Joe warmly enough, flinging her arms round his neck and kissing him on the mouth. Kylie was a beautiful girl with a round face on which good features were set wide apart, giving her a singularly open appearance. Joe had already discovered that Kylie was no mere innocent. She had – beside the considerable fortune accruing from her father's transport business – a sharp and enquiring mind. But for the moment it was enough to feel her slender body against his as he revelled in her sunny good looks and wished her all future happiness.

'Just see that Larry behaves himself,' he said, giving her an extra hug.

Larry overheard the remark. As he shook his father's hand, he said, 'How about behaving yourself, Joe? How come you were late for my wedding? Was that deliberate? We know how irrational you are on the subject of matrimony.'

'Now don't you two start in,' Kylie said. 'Not today of all days.' She raised a hand half-way to her throat, as if to indicate the crucifix hanging there. 'You know my funny religious principles, Joe, and you must honour Larry for respecting them.'

'Well, bless you both, and I hate myself for missing the cere-mony. Don't blame me – blame the Department of the Environ-ment in Washington, who nailed me to this morning's appoint-ment.'

'Family certainly can't compete with a whole Department of the Environment,' Larry said, huffily.

'Joe has to follow his daemon,' Kylie said, winking at her new father-in-law.

'What demon's that?' asked Larry.

'Now, Larry – your pop is a technophile of the old school. He's crazy about machines and you must allow him that.'

'Just as you're crazy about religion, if I can put it that way.'

'Religion still has a place, even in an age of science, and – '

'Spare us!' cried Larry. 'I need another drink. It's my wedding day.' As he turned away, his mother came up, smiling in a brittle way at Joe.

'You missed the ceremony and hit the champagne,' she said angrily. 'Larry and Kylie will never forgive you for this.'

'I'm sorry, Mina.' He took her hand, looking compassionately into her green eyes. For all his kind of hasty blindness, one of his characteristics, he knew very well what was in her mind at that moment. They had had another son, Larry's older brother Dick, killed in an automobile crash together with his young wife Molly. Dick had always been his father's favourite, a brilliant youngster, athletic, and with a deep interest in science, particularly particle physics. Molly too had been clever and high-spirited, a redhead whose body, at the age of twenty-two, had been inextricably merged with her husband's in the fatal crash. It was Molly, not Dick, who returned to Joe in dreams. Dick had gone beyond recall, leaving no space for his younger brother in his father's affections.

With the long habit of a couple who have spent years together, Mina understood something of what passed through Joe's mind. Her mood softened.

She said, 'Odd how Kylie has the religious impulse, just like Molly.' It was the first time Molly's name had passed between them in years. 'I hope that doesn't mean . . .'

'Molly wasn't religious. She just had an intense interest in the supernatural.'

'You've forgotten, Joe. Maybe just as well.' She took his arm. 'Let's take a turn outside. It's not too hot. I'm sorry I flew off the handle earlier. But Larry and Kylie are our only kids now. Let the dead bury the dead.'

As they reached the terrace, he half-turned to her, smiling.

'That's kind of a dumb expression, when you think, isn't it? "Let the dead bury the dead . . ." What a macabre scene that conjures up! They'd have a problem with the shovels, eh?'

She laughed. The terrace, which overlooked the swimming pool, was roofed over with reinforced glass, the supporting pillars of which were entwined with different colours of bougainvillea. He took Mina's hand and they began to stroll, happy to get away from the noise indoors.

A phone on the wall rang as Joe and Mina were passing it. She answered by reflex, then passed the receiver to her husband with a wry look. 'You're wanted, Joe. The world needs you.'

21

He stood in the partial shade, gazing at her face, listening to his old friend Bernard Clift speaking slowly to conceal his excitement.

'Bernie, that can't be,' Bodenland said. 'It's impossible. You must have got it wrong. You know you've got it wrong. Your reputation – '

He listened again, shaking his head, then nodding. Mina watched him with amusement, as his eyes lit up.

'I'll be right over,' he said, finally, 'and I may bring some of the family along.'

As he hung up, Mina said, 'Some fresh madness brewing! Whatever it is, Joe, count me out. I want to take part in an air display over Austin tomorrow.'

'You can freefall any time, Mina. This is terrific. Would you have wanted to have been fishing in Bermuda while the Revolution was going on on the mainland?'

'It was Bernie Clift?'

'Clift doesn't fool around. He's made a find in Utah.'

He explained that Clift had rung to tell him about the discovery of a human-like skeleton. Clift had subjected fragments of bone to carbon-dating analysis. The remains dated out as 65.5 million years BP, before the present. This checked out with their discovery in late Cretaceous rock. They came from a time over sixty million years before mankind in its most primitive form walked the earth.

'That doesn't make any kind of sense,' Mina said.

'It's a revolution in thought. Don't ask me what it means but this we really have to see. It's – well, incredible.' He whistled. 'Just to prove that Larry and Kylie do mean something to me, we're going to take them along too.'

He was already moving back into the house. She caught his sleeve impatiently.

'Joe, easy now. You're so impetuous. Larry's off in a couple of hours to honeymoon in Hawaii. They're not going to want to stop off in Utah, to help us.'

He was looking at his watch.

'They'll love it, and so will you. That's wonderful desert country where Bernie is. Utah's Dixie, they used to call it. If we move, we can be there by nightfall. And remember, tell no one why we are going. Bernie's discovery stays under wraps for now. Otherwise the world's media will be on his back. Okay?'

She laughed, not without a hint of bitterness. 'Oh, Joe – are you allowing me time to pack?'

He kissed her. 'Grab your toothbrush. Tell Kylie to shake the confetti out of her hair.'

CHAPTER II

As the helicopter spiralled downwards over the Escalante Desert, a light flashed up at it, the setting sun reflected from the windscreen of a parked car. Looking down, Joe Bodenland could see cars and trailers clustered round a square of blue canvas. Four minutes later, they were landing nearby in a whirl of dust.

Joe was first from the copter, giving Mina a hand, followed by Kylie, looking around her rather nervously, with Larry, who had piloted them, last. Bernard Clift was standing there, waiting to greet them.

'There's an atmosphere of something here,' Kylie told him, as they were introduced. 'You must feel it, Bernie. I can't explain it. I don't like it. Oppressive.'

Clift laughed shortly. 'That's the Bodenland family, Kylie. You have to get accustomed to them. Now listen, Joe, I'm grateful for your prompt arrival, although frankly I didn't expect you all to show up. We can find a place for you to sleep.' He ran a hand through his hair in a self-conscious gesture. 'This discovery is so important – and top secret. I have shut down our one phone line to Enterprise. The students are forbidden to leave the site, at least without my express permission. No radioing or any form of communication with the outside world. I've made them all swear to keep secrecy on this one, until I'm ready.'

'As a matter of interest, Bernie,' Bodenland said, 'how did you get them to swear?'

He laughed. 'On their mother's virginity. On whatever they took seriously. Even the Bible.'

'I'd have thought that custom had worn thin by now,' Joe said.

'Not with all of us Joe,' said Kylie, laughing.

Clift looked at her approvingly, then said, 'Well, come and see before the light fades. That's what you're here for.'

He spoke jerkily, full of nervous energy.

As they followed him along a narrow track among low sage winding up the mountain, he said, 'Joe, you're a rational man and a knowledgeable one, I figured you'd know what to make of this find. If it's what I think it is, our whole world view is overturned. Humans on the planet sixty million years earlier than any possible previous evidence suggested. A species of man here in North America, long before anything started crawling round Olduvai Gorge . . .'

'Couldn't be a visitor from somewhere else in the universe? There's just the one grave?'

'That's why I'm insisting on secrecy. My findings are bound to be challenged. I'm in for the Spanish Inquisition and I know it. But if we could find a second grave . . . So I don't want anyone inter-fering – at least for a few days.'

Bodenland grunted. 'Our organization has its own security unit in Dallas . . . I could get guards out here tomorrow prompt, if you need them. But you must be wrong, Bernie. This can't be.'

'No, it's like the comic strips always said,' Larry remarked, with a laugh. 'Cavemen contemporary with the brontosaurus and tyran-nosaurus. Must have been some kind of a race memory.'

Ignoring her son's facetiousness, Mina said, 'Bernard, hold it. I'm not prepared for this ancient grave of yours. I'm no dimmer than the next guy, but I can't attach any meaning to sixty-five million years. It's just a phrase.'

Clift halted their ascent abruptly. 'Then I'll show you,' he said.

Bodenland glanced quickly at his friend's face. He saw no impatience there, only the love a man might have for the subject that possessed him and gave his life meaning.

Before them, streaked now by the shades of advancing evening, was a broken hillside, eroded so that strata of rock projected like the ruins of some unimaginable building. Sage grew here and there, while the crest was crowned by pine and low-growing cottonwoods.

'For those who can read, this slope contains the history of the world,' Clift told Mina. 'What interests us is this broken line of deposit under the sandstones. That's what's called the K/T boundary.'

He pointed to a clayey line that ran under all the shattered sandstone strata like a damp-proof course round a house.

'That layer of deposit marks a division between the Cretaceous rocks below and the Tertiary rocks above. It represents one of the most mysterious events in all Earth history – the extinction of the dinosaurs. It's only centimetres thick. Below it lie kilometres of rock which is – as you might say – solidified time, the long millennia of the ages of reptiles. It has been verified beyond doubt that the K/T deposit line was laid down sixty-five million years BP, before present. Our grave lies just below that line.'

'But there were no humans living then,' Mina said, as they started walking again, taking a trail to the left.

'The K/T layer preserves evidence of a worldwide ecological catastrophe. It contains particles of shocked minerals, clues to massive inundations, soot which bears witness to continental-scale firestorms, and so on. Some gigantic impact occurred at that time – scientists guess at a meteorite capable of creating a vast crater, but we don't really know.

'What we do know is that some large-scale event ended a majestic era of brilliant and strange living things.

'Our grave suggests that what perished at the end of the Cretaceous Period – or the Mesozoic Era, which contains all reptilian periods – was not only the dinosaurs but also a human-like race perhaps so thinly distributed that no remains have turned up – till now.'

'Homo Cliftensis,' said Kylie.

They halted where the sandstones had been excavated and there were tokens of human activity, with planks, brushes, jackhammers, and a wheelbarrow incongruous nearby. They stood on a bluff overlooking the desert, across which mesas were sending long fingers of shadow. A well of shadow filled the excavation they now contemplated, as it lay like a pool below the ancient crusts of the K/T boundary.

Kylie shivered. But the air was cooling, the sky overhead deepening its blue.

Two students, a man and a woman, were standing guard by the dig. They moved back as the new arrivals appeared. Clift jumped down into the hole and removed a tarpaulin, revealing the ancient grave. The skeleton remained lying on its side, cramped within the coffin for an unimaginable age. The Bodenland family looked down at it without speaking.

'What's all the red stuff?' Kylie asked, in a small voice. 'Is it bloodstains?'

'Red ochre,' Clift said. 'To bury with red ochre was an old custom. The Neanderthals used it – not that I'm suggesting this is a Neanderthal. There were also flowers in the grave, which we've taken for analysis. Of course, there's more work to be done here. I'm half afraid to touch anything . . .'

They looked down in silence, prey to formless thought. The light died. The skeleton lay half-buried in ochre, fading into obscurity.

Kylie clung to Larry. 'Disturbing an ancient grave . . . I know it's part of an archaeologist's job, but . . . There are superstitions about these things. Don't you think there's something – well, evil here?'

He hugged her affectionately. 'Not evil. Pathetic, maybe. Sure, there's something disconcerting when the past or the future arrives to disrupt the present. Like the way this chunk of the past has come up to disrupt our wedding day.' Seeing Kylie's expression cloud over, he said, 'Let the dead get on with their thing. I'm taking you to have a drink.'

'You'll find a canteen at the bottom of the hill,' said Clift, but he spoke without looking away from his discovery, crouching there, almost as motionless as the skeleton he had disinterred.

The sun plunged down into the desert, a chill came over the world. Kylie Bodenland stood at the door of the trailer they had been loaned, gazing up at the stars. Something in this remote place had woken unsuspected sensibilities in her, and she was trying to puzzle out what it was.

Some way off, students were sitting round a campfire, resurrecting old songs and pretending they were cowboys, in a fit of artificial nostalgia.

City ladies may be fine
But give me that gal of mine . . .

Larry came up behind Kylie and pulled her into the trailer, kicking the door shut. She tasted the whisky on his lips, and enjoyed it. Her upbringing had taught her that this was wickedness. She liked other wickednesses too, and slid her hand into Larry's jeans as he embraced her. When she felt his response, she began to slide herself out of her few clothes, until she stood against him in nothing but her little silver chain and crucifix. Larry kissed it, kissed her breasts, and then worked lower.

'Oh, you beast, you beast,' she said. 'Oh . . .'

She clutched his head, but he got up and lifted her over to the bunk.

Lying together on the bunk later, he muttered almost to himself, 'Funny how the marriage ceremony annoys Joe. He just couldn't face it . . . I had to go through with it to spite him . . . and to please you, of course.'

'You shouldn't spite your father. He's rather a honey.'

Larry chuckled. 'Pop a honey? He's a stubborn-minded old pig. Now I'm adult, I see him in a more favourable light than once I did. Still and all . . . Grocery's a dirty word to him. He resents me being in grocery, never mind I'm making a fortune. I've got a mind of my own, haven't I? It may be small but it's my own. To hell with him – we're different. Let me fix you a drink.'

As he was getting up and walking naked to his baggage, from which a whisky bottle protruded, Kylie rolled on to her back and said, 'Well, it's Hawaii for us tomorrow. It'll be great for you to get from under Joe's shadow. He'll change towards you, you'll see. He may be an old pig but he's a good man for all that.'

Larry paused as he was about to pour, and laughed.

'Lay off about Joe, will you? Let's forget Joe. For sure he's forgotten about us already. Bernie Clift has given him something new to think about.'

Only a few metres away, Clift and Bodenland were walking in the desert, talking together in confidential tones.

'This new daughter-in-law of yours – she is a striking young lady and no mistake. And not happy about what I'm doing, I gather.'

'The religious and the economic views of mankind are always at odds. Maybe we're always religious when we're young. I lost anything like that when my other son died. Now I try to stick to rationality – I hate to think of the millions of people in America who buy into some crackpot religion or other. In the labs, we've also come up against time. Not whole millennia of time, like you, but just a few seconds. We're learning how to make time stand still. As you'd expect, it costs. It sure costs! If only I can get backing from Washington . . . Bernie, I could be . . . well, richer than . . . I can't tell you . . .'

Clift interrupted impatiently. 'Rationality. It means greed, basically . . . Lack of imagination. I can see Kylie is a girl with imagination, whatever else . . .'

'You have taken a fancy to her. I saw that when we met.'

'Joe, listen, never mind that. I've no time for women. And I've got a hold here of something more momentous than any of your financial enterprises. This is going to affect everyone, everyone on earth . . . It will alter our whole concept of ourselves. Hasn't that sunk in yet?'

He started off towards the dark bulk of the mountain. Bodenland followed. They could hear the one group of students who had not yet turned in arguing among themselves.

'You're mad, Bernie. You always were, in a quiet way.'

'I never sleep,' said Clift, not looking back.

'Isn't that what someone once said about the Church? "It never sleeps." Sounds like neurosis to me.'

They climbed to the dig. A single electric light burned under the blue canopy, where one of the students sat on watch. Clift exchanged a few words with him.

'Spooky up here, sir,' said the student.

Clift grunted. He would have none of that. Bodenland squatted beside him as the palaeontologist removed the tarpaulin.

From down in the camp came a sudden eruption of shouts – male bellows and female voices raised high, then the sound of blows, clear on the thin desert air.

'Damn,' said Clift, quietly. 'They will drink. I'll be back.'

29

He left, running down the hill path towards the group of students who had been singing only a few minutes earlier. He called to them in his authoritative voice to think of others who might be sleeping.

Bodenland was alone with the thing in the coffin.

In the frail light, the thing seemed almost to have acquired a layer of skin, skin of an ill order, but rendering it at least a few paces nearer to life than before. Bodenland felt an absurd temptation to speak to the thing. But what would it answer?

Overcoming his reluctance, he thrust his hand down and into the ochre. Although he was aware he might be destroying valuable archaeological evidence, curiosity led him on. The thought had entered his mind that after all Clift might somehow have overstepped the bounds of his madness and faked the evidence of the rocks, that this could be a modern grave he had concealed in the Cretaceous strata at some earlier date – perhaps working alone here the previous year.

Much of Bernard Clift's fame had sprung from a series of outspoken popular articles in which he had pointed out the scarcity of earlier human remains and their fragmentary nature in all but a few select sites round the world. 'Is Humanity Ten Million Years Old?' had been a favourite headline.

Orthodoxy agreed that Homo sapiens could be no more than two million years old. It was impossible to believe that this *thing* came from sixty-five million years ago. Clift was faking; and if he could convince his pragmatic friend Joe, then he could convince the world's press.

'No one fools me,' Bodenland said, half-aloud. He peered about to make sure that the student guard was looking away, watching the scene below.

Crouching over the coffin, he scraped one shoulder against the rock wall and the stained line that was the K/T boundary.

The ochre was surprisingly warm to the touch, almost as if heated by a living body. Bodenland's spatulate fingers probed in the dust. He started to scrape a small hole in order to see the rib cage better. It was absurd to believe that this dust had lain undisturbed for all those millennia. The dust was crusty, breaking into crumbs like old cake.

30

He did not know what he was looking for. He grinned in the darkness. A sticker saying 'Made in Taiwan' would do. He'd have to go gently with poor old Clift. Scientists had been known to fake evidence before.

His finger ran gently along the left floating rib, then the one above it. At the next rib, he felt an obstruction.

Grit trickled between his fingers. He could not see what he had hold of. Bone? Tugging gently, he got it loose, and lifted it from the depression. When he held it up to the light bulb, it glittered dimly.

It was not bone. It was metal.

Bodenland rubbed it on his shirt, then held it up again.

It was a silver bullet.

On it was inscribed a pattern – a pattern of ivy or something similar, twining about a cross. He stared at it in disbelief, and an ill feeling ran through him.

Sixty-five million years old?

He heard Clift returning, speaking reassuringly to the guard. Hastily, he smoothed over the marks he had made in the fossil coffin. The bullet he slipped into a pocket.

'A very traditional fracas,' Clift said quietly, in his academic way. 'Two young men quarrelling for the favours of one girl. Sex has proved a rather troublesome method of perpetuating the human race. If one was in charge one might dream up a better way . . . I advised them both to go to bed with her and then forget it.'

'They must have loved that suggestion!'

'They'll sort it out.'

'Maybe we should hit the sack too.'

But they stood under the stars, discussing the find. Bodenland endeavoured to hide his scepticism, without great success.

'Experts are coming in from Chicago and Drumheller tomorrow,' Clift said. 'You shall hear what they say. They will understand that the evidence of the strata cannot lie.'

'Come on, Bernie, sixty-five million years . . . My mind just won't take in such a span of time.'

'In the history of the universe – even of the earth, the solar system – sixty-five point five million years is but yesterday.'

* * *

They were walking down the slope, silent. A gulf had opened between them. The students had all gone to bed, whether apart or together. Over the desert a stillness prevailed such as had done before men first entered the continent.

The light came from the west. Bodenland saw it first and motioned to his companion to stand still and observe. As far as could be judged the light was moving fast, and in their direction. It made no noise. It extended itself, until it resembled a comet rushing along over the ground. It was difficult to focus on. The men stood rooted to the spot in astonishment.

'But the railroad's miles distant – ' Clift exclaimed trying to keep his voice level.

Whatever the phenomenon was, it was approaching the camp at extreme velocity.

Without wasting words, Bodenland dashed forward, running down the slope, calling to Mina. He saw her light go on immediately in the camper. Satisfied, he swerved and ran towards the trailer his son occupied. Banging on the door, he called Larry's name.

Hearing the commotion, others woke, other doors opened. Men ran naked out of tents. Clift called out for calm, but cries of amazement drowned his voice. The thing was plunging out of the desert. It seemed ever distant, ever near, as if time itself was suspended to allow it passage.

Bodenland put his arm protectively round Mina's shoulders when she appeared.

'Get to some high ground.' He gave Larry and Kylie similar orders when they came up, dishevelled, but stood firm himself, unable not to watch that impossible progress.

The notion entered his head that it resembled a streamlined flier viewed through thick distorting glass. Still no sound. But the next moment it was on them, plunging through the heart of the little encampment – and all in silence. Screams rose from the Dixie students, who flung themselves to the ground.

Yet it had no impact, seemed to have no substance but light, to be as insubstantial as the luminescence it trailed behind it, which remained floating to the ground and disappeared like dying sparks.

Bodenland watched the ghastly thing go. It plunged right into and through one of the mesas, and finally was swallowed in the distances of the Utah night. It had appeared intent on destruction, yet not a thing in the camp was harmed. It had passed right through Larry's trailer, yet nothing showed the slightest sign of disarray.

Larry staggered up to his father and offered him a gulp from a silver hip flask.

'We've just seen the original ghost train, Joe,' he said.

'I'll believe anything now,' said Bodenland, gratefully accepting the flask.

When dawn came, and the desert was transformed from shadow to furnace, the members of the Old John encampment were still discussing the phenomenon of the night. Students of a metaphysical disposition argued that the ghost train – Larry's description was generally adopted – had no objective reality. It was amazing how many of these young people, scientifically trained, the cream of their year, could believe in a dozen wacky explanations. Nearly all of them, it seemed to Bodenland as he listened and sipped coffee from the canteen, belonged to one kind of religious cult or another. Nearly all espoused explanations that chimed with their own particular set of beliefs.

Larry left the discussion early, dragging Kylie away, though she was clearly inclined to pitch into the debate.

One of the students who had been engaged in the previous night's scuffle increasingly monopolized the discussion.

'You guys are all crazy if you think this was some kind of an enemy secret weapon. If there was such a thing, America would have had it first and we'd know about it. Equally, it ain't some kind of Scientology thing, just to challenge your IQs to figure it out or join the Church. It's clear what happened. We're all suddenly stuck here in this desert, forbidden to communicate with our parents or the outside world, and we're feeling oppressed. Insecure. So what do we do? Why, it's natural – we get a mass-hallucination. Nothing but nothing happened in Old John last night, except we all freaked out. So forget it. It'll probably happen again tonight till we all go crazy and get ourselves shipped to the funny farm.'

Bodenland stood up.

'People don't go crazy so easily, son. You're just shooting your mouth off. Why, I want to know, are you so keen to discount what you actually saw and experienced?'

'Because that thing couldn't be,' retorted the student.

'Wrong. Because you try to fit it in with your partial systems of belief and it won't fit. That's because of an error in your beliefs, not your experience. We all saw that fucking thing. It exists. Okay, so we can't account for it. Not yet. Any more than we can account for the ancient grave up there on the bluff. But scientific enquiry will sort out the truth from the lies – *if* we are honest in our observations!'

'So what was that ghost train, then?' demanded one of the girls. 'You tell us.'

Bodenland sat down next to Mina again. 'That's what I'm saying. I don't know. But I'm not discounting it on that account. If everything that could not be readily understood was discounted by some crap system of belief, we'd still be back in the Stone Age. As soon as we can talk to the outside world again, I'm getting on to the various nearby research establishments to find who else has observed this so-called ghost train.'

Clift said quietly, 'I've been working this desert fifteen years, Joe, and I never saw such a thing before. Nor did I ever hear of anyone else who did.'

'Well, we'll get to the bottom of it.'

'Just how do you propose to do that, Mr Bodenland?' asked the girl who had spoken up before. Supportive murmurs came from her friends.

Bodenland grinned.

'If the train comes again tonight, I'm going to be ready to board it.'

The students set up such a racket, he hardly heard Mina say at his side, 'Jesus, Joe, you really are madder than they are. . . .'

'Maybe – but we've got a helicopter and they haven't.'

Towards evening, Mina climbed with Bernard Clift to an eminence above the camp, and looked westwards.

Joe had been away most of the day. After having persuaded Larry and Kylie to stay on a little longer, he had ridden out with them to see if they could track down any signs of the ghost train.

'What's out there?' Mina asked, shielding her eyes from the sun.

'A few coyotes, the odd madman rejecting this century, preparing to reject the next one. Not much else,' Clift said. 'Oh, they'll probably come across an old track leading to Enterprise City.'

She laughed. 'Enterprise City! Oh, Joe'll love the sound of that. He'll take it as an omen.'

'Joe doesn't believe what we've got here, does he? That's why he's allowing this train thing to distract him, isn't it?'

Mina continued to stare westwards with shielded eyes.

'I have a problem with my husband and my son, Bernard. Joe is such an achiever. He can't help overshadowing Larry. I feel very sorry for Larry. He tried to get out from his father's shadow, and rejected the whole scientific business. Unfortunately, he moved sideways into groceries, and I can see why that riles Joe. No matter he's made a financial success, and supplies a whole south-eastern area of the USA. Now marrying into Kylie's family's transport system, he'll be a whole lot more successful. Richer, I should say.'

'Doesn't that please Joe?'

She shook her head doubtfully. 'Whatever else Joe is, he's not a mercenary man. I guess at present he's just waiting to see if a nice girl like Kylie can cure Larry of his drinking habits.'

'As you say, she's a nice girl right enough. But can she?'

She looked straight at Clift. 'There's danger just in trying. Still, there's danger in everything. I should know. My hobby's freefall parachuting.'

'I remember. And I've seen the articles on you in the glossies. Sounds like a wonderful hobby.'

She looked at him rather suspiciously, suspecting envy. 'You get your kicks burrowing into the earth. I like to be way above it, with time and gravity in suspense.'

He pointed down the trail, where three figures on mules could be discerned in a cloud of dust.

'Your husband's on his way back. He was telling me he's also got time in suspense, in his laboratories.'

'Time isn't immutable, as the science of chaos proves. Basically Joe's inertial disposal system is a way of de-stabilizing time. Ten years ago, the principles behind it were scarcely glimpsed. I like that. Basically, I'm on Joe's side, Bernard, so it's no good trying to get round me.'

He laughed, but ignored the jibe.

'If time isn't immutable, what is it? Being up against millions of years, I should be told.'

'Time's like a fog with a wave structure. It's all to do with strange attractors. I can send you a paper about it. Tamper with the input, who knows what output you'll get.'

Clift laughed again.

'Just like life, in fact.'

'Also subject to chaos.'

They climbed down the hill path to meet Bodenland and his companions, covered in dust after the ride.

'Oh, that was just wonderful,' Kylie said, climbing off her mule and giving Mina a hug. 'The desert is a marvellous place. Now I need a shower.'

'A shower and a dozen cans of beer,' supplemented Larry.

'It was wonderful, but it achieved nothing,' Bodenland said. 'However, we have left a pretty trail of flags behind. All I hope is that the ghost train calls again tonight.'

'What about Larry?' she asked, when they were alone.

'He's off with Kylie tomorrow, whatever happens tonight.'

'Don't look so sour, Joe. They are supposed to be on honeymoon, poor kids. Where would you rather be – on a beach in Hawaii, or in this godforsaken stretch of Utah?'

He smiled at her, teasingly but with affection. 'I'd rather be on that ghost train – and that is where I'm going to be tonight.'

But Bodenland was in for disappointment.

The night brought the stars, sharp as diamonds over the desert, but no ghost train. Bodenland and his group stayed by the mobile canteen, which remained open late to serve them. They drank coffee and talked, waiting, with the helicopter nearby, ever and again looking out into the darkness.

'No Injuns,' Kylie said. 'No John Wayne stagecoach. The train made its appearance and that was it. Hey, Joe, a student was telling me she saw ghostly figures jumping – no, she said floating – off the train and landing somewhere by the dig, so she said. What do you think of that?'

36

'Could be the first of later accretions to what will be a legend. Bernie, these students are going to want to bring in the media – or at least the local press. How're you going to handle that?'

'I rely on them,' Clift said. 'They know how things stand. All the same . . . Joe, if this thing shows up tonight, I want to be on that helicopter with you.'

'My god, here it comes,' Mina screamed, before Bodenland could reply.

And it was there in the darkness, like something boring in from outer space, a traveller, a voyager, an invader: full of speed and luminescence, which seemed to scatter behind it, swerving across the Escalante. Only when it burst through mesas did its lights fade. This time it was well away from the line of flags planted during the day, heading north, and some miles distant from the camp.

Bodenland led the rush for the helicopter. Larry followed and jumped into the pilot's seat. The others were handed quickly up, Mina with her vidcam, Clift last, pulling himself aboard as the craft lifted.

Larry sent it scudding across ground, barely clearing the camper roofs as it sped up into the night air.

'Steady,' Kylie said. 'This isn't one of your models, Larry!'

'Faster,' yelled Mina. 'Or we'll lose it.'

But they didn't. Fast though the ghost train sped, the chopper cut across ground to it. Before they were overhead, Joe was being winched down, swinging wild as they banked.

The strange luminous object – strangely dull when close, shaped like a phosphorescent slug – was just below them. Bodenland steadied himself, clasped the wire rope, made to stand on the roof as velocities matched – and his foot went through nothingness.

He struggled in the dark, cursing. Nothing of substance was below his boots. Whatever it was, it was as untouchable as it was silent.

Bodenland dangled there, buffeted by the rotors overhead. The enigmatic object tunnelled into the night and disappeared.

The shots of the ghost train in close up were as striking as the experience had been. Figures were revealed – revealed and con-cealed – sitting like dummies inside what might have been carriages.

They were grey, apparently immobile. Confusingly, they were momentarily replaced by glimpses of trees, perhaps of whole forests; but the green flickered by and was gone as soon as seen.

Mina switched the video off.

'Any questions?' she asked, flippantly.

Silence fell.

'Maybe the trees were reflections of something – on the windows, I mean,' Larry said. 'Well, no . . . But *trees*. . . .'

'It was like a death train,' Kylie said. 'Were those people or corpses? Do you think it could be . . . No, I don't know what we saw.'

'Whatever it was, I have to get back to Dallas tomorrow,' Joe said. 'With phantom trains and antediluvian bones, you have a lot of explaining to do to someone, Bernie, my friend.'

Next morning came the parting of the ways at St George airport. Bodenland and Mina were going back to Dallas, Larry and his bride flying on to their Hawaii hotel. As they said their farewells in the reception lounge, Kylie took Bodenland's hand.

'Joe, I've been thinking about what happened at Old John. You've heard of near-death experiences, of course? I believe we underwent a near-death experience. There's a connection between what we call the ghost train and that sixty-five-million-year-old grave of Bernard Clift's. Otherwise it's too much of a coincidence, right?'

'Mm, that makes sense.'

'Well, then. The shock of that discovery, the old grave, the feeling of death which prevailed over the whole camp – with vultures drifting around and everything – all that precipitated us into a corporate near-death experience. It took a fairly conventional form for such experiences. A tunnel-like effect, the sense of a journey. The corpses on the train, or whatever they were. Don't you see, it all fits?'

'No, I don't see that anything fits, Kylie, but you're a darling and interesting girl, and I just hope that Larry takes proper care of you.'

'Like you take care of me, eh, Pop?' Larry said. 'I'll take care of Kylie – and that's my affair. You take care of your reputation, eh? Watch that this ancient grave of Bernie's isn't just a hoax.'

38

Bodenland clutched the silver bullet in his pocket and eyed his son coldly, saying nothing. They parted without shaking hands.

No word had come from Washington in Bodenland's absence. Instead he received a phone call from the *Washington Post* wanting an angle on governmental procrastination. Summoning his Publicity Liaison Officer, Bodenland had another demonstration arranged.

When a distinguished group of political commentators was gathered in the laboratory, clustering round the inertial disposal cabinet, Bodenland addressed them informally.

'The principle involved here is new. Novelty in itself takes a while for governmental departments to digest. But we want to get there first. Otherwise, our competitors in Japan and Europe will be there before us, and once more America will have lost out. We used to be the leaders where invention was concerned. My heroes since boyhood have been men like Alexander Graham Bell and Thomas Alva Edison. I'm going to do an Edison now, just to prove how safe our new principle of waste disposal is.'

He glanced at Mina, giving her a smile of reassurance.

'My wife's anxious for my safety. I welcome that. Washington has different motivations for delay.'

This time, Bodenland was taking the place of the black plastic bag. He nodded to the technicians and stepped into the cabinet. Waldgrave closed the door on him.

Bodenland watched the two clocks, the one inside the cabinet with him and the one in the laboratory, as the energy field built up round him. The sweep hand of the inside clock slowed and stopped. The blue light intensified rapidly, and he witnessed all movement ceasing in the outside world. The expression on Mina's face froze, her hand paused halfway to her mouth. Then everything disappeared. It whited out and went in a flash. He stood alone in the middle of a greyish something that had no substance.

Yet he was able to move. He turned round and saw a black plastic bag some way behind him, standing in a timeless limbo. He tried to reach it but could not. He felt the air grow thick.

The stationary clock started to move again. Its rate accelerated. Through the grey fog, outlines of the laboratory with its frozen

39

audience appeared. As the clock in the cabinet caught up with the one outside, everything returned to normal. Waldgrave released him from the cabinet.

The audience clapped, and there were murmurs of relief.

Bodenland wiped his brow with a handkerchief.

'I became stuck in time, just for five minutes. I represented a container of nuclear waste. Only difference, we would not bring the waste back as Max Waldgrave just brought me back. It would remain at that certain time at which it was disposed of, drifting even further back into the past, like a grave.

'This cabinet is just a prototype. Given the Department of the Environment's approval, Bodenland Enterprises will build immense hangars to cope with waste, stow it away in the past by the truckload, and become world monopolists in the new trade.'

'Could we get the stuff back if we ever wanted to?' someone asked. 'I mean, if future ages found what we consider waste to be valuable, worth reclamation.'

'Sure. Just as I have been brought back to the present time. The point to remember is that at the moment the technology requires enormous amounts of energy. It's expensive, but security costs. You know we at Bodenland Enterprises are presently tapping solar energy, beamed down from our own satellite by microwave. If and when we get the okay from the DoE, we can afford to research still more efficient methods of beaming in power from space.'

The two men from the *Post* had been conferring. The senior man said, 'We certainly appreciate the Edison imitation, Mr Bodenland. But aren't you being unduly modest – haven't you just invented the world's first time machine? Aren't you applying to the wrong department? Shouldn't you be approaching the Defence top brass in the Pentagon?'

Laughter followed the question, but Bodenland looked annoyed. 'I'm against nuclear weapons and, for that matter, I'm enough of a confirmed Green to dislike nuclear power plants. Hence our research into PBSs – power-beam sats. Solar energy, after many decades, is coming into its own at last. It will replace nuclear power in another quarter century, if I have anything to do with it.

'However, to answer your question – as I have often answered it before – no, I emphatically reject the idea that the inertial principle has anything to do with time travel, at least as we understand time travel since the days of H. G. Wells.

'What we have here is a form of time-stoppage. Anything – obviously not just toxic wastes – can be processed to stay right where it is, bang on today's time and date, for ever, while the rest of us continue subject to the clock. That applies even to the DoE.'

As the last media man scooped up a handful of salted almonds and left, Mina turned to Bodenland.

'You are out of your mind, Joe. Taking unnecessary risks again. You might have been killed.'

'Come on, it worked on mice.'

'You should have tried rats.'

He laughed.

'Birdie, I had an idea while I was in limbo. Something Kylie said stuck in my mind – that the ghost train and the discovery of Bernie Clift's grave were somehow connected. Suppose it's a time connection . . . That train, or whatever it is, must have physical substance. It's not a ghost. It must obey physical laws, like everything else in the universe. Maybe the connection is a time connection. If we used the inertial principle in a portable form – rigged it up so that it would work from a helicopter – '

'Oh, shucks!' she cried, seeing what was in his mind. 'No, no more funnies, please. You wouldn't want to be aboard that thing even if you could get in. It's packed with zombies going God knows where. Joe, I won't let you.'

He put his hands soothingly on her shoulders. 'Mina, listen – '

'How many years have I listened? To what effect? To more stress and strain, to more of your bullshit?'

'I have to get on that train. I'm sure it could be done. It's no worse than your sky-diving. Leap into the unknown – that's what we're all about, darling.'

'Oh, shit,' she said.

CHAPTER III

At some time in the past, the cell had been whitewashed in the interests of cleanliness. It was now filthy. Straw, dust, pages of old newspaper, a lump of human ordure, littered the stone-paved floor.

A mouse ran full tilt along one of the walls. Its coat was grey, with longer russet hair over the shoulders. It moved with perfect grace, its small beady eyes fixed on the madman ahead, and more particularly on his open mouth.

Strapped within a straitjacket, the lunatic lay horizontal on the floor. The straitjacket was of canvas, with leather straps securing it, imprisoning the arms of the madman.

He had kicked his semen-stained grey mattress into a corner, to lie stretched out on the stones, his head wedged in another corner.

He was motionless. His eyes gleamed as he kept his gaze on the mouse, never blinking. His chops gaped wide, his tongue curled back. Saliva dripped slowly to the ground.

The mouse had been foraging in one of the holes in the old mattress when the madman fixed it with his gaze. The mouse had remained still, staring back, as if undergoing some internal struggle. Then its limbs had started to twitch and move. It had slewed round, squealing pitifully. Then it began its run towards the open jaws.

There was no holding back. It was committed. Scuttling along with one flank close to the wall, it ran towards the waiting face. With a final leap, it was in the mouth. The madman's jaws snapped shut.

His eyes bulged. He lay still, body without movement. Only his jaws moved as he chewed. A little blood leaked from his lips to the floor.

With much cracking of tiny bones, he finished his mouthful. Then he licked the pool of blood from the stained stones.

Outside the cell stretched a long corridor, a model of cleanliness compared with the cell in which the madman was imprisoned. At the other end of the corridor, Doctor Kindness had his office, which connected with a small operating room.

The office was furnished with phrenological and anatomical charts. On one of the wood-panelled walls hung a day-to-day calendar for the current year, 1896, with quotations from Carlyle, Martin Tupper, Samuel Smiles, and other notables.

The furniture was heavy. Two armchairs were built like small fortresses, their soiled green leather bulging with horsehair, their mahogany shod with brass studs.

A general air of heaviness, of a place where, in the interests of medicine, oxygen was not allowed to enter, hung about the room. In the black lead grate, a coal fire had died, in despair at the retreat of the last of the oxygen. Only the black meerschaum pipe of the doctor glowed, sucking oxygen from the lungs of this pillar of the asylum. Clouds of smoke ascended from the bowl of the pipe to the ceiling, to hang about the gas brackets looking for release.

In order to make the room less inviting, a row of death masks stood on the heavy marble mantleshelf above the dead fire. The masks depicted various degrees of agony, and were of men and women who, judging by this plaster evidence involuntarily left behind, had found life with all its terrors preferable to what was imminently to come.

The doctor was perfectly at home in this environment. As he sauntered through, smoking, from the operating room, he set a blood-stained bone-saw down among the papers of his desk before turning to his visitor.

Dr Kindness was pale and furrowed, and enveloped almost entirely in a blood-stained white coat. In his prevailing greyness, his only vigorous signs of life were exhibited through his pipe.

His visitor was altogether of a different stamp. His most conspicuous characteristic was a bushy red beard, which flowed low enough over the lapels of a suit of heavy green tweed to make it impossible to tell if he was wearing a tie. He was of outdoor appearance, solid, and with a normally pleasant expression on his broad face. At this moment, what with the smoke and the bone-saw and the oppressive atmosphere of the asylum, he looked more apprehensive than anything else.

'Well, it's done,' said Dr Kindness, removing the pipe for a moment. 'If you'd like to come and have a look. It's not a pretty sight.'

'Sure, sure, I'd be glad. . . .' But the ginger man rose from his armchair by the dead fire with reluctance, and was aided into the operating room only by Dr Kindness's pressure behind him.

The reason for Dr Kindness's heavy generation of smoke-screen was now apparent. The stench in the operating room was pervasive. To breathe it caused an agitation in the heart.

On a large wooden table much like a butcher's slab lay a naked male body streaked with dirt. The genitals were scabbed, and whole areas of stomach and chest were so mottled with rashes and ulcers they resembled areas of the Moon's surface.

The doctor had sawn off the top of the skull, revealing the brain. Blood still seeped from the cavity into a sink.

'Get nearer and have a good look,' Dr Kindness said. 'Light's rather bad in here. It's not many people who get the chance to see a human brain. Seat of all wisdom and all wickedness . . . What do you observe?'

The ginger man leaned over and peered into the skull.

Rather faintly, he said, 'I observe that the poor feller's good and dead, doctor. I suppose the corpse will get a decent burial?'

'The asylum will dispose of it.'

'I also observe that the brain seems to be rather small. Is that so?'

Dr Kindness nodded. 'Poke about in there if you wish. Here's a spatula. You're correct, of course. That's an effect of tertiary syphilis. The brain shrivels in many cases. Like an orange going bad. GPI follows – General Paralysis of the Insane.'

The doctor smote himself on the chest and, in so doing, awoke a husky cough. When he had recovered, he said, 'We doctors are fighting one of mankind's ancient scourges, sir. Satan and his legions now descend on us in modern form, as minuscule protozoa.

As you probably know, this disease threatens the very foundations of the British Empire. Indeed, the Contagious Diseases Acts of the 1860s were passed in order to protect the young men of our army and navy from the prostitutes who spread VD.'

At the mention of prostitutes, the ginger man did a lot of head shaking and tut-tutting. 'Terrible, terrible it is. And the prostitutes must get it from the men.'

'The men get it from the prostitutes,' said Dr Kindness, sternly.

A small silence fell, in which Dr Kindness cleared his throat.

'And there's no cure once you've contracted it?' said the ginger man, with a terrified expression.

'If treated early enough . . . Otherwise . . .' The doctor removed his pipe to utter what was intended to be a laugh. 'Many of the inmates of this institution die of GPI. Men and women. If you'd like to come back tomorrow, I'll be able to show you a really excellent corpse of an old woman in her sixties. Mad as a hatter the last eight years.'

'Thanks, doctor, but I'm busy tomorrow. Sorry to take up so much of your time.' He thrust his hands deep in his pockets, in an effort to still their trembling.

As he hurried from the bleak building with all its stone wings and stone walls and stony windows, he muttered a verse from Psalm XXVI to himself. 'Oh shut not up my soul with the sinners: nor my life with the bloodthirsty . . .'

And as he climbed into his waiting carriage, he said aloud, 'Holy Lord, but I need a drink. It's a terrible way for a man to end up.'

Bodenland and Waldgrave were in the construction wing consulting with senior mechanics when a call came through from Bodenland's secretary, Rose Gladwin, that Bernard Clift wanted to see him urgently.

'I'll be there, Rose.'

He could see Clift through a glass door before Clift saw his approach. The younger man still wore the dusty clothes he had had on at Old John in Utah. His whole manner suggested excitement, as he paced back and forth in the waiting room with a springy step, punching the palm of one hand with the fist of the other, and talking to himself with downward gaze as if rehearsing a speech.

'You'll wonder what I'm doing in Dallas,' he began, almost without preamble, as Bodenland went in. 'I'm on my way to PAA '99 in Houston. Progress in Advanced Archaeology. We're still fighting a rump of idiots who think Darwin was the devil. I've been scheduled to speak for some months. Well, I'm going to announce that I've uncovered a humanoid creature going back some sixty-five million years. I'm in for the Spanish Inquisition, and I know it.'

'I thought you'd come to inspect our inertial project,' Bodenland said, smiling.

Clift looked blank. 'I wanted to see you because I've had a rethink about secrecy in the last forty-eight hours. Our security broke down. The students told the tale to a local radio station. I don't want a garbled message getting about. I have to ask you for some support, Joe – I mean financial. My university won't fund me on this.'

'You asked them and they turned you down?' He saw by Clift's expression that his guess was correct. 'They said you were crazy? What makes you think *I* don't think you're crazy? Come and have a coffee, Bernie, and let me talk you out of this.'

Clift shook his head exasperatedly, but allowed himself to be led into the secretary's room, where he sank into a chair and sipped black coffee.

'The experts I told you about – both able young men from the archaeological research departments of the museums in Chicago and Drumheller – took a look at the evidence. Of course they're cautious. They have to make reports. But I think I have won their backing. They will be at Houston, at PAA '99. Don't shake your head, Joe. Look at this.'

He jumped up, almost upsetting his cup. From his briefcase he spilled on the table black-and-white photos of the site and the grave, taken from all angles.

'There's no way this can be a hoax, Joe.' He made an agitated movement. 'It would be to your company's advantage to associate yourself with this momentous discovery. I'm positive there was a – at least a pseudo-human species contemporaneous with the duck-billed dinosaurs and other giant herbivores and, of course, with major predators such as Tyrannosaurus Rex. I'm going to overturn scientific knowledge just as Lyell and Darwin and others overturned the grip of false religion in the nineteenth century. You realize the amount we know for sure about the Cretaceous is virtually all contained in a lorry-load of old bones? The rest is guesswork. Inspired imagination.'

Bodenland interrupted his eloquence. 'Look beyond your personal excitement. Suppose you were taken seriously in Houston. Think of the effect on the stock market – '

Clift jumped up, heedlessly upsetting his coffee. 'I change the world and you worry about the Dow Jones Index? Joe, this isn't like you! Grasp the new reality.'

'My shareholders would shoot me if – '

'Here's a kind of human with burial customs not unlike ours – flowers in the grave, ochre, even some kind of meaningful symbol on the coffin lid – but below the K/T boundary. Maybe it developed from some offshoot of early dinosaurs. I don't know, but I tell you that this is – well, it's greater than the discovery of a new planet, it's – '

'Hold it, Bernie,' said Joe, laughing. 'I do see that it might be all you say, and more – if it proved to be true. But how could it be true? You want it to be true. But suppose it's like the Piltdown man, just a hoax. Something some of those brighter students of yours tried on for fun . . . I can't possible associate this organization with it at this early stage. We've got responsibilities. If you want a few hundred bucks, I'd be glad – '

Clift looked angry. 'Joe, are you hearing me? I just told you, this is no fucking hoax. How many of the world's great discoveries have been laughed at on first appearance? Remember how men thought that flying machines were impossible – and continued to do so even after the first flying machine had left the ground? Remember how the great Priestley discovered the role of oxygen in combustion – yet still believed in the old phlogiston theory?'

'Okay, okay.' Bodenland raised his hands for peace. 'Quite contrary to Priestley's case, in this case popular mythology is entirely on your side. The comic strips and movies have always pretended that mankind and dinosaurs co-existed. You're just claiming that Fred Flintstone was a real live actual person.'

He saw this remark was not appreciated, and went on hurriedly, 'Bernie, honestly, I'd be happy if I could swallow all this. Seeing

47

orthodoxies overturned is my kind of meat. But you don't stand a chance on this one. Go back to the goddamned Escalante, find a second grave in that same stratum. Then I'll take you seriously.'

'You will? Okay.' He paused dramatically and gestured towards the table. 'Take a look at the photos. You've scarcely glanced at them. You're like the Italian authorities, refusing to look through Galileo's telescope. You've taken it for granted you know what the photos are all about. These are shots of a second grave, Joe. We struck it even when you were leaving to get your plane.'

Bodenland gave his friend one baffled look, then peered at the plates.

The grave much resembled the first, which was why he had hardly bothered to look at the photos. The remains were enclosed in a similar coffin, with the same mysterious sign on the lid. In this case, the lid had been removed with little damage.

The skeleton, sunk in red ochre, lay on its side, in the same position as the first skeleton. Distance shots showed that this grave was no more than fifty metres from the first, still just below the K/T boundary, but deeper into the hill, where the strata curved inward.

'You observe,' Clift said, now using his voice of icy calm. 'The second grave. There are two significant differences compared with our first discovery. In this case, the skeleton is of a female. And she lies with a wooden stake through what was her heart.'

'I'm sure your beautiful young daughter-in-law would tell you that you know nothing about human nature, Joe,' Clift said, as they walked through the building. 'I can't keep this secret. I'm bursting with it. There's the scientific aspect, and that's predominant. This is something that is going to cause shock waves. It'll be hotly contested. I'm in for the Spanish Inquisition and I know it. I also know I can defend my case.

'But there's more to it than that. You've had plenty of publicity in your time, what with your association with Victor Frankenstein and Mary Shelley and all that. I also want publicity. I want recognition, as every man does, if he's honest. Publicity will give me the funding I require.

'Millions of dollars are needed. Millions. The whole Iron Hills area must be torn apart. We've got a new civilization to explore – beyond our dreams. Imagine, civilization started here, in the USA, long before apes came out of the African jungles!'

'Yes, and when this hits the media, you're going to have the whole universe invading your pitch. You're not going to be able to work. The site will be ruined. And I won't be able to chase that phantom train.'

'That's where you can help. If your organization will back me, I want you to get an army of security personnel down at Old John straight away.'

'Do you want a bed for the night? I'll ring Mina, if she isn't twenty thousand feet up.'

'I'll ring her, Joe, thanks. And Joe – thanks a million. I know you'll be in the hot seat too. One day, I'll return this favour.'

They shook hands.

Joe said, 'Mina will take care of you. I may be a little hard to contact, just for a while.'

'How's that?'

'Never mind. Up guards and at 'em, Bernie. Shake the world! I'm on your side.'

The great green-and-white waves of the Pacific came curling into Hilo Bay, Hawaii. The foam scattered in the sunlight, the water lost its power, crawled up the volcanic sands, sank down again, and miraculously revived, to make another assault on the beaches.

Larry and Kylie came out of the ocean shaking the water from their hair.

'I just know something is wrong, Larry. Please let's get back to the hotel,' she said.

'Nothing's wrong, sweetie. Forget your intuitions. It's something you ate. How can anything be wrong? We've only been down on the beach an hour.'

'I'm sorry, Larry,' Kylie said, reaching for a towel. 'I just feel kind of edgy inside. I need to get back to the hotel to see if there's a message or something. You don't have to come. I can go on my own.'

'Oh, shit, I'll come. You'll be making me nervous next.'

Back in the Bradford Palace, where they had now been staying for three days, everything was normal. Phoning down from their room to Reception revealed no message. Nothing had happened.

'I'm sorry, darling,' Kylie said, nuzzling him. 'I just had that silly feeling. You want to go back to the beach?'

'No, I don't want to go back to the beach. Supposing you get another funny spell directly we're down there. We could be bouncing back and forth like yo-yos all day. I'm going to drag a six-pack on that balcony and tan. Forget it.'

'Don't be like that, Larry. I wish you wouldn't drink so much.'

He turned and grinned as he headed for the fridge. 'You got some religious objections or something?'

She stood in the middle of the room, nibbling an index finger. She said nothing to him when he returned, switching on the TV too loud on his way to a cushioned lounger on the balcony of the suite. She looked out past him, through the tall palms, past the busy road and the other hotels and the whole vulgar commercial razzmatazz of Hilo Bay, to where there was the green line of the ocean, beyond the shallows where the swimmers and surfers sported, a line that offered at least the prospect of infinity.

Sadly, she turned away, changed into a loose caftan, and took a copy of Bram Stoker's novel *Dracula* over to a side-sofa to read, out of range of the TV screen.

She had marked her place with the wrapper of a Hershey bar.

With a part of her mind, Kylie was aware of a commercial on television for the local Hedge's Beer. It's slimming, it's trimming – get a Hedge against inflation. A news bulletin followed.

Absorbed in her reading, she hardly took it in until Larry yelled from the balcony: 'Bernie Clift!'

There was Clift's face on the screen.

Against library pictures of desert, the announcer was speaking. 'The scientific world – or at least that part of it meeting yesterday at a conference in Houston – was in uproar over a statement made by famous palaeontologist, Bernard Cliff. Cliff claims he has discovered a race of human-like beings who lived millions of years before the Stone Age, in the time of Ally Oop.'

Clift was seen at a microphone, brushing back a lock of hair from his forehead and speaking above a hubbub. 'On the evidence

50

of a pair of graves in Utah we cannot generalize too freely. But the workmanship of the coffins, which is surprisingly modern in technique, suggests a high degree of culture. Dating methods indicate beyond doubt a date of some 65.5 million years ago. This clearly places the coffins and the bodies they contain back at a period when the tyrannosaur and other giant dinosaurs were still roving the continents.'

The clip ended. Back came the announcer, saying, 'Later, Cliff revealed that a preliminary analysis of the two fossilized bodies indicates strong shoulder development with much enlarged shoulder blades. Which leads to the hypothesis that Cliff's new discoveries could possibly have evolved from a flighted species, such as the pterodactyl or pteranodon. As shown in this artist's impression.'

Over the sketch, his voice continued, 'A natural wave of scepticism greeted the Utah announcement . . .' By this time, Larry and Kylie were arm in arm before the TV set, exclaiming in excitement.

'Scepticism!' Larry exclaimed. 'What else?'

'. . . and it's not from the Bible Belt only that these protests have come. Within the last hour, Professor Danny Hudson of the Smithsonian Institute has issued a challenge to Bernard Cliff to put up or shut up. He is reported as saying he expects the evidence to become available to quote unbiased scientific examination unquote.'

Mina's face appeared on the screen.

She was in mid-spate. This was evidently an excerpt from a longer interview in Clift's defence. She had time to say only, 'They all laughed at Christopher Columbus, remember? Columbus thought the world was round, the idiot.'

She laughed and was faded. The station announcer reappeared.

'Professor Cliff is unavailable for further comment. That was attractive green-eyed 46-year-old Mina Legrand, close associate and intimate friend of legendary Joe Bodenland, who once claimed he had gone back in time to shake hands with Frankenstein. Bodenland now heads the multi-national Bodenland Enterprises.

'Our sources report that Bodenland himself is missing. Mina Legrand could not comment, beyond stating Bodenland was interested in the amazing new discovery. Meantime, let's hope all those Utah critters are well and truly extinct . . .'

'Oh God . . .' Kylie switched off the power before the commercials popped up, and turned to Larry.

He set down his half-empty glass.

'You were right all along, sweetie. Something is wrong. My father needs me. We're going to have to catch the next plane.'

'Oh, no, Larry. Your father has to look after himself, just as you say he always made you look after yourself. You're only going to lay yourself open to a snub if you interfere now. He'll be okay. Joe'll be okay. Let's go back to the beach.'

'Jesus!' He waved his hands above his head. 'Who just now wanted to get off the beach? Women – I'll never understand them. Pack, Kylie. We're off. Utah. That's where Joe'll be. Old John.'

She blocked his way to the bedroom, angry and pugnacious.

'I'm not going back to Old John. Nor are you. Screw Old John. Think, will you? You are married to me. You are no longer going to live under your father's shadow. I love the old boy, but he is going to ruin your life if you are weak. Can't you understand that? Everyone else does.'

'Weak, am I? We'll see about that.' He grabbed her wrist and twisted her round until she sank to the ground. 'Baby, I'm all action when I get going, and I'm going right now.'

As he ran into the bedroom, Kylie got to her knees and shouted, 'Buster, if you go you're gone for good, get that? Your parents have already loused up our honeymoon once. I'm not having it again. Ring your mother if you're so anxious about your father. But if you leave this hotel, you leave it on your own, and our marriage is a dead duck.'

Striding by her with a hastily packed overnight bag, he stared at her bitterly, and made a threatening gesture.

' "Goodbye was all he wrote", ' he said. The suite door slammed behind him.

Kylie walked about the suite for a while. She went into the bedroom and collected up all of her husband's clothes from the cupboards and elsewhere, stuffing them into his travel case. When she had cleared the room of his belongings, she took the case to the window and flung it out into the gardens below.

She stripped down until she wore nothing but her crucifix, where-upon she took a shower. After that, she sat in her caftan and attempted to read *Dracula* for a while. But her mind was elsewhere.

When the time came, she put on a cocktail dress in which to go down to dinner. In the Bradford's outdoor restaurant, she ate a lobster thermidor and drank half a bottle of white Australian wine.

Thus fortified, she went into the ballroom, where a blond-haired young man on vacation from Alaska immediately asked her to dance.

She did dance.

CHAPTER IV

In the night that enveloped Utah, Larry was half-drunk. 'This chopper's easier to fly 'n one of my model planes,' he called to Bodenland.

Neither Bodenland nor Clift made any response, if they heard.

'I've got a World War Two Boeing I just made,' Larry shouted. 'A beauty. Fifteen feet wing-span. You should see it. Goes faster than the real thing!' He roared with laughter.

Beneath them went the rushing phantom of the ghost train, its eerie luminence shining from the roof as from its sides.

Bodenland lowered himself cautiously, with Bernard Clift just behind, his boots almost touching Bodenland's helmeted head. When Bodenland gave the Thumbs Up signal, Larry switched on the improvised inertial beam. It shone down, vividly blue, encompassing the two men and the top of the train. From Larry's careering viewpoint, they disappeared.

'You've gone!' he yelled to the rushing air. 'Gone! The invisible men . . . That's you and Kylie – both gone!' The train was getting away from him. Cursing, he tried to kick more power from the labouring engines, but it was not there.

The train pulled away ahead, and he gave up trying. When he switched off the inertial beam, the wire rope was empty. Bodenland and Clift had indeed gone. He wound in the rope.

Larry's feelings were mixed. He had had no opportunity to say anything about the quarrel with Kylie. His father had been too absorbed in this venture. His arrival had been taken for granted, to Larry's mixed relief and disappointment. He had found Old John surrounded by vehicles and uniformed personnel from Bodenland Enterprises. The students were gone. Now the site of the two graves more resembled an armed camp than a dig.

Only now, as he headed back alone to the camp and another drink did it occur to Larry that perhaps his mother was feeling the same kind of anger with Joe as Kylie felt for him.

'Ah, I'll phone her in the morning, damn her,' he said. He sensed Joe's warmth for Kylie, and dreaded his rebuke.

Directly the beam was off them, the outside world disappeared. They clung to the train roof, and edged themselves carefully through an inspection hatch, to drop down into a small compartment.

Neither Bodenland nor Clift had any notions of what to expect. Such vague anticipations as they held were shaped by the fact that they were boarding what they had casually christened a ghost train.

There was no way in which they could have anticipated the horrific scene in which they found themselves. It defied the imagination – that is, the everyday imagination of waking life: yet it some way resembled a nightmare scene out of the writings of Edgar Allan Poe. Something in some horrible way prepared for.

They had lowered themselves into a claustrophobic little den lined with numbers of iron instruments carefully stowed in cabinets behind glass doors. Separately, scarcely a one would have been recognized for what it was by an innocent eye. Ranked together, they presented a meaning it was impossible to mistake. They were torture instruments – torture instruments of a primitive and brutal kind. Saws, presses, screws and spikes bristled behind their panes of glass, which gave back a melancholy reflection of the subdued light.

Most of the compartment was filled by a heavily scarred wooden table. Pressed against the top of the table by a complex system of bars was a naked man. Instinctively, the two men backed away from this terrifying prisoner.

His limbs were distorted by the pressure of the bars cutting into his flesh. The gag in his mouth was kept in place by a metal rod, against which his yellowed and fanglike teeth had closed.

His whole body colour was that of a drowned man. The limbs –

where not flattened or swollen – were pallid, almost green, his cheeks and lips a livid white. Beyond the imprisoned wrists curled broken and bloody fingers.

His head had been shaved and was scarred, as by a carelessly wielded open razor. A purple line had been drawn round the equator of his head, above his eyebrows.

Bodenland and Clift took a moment to realize that the prisoner was living still. Dull though his eyes were, he made a stir, the fangs in the flattened mouth clicked as if ravenous against their containing bar, the limbs trembled, one oedematous foot twitched.

Clift started to retch.

'Let's get out of here,' he said. 'We should never have come.'

Bodenland would say nothing. They edged round the table. The fish gaze of the victim on the table followed them, eyeballs palely bulging.

Twisting an unfamiliar type of latch on the door, they moved out into a corridor. Bodenland covered his eyes and face with a broad hand.

'I'm sorry I got you into this, Bernie.'

The corridor was even darker than the torture compartment. No sense of movement reached them, though every now and again the corridor swerved, challenging their balance, as if it was rounding a bend at speed.

No windows gave to the outside world. At intervals, glass doors led to compartments set on the left of the corridor as they progressed.

Inside these compartments, dark and dreary, sat immobile figures, their bodies half embedded in moulded seating. The whole ambience was of something antique and underground, such as a long forgotten Egyptian tomb, in which the spirits of the dead were confined. The mouldings of the heavy wooden doors, the elaborate panelling, all suggested another age: yet the tenebrous scene was interspersed by tiny glitters at every doorway, where a panel of indicators kept up a code of information.

The men moved down the corridor, and came to an unoccupied compartment, into which they hastened with some relief. They shut themselves in, but could find no lock for the door.

'We didn't come armed,' Bodenland said, with regret.

When their eyes had adjusted to the dimness, they saw plush mummy-shaped recesses in which to sit. Once seated, they had in front of them a control touch-panel – electronic but clearly of another age, and made from a material fatty in appearance. Bodenland started to fiddle with the controls.

'Joe – suppose you summon someone . . .'

'We can't just sit around like passengers.'

He began to stab systematically with his middle finger.

A lid shot up like an eyelid on the wall facing them, and a VDU lit. Colours flowed hectically, then a male face snapped into view, a heavy aquiline face that looked as if it had been kept in deep freeze. Seeming to press its nose against the glass screen, it opened its mouth and said, 'Agents of Group 16, prepare to leave for —— Agents of Group 16.'

'Where did he say?' asked Clift.

'Never heard of the place. How come we can't see through this window?' Bodenland ran his hand over a series of pressure plates. The window on his left hand turned transparent. It was barred, but permitted a distorted view of the outside world in tones of grey. With this view, a sense of movement returned; they could see what looked like uncultivated prairie flashing by.

And at the same time, phantasmal figures, looking much attenuated, drifted from the train, to land on a grass mound they were passing.

'There go the agents of Group 16,' commented Bodenland. 'Whoever the hell they are.'

The train then appeared to gather speed again.

More investigation of the control panel brought forth from its socket a small terrestrial globe. A thread-thin trace light revealed what they could only believe was their course, heading north-west. But the continents were subtly changed. Florida had extended itself to enclose the Caribbean. Hudson Bay did not exist. Indications were that the train was now crossing what should have been the waters of Hudson Bay; all that could be seen were forests and undulating savannah lands.

Numerals flashed across the VDU. Clift pointed to them with some excitement. He seemed to have recovered from his shock of fear.

'Read those figures, Joe. They could be calibrated in millions of years. They certainly aren't speeds or latitudes.'

'You think that's where we are – or *when* we are? Not simply moving through distance, but some time before Hudson Bay was formed . . .'

'Before Hudson Bay . . . and when the climate was milder . . . In a forgotten epoch of some early inter-glacial . . . Is it possible?'

Bodenland said, 'So we're travelling on – a time train! Bernard, what wonderful luck!'

Clift looked at him in surprise. 'Luck? Who knows where we're heading? More to the point, who controls the train?'

'We'll have to control the train, Bernie, old sport, that's who.'

As he rose, a last group of zombie figures could be seen to leave the train, drifting like gossamer with outspread arms, to land safely among tall grasses and fade into night.

At which point, the train swerved suddenly eastwards, throwing Bodenland back into his seat. The thread indicator also turned eastwards, maintaining latitude. The electronic numbers on the screen diminished rapidly.

'Well, that's something,' Clift said. 'We're coming nearer to the present instead of disappearing into the far past. If our theory's right.'

'Let's move. There must be a cab or similar up front.'

As they rose, the aquiline face returned to their VDU.

'Enemy agents boarded the train at Point 656. They must be terminated. Believed only two in number. They must be terminated. Group 3 also organize death-strikes against their nearest and dearest.'

'Hell,' said Clift. 'You heard that. We have to get off this thing.'

'You want to jump? I don't like this either, but our best hope is to try and hijack the train, if that's possible.'

'And get ourselves killed?'

'Let's hope that won't be necessary. Come on.'

He opened the door. The corridor appeared empty. After only a moment's hesitation, he eased himself through the door. Clift followed.

Larry had bought himself a big white cowboy hat in Enterprise, after taking a few drinks in a bar. He drove in his hired car back to the Old John site.

The change in three days, since the news of the strange grave had been given to the world, was dramatic. There was no way in which the Bodenland security force could keep everyone away. As Bodenland had predicted, the world had descended on this quiet south-west corner of Utah. The media were there in force, not only from all over the States but from Europe, Japan, the Soviet Union, and elsewhere. Hustlers, hucksters, and plain sightseers rubbed shoulders. Big mobile diners had rolled in from St George and Cedar City, bars had been set up. It was like a gold rush. Chunks of plain rock were selling fast.

Temporary TV studios had been established, comfort stations, mobile chapels, all kinds of refreshment stalls and marquees. The actual digs were barricaded off and protected by state police.

Larry made his way through the thick traffic, yelling cheerfully to other drivers out of the window as he went. Once he had parked, he fought his way through to the trailer he had hired.

There Kylie was awaiting him, her fair hair capturing the sun.

She threw her arms round him. 'I've been here all day. Where've you been?'

'I was drowning my sorrows in Enterprise.'

'You got a girl there?'

'I ain't that enterprising. Listen, Kylie, forgive me, sweet. I shouldn't have walked out on you as I did, and I've felt bad ever since.'

She was happy to hear him say it.

'We were both too hasty.' She stuck her tongue in his mouth.

'Come on the bed,' he said. 'I'll show you how I feel about you. I've had three days here, kicking my heels and feeling bad.'

'Bed later. I got in this morning with Mina. I flew to Dallas and she flew me here in her plane.'

'That old Bandierante? It'll fall to pieces in the air one day.'

'Come and see her. She's worried crazy about Joe. You'll have to tell her – and me – exactly where he is and what happened.'

He made a face, but was in no mood to argue.

The Bandierante was the plane from which Mina Legrand liked to sky-dive. She had left it on an improvised landing field on the edge of the desert, five miles away. She had paid over the odds for a rusty old Chevvy in order to be mobile. They caught up with her in a mess of traffic on what had become Old John's main street. Mina had climbed out of the car to argue more effectively with a cop trying to control the flow of automobiles, one of which had, perhaps inevitably, broken down.

She turned an angry face to her son.

'And where have you been? What have you done with your father?'

He explained how Joe and Clift had disappeared in the inertial beam. There was every reason to believe that by that means they had managed to get aboard the train.

'And where are they now?' she snapped.

'Look, lady,' said the cop, 'now it's you holding up the traffic flow.'

'Oh, shut up!' she snapped.

'I been here three days, Mom. Three days and three nights I waited in the desert by our flags,' Larry said. 'No sign of anything.'

'You're as big an idiot as your father.'

'Gee, thanks, Mom. I'm not responsible. You're responsible – you made the news announcement.'

'When have you ever been responsible! What you think, Kylie?'

Ever tactful, Kylie advised her mother-in-law to take things easy, shower, and maybe do a little sky-diving, since she had her plane. Joe could surely look after himself.

'Well, I'm just worried crazy,' Mina said. 'You'll find me in the Moonlite Motel in Enterprise if you want me. I can't face going back to Dallas.'

'Dallas, anywhere, lady,' said the cop. 'Just get moving, will you, please?'

Mina jumped into the driving seat and accelerated sharply, bashing another automobile as she left.

The cop glared at Larry as if he was responsible.

'Thanks for your help, officer,' Larry said.

CHAPTER V

The institution stood in parkland, remote from the town. It was four storeys tall, all its windows were barred, and many white-washed in addition. With its acres of slate roof, it presented a flinty and unyielding appearance.

If its front facade had a Piranesi-like grandeur, the rear of the building was meagre, cluttered with laundries, boiler-rooms, stores for coal and clinker, and a concrete exercise yard, like a prison. In contrast was the ruin of an old abbey standing some way behind the asylum. Only the ivy-clad tower, the greater part of a chapel, with apse and nave open to the winds, remained. The once grand structure had been destroyed by cannonfire at the time of Cromwell. Nowadays, its crypt was occasionally used by the institution as a mortuary, particularly when – as not infrequently happened – an epidemic swept through the wards and cells.

At this time of year, in late summer, the ivy on the ruin was in flower, to be visited by bees, wasps and flies in great profusion. Inside the institution, where the prevailing colour was not green but white and grey, there was but one visitor, a ginger man stylishly dressed, with hat and cane.

This visitor followed Doctor Kindness down a long corridor, the chilly atmosphere and echoing flagstones of which had been expressly designed to emphasize the unyielding nature of the visible world. Dr Kindness smoked, and his visitor followed the smoke trail humbly.

'It's good of you to pay us a second visit,' said Dr Kindness, in a way that suggested he meant the opposite of what he said. 'Have you a special medical interest in the subject of venereal disease?'

'Er – faith, no, sir. It's just that I happen to be in the theatrical profession and am at present engaged in writing a novel, for which I need a little first-hand information. On the unhappy subject of . . . venereal disease . . .'

'You've come to the right place.'

'I hope so indeed.' He shivered.

The doctor wore his habitual blood-stained coat. His visitor wore hairy green tweeds with a cloak flung over them, and tugged nervously at his beard as they proceeded.

During their progress, a lanky woman in a torn nightshirt rushed out from a door on their right hand. Her grey staring eyes were almost as wide as her open mouth, and she uttered a faint stuttering bird cry as she made what appeared to be a bid for freedom.

Freedom was as strictly forbidden as alcohol or fornication in this institution. Two husky young attendants ran after her, seized hold of her by her arms and emaciated body, and dragged her backwards, still stuttering, into the ward from which she had escaped. The door slammed.

By way of comment, Dr Kindness waved his meerschaum in the general direction of the ceiling, then thrust it back into his mouth and gripped it firmly between his teeth, as if minded to give a bite or two elsewhere.

They came to the end of the corridor. Dr Kindness halted in a military way.

'You're sure you want to go through with this?'

'If it's not a trouble. "Some put their trust in chariots . . ." I'll put my trust in my luck.' He gave as pleasant a smile as could be. 'The luck of the Irish.'

'Please yourself, certainly.'

He stood to one side, and gestured to the ginger man to approach the cell door at which they had arrived.

A foggy glass spyhole the size of a saucer punctuated the heavy panels of the door. The ginger man applied his eye to it and stared inside. 'For now we see through a glass darkly,' he muttered.

The cell was bare and of some dimension, perhaps because it occupied the corner of the building. Such light as it enjoyed came from a small window high in an outer wall. The only furnishing of the cell was a mattress rumpled in a corner like a discarded sack.

A madman sat on the mattress, combing his hair thoughtfully with his nails. He was dressed in a calico shirt, trousers, and braces.

'This fellow is Renfield by name. He has been with us a while. Murdered his baby son and was caught trying to eat its head. Quite a pleasant fellow in some moods. Some education, I suppose. Came down in the world.'

The ginger man removed his eye from the glass to observe the doctor.

'Syphilitic?'

'Tertiary stage. Dangerous if roused.'

The ginger man looked down at his shiny boots.

'Forgive me if I ask you this, doctor, but I was wondering if you felt pity for your patients?'

'Pity?' asked the doctor with some surprise, turning the word over in his mind. 'Pity? No. None. They have brought their punishment on themselves. That's obvious enough, isn't it?'

'Well, now, you say "punishment".' A tug at the beard. 'But suppose a man was genuinely fond of a woman and did not know she had any disease. And suppose he was in error just once, giving in to his passions . . .'

'Ah, that's the crux of the matter,' said the doctor, removing his pipe to give a ferocious smile. 'It's giving in to the passions that's at the root of the trouble, isn't it? Let me in turn pose you a question, sir. Do you not believe in Hellfire?'

The ginger man looked down at his boots again, and shook his head.

'I don't know. That's the truth. I don't know. I certainly *fear* Hellfire.'

'Ah. Most of the inhabitants of this mental institution know the answer well enough. Now, if you're ready to go in – '

The doctor produced a key, turned it in the lock, slid back two large bolts and gestured to the ginger man to enter.

The madman, Renfield, sat motionless on his mattress, giving no sign. A fly, buzzing aimlessly about like a troubled thought, made the only noise. It spiralled down and landed on a stain on the mattress.

The ginger man took up a position with his back against the wall by the door. After the door closed behind him, he sank slowly down, to balance on his heels. He smiled and nodded at Renfield, but said nothing. The madman said nothing and rolled his eyes. The fly rose up and buzzed against the square of window, through which clear sky could be glimpsed.

'It's a lovely day outside,' said the ginger man. 'How would you like a walk? I could come with you. We'd talk.'

After a long silence, Renfield spoke in a husky voice. 'Nobody asked you, kind sir, she said. I'm all alone. There once was ten of us. Now no one knows the where or when of us.'

'It must be very lonely.'

The madman roused himself, though still without observing his visitor direct.

'I'm not alone. Don't think it. There's someone always watching.' He raised a finger to the level of his head, pointing to the ceiling. Then, as if catching sight of an alien piece of food, he reached forward quickly and bit the finger till it bled.

The ginger man continued to squat and observe.

'Do you realize what you're suffering from?' he asked softly. 'The name of the ailment, I mean.'

Renfield did not reply. He began to hum. 'Ummm. Ummm.'

The bluebottle spiralled down again. He had his eye on it all the way. Directly it landed on his shirt, he grabbed it and thrust it into his mouth.

Only then did he turn and smile at his visitor.

'Life,' he said conversationally. 'You can never get enough of it, don't you find that, kind sir? It's eat or be eaten, ain't it?'

As they advanced along the corridor, it became darker and smokier. Both Bodenland and Clift decided that their chances of survival were thin.

The dimensions of the corridor altered in an alarming fashion. The way ahead twisted like a serpent. It appeared as if infinity stretched before them – grand and in some way elevating, but nevertheless formidable.

And then suddenly at infinity the air curdled, like milk in a thunderstorm, and an atmospheric whirlpool formed. From that whirlpool emerged a terrifying figure, beating its way towards them.

'Joe!' yelled Clift. The sound echoed in their ears.

A great leathery winged thing, its vulpine head plumed like something from a Grünewald painting, thrashed towards them. It had an infinite distance to go, yet it moved infinitely fast, despite the wounded slow-motion flap of its pinions. Its eyes were dead. Its mouth blazed. It had scaly claws, like the feet of a giant bird. In those claws it carried a brutal blunt gun of matt metal. It raised this weapon and began firing at the two men as it progressed.

Phantasm though it seemed, the monster's bullets were real enough. They came in a hail, screaming as they came. Bodenland dived into a shallow guard's blister to one side of the passage. Clift fell, kicking, with a bullet in his shoulder.

Hardly conscious of what he was doing, Bodenland scrambled halfway to his feet. The blister contained a wheel, perhaps a brake-wheel, and little else – except an emergency glass panel with something inside he could not see for shadow. A hatchet? Swinging his fist, he shattered the glass. Inside the case was nothing more formidable than a torch.

In those few seconds when death was coming upon him, Bodenland's brain seized on its final chance to function. From its remotest recesses, from below a conscious level, it threw out a picture – clear and chill as if forged of stained glass in some ancient chapel.

The picture was of a great artery stretching through the body of planetary time. And up that artery to the throat of it where Bodenland crouched swam terrible creatures from the very bowels of existence, ravenous, desperate for a new chance at life, stinking from the oblivion that had shrouded them.

This avenging thing on its pterodactyl wings – so the picture depicted it – was no less mythological than real. Alien, yet immediately recognizable. One of its talons screeched against wood as it slowed in the corridor to turn on him. So monstrous was it, it seemed the train could never contain the wooden beat of its wings. They burned with dark flame.

And it keened on a shrill note, cornering its prey.

Clouds of murk rolled with it as it swerved upon the blister. Bodenland had dropped to one knee. With his left arm raised protectively above his head, he held the torch in his right hand and shone it at the predator.

The beam of light pierced through murk to the red eyes of it. Abruptly, its singing note hit a higher pitch, out of control. It began to smoulder inside wreaths of biscuit wrack. It recoiled. The leather wings, fluttering, banged woodenly against imprisoning walls. The immense veined claws opened convulsively, letting drop its weapon, as faster went the beat of the wings.

Just for a moment, in place of horror, a vision of a fair and beautiful woman appeared – dancing naked, shrieking and writhing as if in sexual abandon – couched on gaudy bolsters. Then – dissolved, faded, gone, leaving only the monster again, to sink smoking to the floor.

A great wing came up, fluttered, then broke, to join the crumble of ashes which strewed themselves like a shawl along the train corridor.

Bodenland switched off the torch. He remained for a moment where he was.

Another moment and he forced himself to rise. He placed a hand over his heart as if to still its beating. Then he went to see his friend.

Clift had dragged himself into a sitting position. Blood oozed from under his shirt.

'You know what it was?' he gasped.

'I know it was most ancient and most foul. Are you okay, Bernard? It seemed to dissolve into a – well, into a woman. An illusion. The perspective and everything. Terrifying.'

'It was a lamia, a female monster. There's a literature about it.'

'Fuck the literature. We've got to get out of this corridor. Brace yourself, buddy.'

As he dragged Clift to his feet, the latter gasped with pain. But he stood, clutching his shoulder and managing a grin.

'God knows where we've got ourselves, Joe. Maybe I shouldn't take the name of the Lord in vain . . .'

'We've got ourselves into more than we bargained for,' Bodenland said. Half-supporting his friend, he started down the corridor, which had now regained normal dimensions.

Moving steadily, they made it to the cab in the front of the train.

Bodenland propped Clift in the corridor, and made a sudden rush in, where a man in overalls worked in the greyness.

He sat on a swing stool, handling controls. He was shadowy, his age impossible to tell. And when Bodenland jumped in on him, he swivelled round to exclaim in astonishment, 'No, no – you're the man with the bomb!'

This stopped Bodenland in his tracks.

But the driver raised his hands, saying, 'I'm still afraid – don't attack me.' He made no attempt to escape.

'You know who I am?' Bodenland asked. But even as he spoke, he heard the sound of someone approaching down the corridor. Dreading another monstrous apparition, he snatched the driver's gun, which the man made no attempt to draw.

As he did so, Clift looked into the cab.

'Joe, dozens of them. Second line of defence. The gun, quick!'

He grabbed the gun from Bodenland and at once began firing down the corridor. Bullets from the enemy spanged by. There were cries in the corridor, then silence.

Bodenland went out to see. Whoever the assailants were, they had disappeared. Two dead lay a few yards away. Clift lifted himself on one elbow.

Kneeling down by him, Bodenland asked him gently how it was.

'The grave – ' Clift said, then could speak no more. Bodenland caught him as his head fell, and hauled him up into a more comfortable position. Blood welled from the palaeontologist's chest. He looked up into Bodenland's face, smiled, and then his face contorted into a rictus of pain. He struggled furiously as if about to get up, and then dropped back, lifeless. Bodenland looked down at him, speechless. Tears burst from his eyes and splattered Clift's cheeks.

He dragged his dead friend into the driver's cabin.

'I'll get you bastards if it's the last thing I do,' he said.

CHAPTER VI

The little Brazilian-made plane, a vintage Bandierante, winged high above the eroded Utah landscape, and released its passenger from a rear door, like some hypothetical bird of prey launching an embryo into the wind.

Mina floated away from the plane, arms outstretched, knees bent, riding the invisible steed of air, controlling it with her pubic bone, steering it with the muscles of her thighs. This was her element, here was her power, to soar above the mist-stricken earth.

No sell-by dates existed up here. It was neutral territory. Even her snug green cover-all she chose to regard as her skin, making her an alien visitor to the planet.

And if there were aliens on other planets in the galaxy, let them stride their own skies. Let them not discover Earth; let them not, she thought, disclose themselves to the peoples of Earth. It was difficult enough to find meaning to life in a non-religious age; how much more difficult if you knew that there were a myriad other planets choked with living creatures like humans, facing the same day-to-day struggles to survive – to what end?

The image came back to her, as it often did when she steered her way through the atmosphere by her pubis, of herself as a small straggly girl, oldest daughter of a poor family in Montana, when she had gone out at her mother's behest to hang freshly washed sheets on a clothes line. The wind blew, the sheets tugged, she struggled. At a sudden freak gust, a still wet sheet curled itself round her thin body and carried her, half-sailing, down the hill. Was that when she had first yearned for an accidental freedom?

For her, the zing of high altitude could wash away even memories, including more recent ones. The hollowness she felt encroaching on her life could not reach her here. Nor could thoughts of how things were with Joe.

Now the sheets of the wind were snug about her again. She knew no harm. But Utah was coming closer, tan, intricate, neat. There was no putting off for long the demands of gravity, the human condition.

As he laid Clift's body down in the cab, Bodenland felt utterly detached from his own body. The conscious part of him floated, as a goldfish might watch from its bowl the activities in the room to which it was confined, while his body went about setting his dead friend out straight, pretending that comfort was a matter of reverent attention to a corpse. The death, the apparition which had attacked him, not to mention the horrific novelty of the vehicle in which he was trapped, had brought about the detachment. The shock of fear had temporarily disembodied him.

He straightened in slow motion and turned towards the driver. The driver stood tense against a wall, hands by his side. His riven face, grey and dusty, trained itself watchfully on Bodenland. He made no attempt to attack or escape. Only his eyes were other than passive. *Molten zinc*, thought Bodenland, a part of his mind reverting to laboratory experiments.

'You know me? You recognize me?'

'No, no.' The man spoke without moving his head. His jaw hung open after uttering the two syllables, revealing long canines in his upper jaw and a white-coated tongue.

'You said I was the man with the bomb. What did you mean by that?'

'No, nothing. Please . . .'

Bodenland saw his right hand come up and grab the man by his throat. When the hand began to shake him, the driver almost rattled. He put his hands up feebly to protect himself. His skin appeared made of some frowsty old material, as if he were a cunningly stitched rag doll.

'Tell me what this train is we're on. Where are we? Who are you?'

When he let go of the creature, the driver sank to his knees. Bodenland had done him more damage than he intended.

'The Undead – the Undead, sir. I won't harm you . . .'

'You sure won't.' He bent over the driver, catching a whiff of his carrion breath as the man panted. 'What are you talking about?'

'I was an airline pilot in life,' said the driver faintly. 'You will become like us. You are travelling on the train of the Undead and our Lord will get you sure enough.'

'We'll see about that. Get up and stop this train.' He wrenched the man to his feet, thrusting him towards the controls. The driver merely stood wretchedly, head bowed.

'Stop the train. Move, you rat. Where are we? *When* are we?'

The driver moved. He pulled open his tunic, ripped his shirt in two with sudden strength and turned to face Bodenland.

He pointed to his naked chest. So extreme was its emaciation that rib bones stuck out white as if frosted from their cyanotic covering of skin.

'Look,' he said. 'Get an eyeful of this, you fool. Do you see any heartbeat here?'

In disgust, Bodenland stared at the dead barrel of chest. He caught the man a blow across the side of his face, sending him reeling.

'You can still feel pain? Fear? You're human in that, at least. I will break open your chest and wrench out that dead heart unless you stop this train.'

Holding his face, the driver said, 'The next programmed stop is in what you call 2599 AD, the Silent Empire. I'm unable to alter the programming.'

'You slowed in Utah.'

'Utah? Oh, Point 656, yes . . . That's a sacred site to the Undead. We had to let agents off the train.'

'Okay, you can let me off there. That's where I need to be. How many time trains are there?'

'One, sir, just this one.'

'Don't lie to me.'

'There's just one.' He spoke without emphasis, leaning lightly against the control panels, holding his face, letting the faint illumination turn his body into a seemingly abandoned carcass. 'This train shuttles back and forth on scheduled time routes. All

programmed. I'm not much more than a supervisor. It's not lik
piloting an airliner.'

'There must be other trains.'

'There's just the one. To ride time quanta you gobble vast
amounts of energy. Solar energy. Very extravagant. Reverse relativism. Trains can't be seen by the outside world – not unless we're
slowing to let agents off.'

The driver smiled showing the canines more fully. No humour
warmed the smile. The lips simply peeled back in memory of
something that might once have amused.

'The sheep asks the wolf what it does . . .'

The detached part of Bodenland watched as he attacked the driver
and fell to the floor with him. In their struggle, they kicked Clift's
body, making it roll on to its face.

And Bodenland was demanding who had invented this cursed
train. The answer was that, as far as the driver knew, the train was
the invention of the Fleet Ones.

'The Fleet Ones, sir, are the Undead – the vampires – who rule
the world in its last days. This is their train, sir, you've ventured
on.'

'I'm borrowing it, and it's going to get me back home to 1999.
You're going to show me how.'

The detached viewpoint saw how the creature made to bite
Bodenland in the upper arm. But Bodenland took a firm grip of his
throat and dragged him to the controls.

'Start explaining,' he said.

'Ummmm ummmm ummmmmmmm. Moon and Mercury, Moon
and Mercury, Romance and Remedy . . . Ummmm.'

The madman Renfield rocked himself in a tight bundle and
hummed as if he were full of bluebottles.

The ginger man squatted stolidly in his corner by the cell door,
watching, nodding in time with the humming, alert to the fact
that Renfield was rocking himself closer. Above them, against the
square of window showing blue sky, a spider hung by a thread,
well out of the madman's way.

'Ummmm, you're one of us, kind sir, she said, one of the fallen.
May I ask, do you believe in God?'

Having uttered the Almighty's name, he fell into fits of laughter, as if the hallowed syllable contained all the world's mirth.

'Yes, I do believe,' said the ginger man. 'I think.'

'Then you believe in Hell and Hellfire.'

'That I certainly do believe in.' He smiled wanly, and again the madman laughed.

'I'm God. I'm God and I'm Hellfire. And where are these items contained? Why – in blood!' He pronounced the word in savage relish, striking his skull violently as he did so. 'In blood, in the head, the head, kind sir, the napper. The napper's full of blood. There are things that peer in here of a night . . . things which cry and mew for the blood. You see, it's scientific, kind sir, she said, because . . . because you need the blood to drown out the thought. You don't need thought when you're dead, or silver bells or cock-hole smells or pretty maids all in a row, because when you're dead you can do anything. You can do anything, kind sir, I assure you. The dead travel fast. Ummmm.'

The ginger man sighed, as if in at least partial agreement with these crazed sentiments.

'Can you tell me what these things look like which peer in at you at night?'

Renfield had rocked himself very close now.

He put a dirty finger against the wall, as if pointing to something unseen by others.

'There, you see? They come from dead planets, kind sir. From the Moon and Mercury.' He ground his teeth so violently that his intention might have been to eat his own face. 'Ummmm, they're a disease, wrapped in a plague, masquerading as life. Life – yes, that's it, life ummmm. And we shall all become like them, us, by and by, if God so wills.'

On the last word, he sprang at the ginger man, screaming, 'Give me a kiss of life, kind sir, she said!'

But the ginger man was alert, leaped to his feet in time, fended off the madman with his silver-headed cane.

'Down, dog. Back to your kennel, beast, Caliban, or I'll call in the warden and have you beaten black and blue.'

The madman retreated only a step and stood there raging or pretending rage, showing teeth, brandishing claws. When the ginger man caught him lightly over the shoulders with his cane, he desisted and crawled on hands and knees back to the far corner, by his mattress. There he sat, looking upward, innocent as a child, one finger stuck deep into his ear.

A rhombus of sunlight crept down the wall, making for the floor as noon approached, slow as time and as steady. The ginger man remained by the door, unmoving, in a less threatening attitude, though he still had his stick ready.

Almost as stealthily as the sunbeam, the madman began to roll on the stone floor. His movements became more exaggerated as he tried to tie himself into knots, groaning at the same time.

The normally genial face of Renfield's visitor was grave with compassion.

'Can I help in any way?' he asked.

'Why do you seek my company in this fortress?'

'It's a fair question, but I cannot deliver you the answer. Tell me if I can help you.'

Renfield stared at him from an upside-down viewpoint.

'Bring me boxes of spiders to eat. Spiders and sparrows. I need the blood. It's life, kind sir. Life's paper. Seven old newspapers make a week in Fleet Street. The Fleet Ones can eat up a week with their little fingers, this little finger on the right.'

He started to scratch a figure with sharp teeth on the wall as he spoke.

'Talk sense, man,' said the ginger man, sternly.

'There soon will come a scientist who will say even stranger things about space and time. We can't comprehend infinity, yet it's in our heads.'

'Together with the blood?' He laughed impatiently, turning to the door to be released.

As he rapped on the panel, the madman said, 'Yes, yes, with the blood, with a whole stream of blood. You'll see. It's in your eyes, kind sir, she said. A stream of blood stretching beyond the grave, beyond the gravy.'

He made a jump for the distant spider as the door slammed, leaving him alone.

The ginger man walked with the doctor in the bloodstained coat. The doctor accompanied him gravely to the door of the asylum, where a carriage waited. As the ginger man passed over a guinea, he said, with an attempt at casual small talk, 'So I suppose there's no cure for dementia praecox, is that so?'

The doctor pulled a serious face, tilted his head to one side, gazed up into the air, and uttered an epigram.

'I fear a night-time on Venus means a lifetime on Mercury.'

'You wretches live in the dark,' Joe Bodenland said. 'Don't you hate your own sickness.'

He expected no answer, speaking abstractedly as he finger-tipped the keyboard in the train's chief control panel. The driver stood by, silent, offering no reply. The information had been squeezed out of him, like paste from a half-empty tube.

'If you've told me right, we should be back in 1999 any minute.'

Bodenland watched the scattering figures in a globe-screen, peering through the half-dark.

As the time train slowed, the grey light lifted to something brighter. The driver screamed with fear, in his first real display of emotion.

'Save me – I'm photophobic. We're all photophobic. It would be the end – '

'Wouldn't that be a relief? Get under that tarpaulin.'

Even as he indicated the tarpaulin stacked on a rack with fire-fighting equipment, the driver pulled it out and crawled under it, to lie quaking on the floor near Clift's body.

The light flickered, strengthened. The train jerked to a halt. Generators died. Silence closed in.

Rain pattered softly against the train body. It fell slowly, vertically, filtering down from the canopy of foliage overhead. All round the train stood mighty boles of trees, strong as stone columns.

'What . . .' Pulling down a handle, Bodenland opened the sliding door and stared out.

They had materialized in a swamp. Dark water lay ahead, bubbles rising slowly to its surface. Everywhere was green. The air hummed with winged life like sequins. He stared out in amazement, admiration mingling with his puzzlement.

The rain was no more than a drip, steady, confidential. The moist warm air comforted him. He stood looking out, breathing slowly, returning to his old self.

As he remained there, taking in the mighty forest, he became aware of the breath going in and out at his nostrils. The barrel of his chest was not unmoving; it worked at its own regular speed, drawing the air down into his lungs. This reflex action, which would continue all his days, was a part of the biological pleasure of being alive.

A snake that might have been an anaconda unwound itself from a branch and slid away into the ferns. Still he stared. It looked like the Louisiana swamps, and yet – a dragonfly with a five foot wingspan came dashing at him, its body armoured in iridiscent green. He dashed it away from his face. No, this wasn't Louisiana.

Gathering his wits, he turned back into the cab. The train gave a lurch sideways.

The LCD co-ordinates had ceased to spin. Bodenland stared at them incredulously, and then checked other readings. They had materialized some 270 million years before his present, in the Carboniferous Age.

The cab rocked under his feet and tilted a few more degrees to one side. Black water lapped over the lip of the door up to his feet. Staring out, he saw that the weight of the train was bearing it rapidly down into the swamp.

'You,' he said, shaking the supine driver under his cover. 'I'm going to pitch you out into that swamp unless you tell me fast how we get out of here.'

'It's the secret over-ride. I forgot to tell you about it – I'll help you all I can, since you were merciful to me . . .'

'Okay, you remember now. What do we do?'

The dark water came washing in as the driver said, 'The over-ride is designed to stop unauthorized persons meddling with the time-controls. Only the space controls responded to your instructions, the rest went into reverse.'

While he was speaking, the train tilted again and Clift's body slid towards the door.

'What do we do, apart from drown?'

'The train is programmed for its next stop and I can't change that. Best thing is to complete that journey, after which the programme's finished and the over-ride cuts out. So you just switch on, cancelling the previous co-ordinates you punched in.'

The water was pouring in now, splashing the men. A bejewelled fly swung in and orbited Bodenland's head.

'Where's this pre-programmed journey taking us?'

With an extra surge of water, a warty shape rose from the swamp, steadying itself with a clumsy foot at the doorway. A flat amphibian head looked at them. Two toad eyes stared, as if without sight. A wide mouth cracked open. A goitre in the yellow throat throbbed. The head darted forward as Bodenland instinctively jumped back, clinging to a support.

The lipless frog mouth fastened on Clift's body. With a leisurely movement, the amphibian withdrew, bearing its meal with it down into the waters of the swamp. It disappeared from view and the black surface closed over it.

Bodenland slammed the sliding door shut and staggered to the keyboard. He punched on the Start pressurepads, heard the roar of generators, which died as the engine seemed to lift.

The outer world with its majestic colonnades of trees blurred, whited out, faded to grey and down the colour spectrum, until zero-light of time quanta came in. The driver sat up in the dirty water swilling about him and peered haggard-faced from his tarpaulin.

Drained by the excitements of the last few hours, appalled by the loss of his friend, Bodenland watched the numerals juggling with themselves in the oily wells of the display panel. He came to with a start, realizing he might fall asleep.

Making an effort, he got down a length of thin cable and secured the driver with it, before locking the door to the corridor.

He stood over his captive, who began to plead for mercy.

'You don't have a great store of courage.'

'I don't need courage. You need the courage. I know you have ten thousand adversaries against you.'

Bodenland looked down, contemplating kicking the creature, before overcoming the impulse.

'Where are we programmed for?' he asked, thinking that almost anywhere was preferable to the Carboniferous.

'We have to visit Transylvania,' said the driver. 'But the programme is set only as far as London, in year 1896, where we let off a powerful female agent.'

'Oh yes? And what's she up to?'

'She has business at the home of a man living near London, a man by the name of Bram Stoker.'

CHAPTER VII

She went over to look at the little glass panel of the air-condition-ing unit. It was functioning perfectly. Nevertheless, the motel suite felt arid to her, lifeless, airless, after her flight through the sky.

Mina Legrand's rooms were on the second floor. Her years in Europe prompted her to open a window and let in a breeze, sanit-ized by the nearby desert. Enterprise sprawled out there, the park and sign of the Moonlite Motel, and, beyond them, the highway, on which were strung one-storey buildings, a store or two, and a used car lot, with a Mexican food joint marking the edge of town. Pick-ups drove by, their occupants preparing to squeeze what they could from the evening. Already dusk was settling in.

Turning from the window, she shucked off her green cover-alls and her underwear and stepped into the shower.

Despite the pleasure of the hot water coursing over her body, gloom settled on her. She hated to be alone. She hated solitude more of late. And perhaps Joe had been absent more of late. Now she would be seeing less of Larry, too. And there were the deaths in the back of her mind, never to disappear. Sky-diving was different; paradoxically, it took her away from loneliness.

She was at that age when wretchedness seeped very easily through the cracks in existence. A friend had suggested she should consult a psychoanalyst. That was not what she wanted. What she wanted was more from Joe, to whom she felt she had given so much.

She discovered she was singing in the shower.

'Well, what did I do wrong
To make you stay away so long?'

The song had selected itself. To hell with it. She cut it off. Joe
had let her down. What she really needed was a passionate affair.
Fairly passionate. Men were so tiresome in so many ways. In her
experience, they all complained. Except Joe, and that showed his
lack of communication . . .

With similar non-productive thoughts, she climbed from the
shower and stood under the infra-red lamp.

Later, in a towelling robe, she made herself a margarita out of
the mini-bar, sat down, and began to write a letter to Joe on the
Moonlite Motel notepaper. 'Joe you bastard – ' she began. She sat
there, thinking back down the years.

Finishing the drink, she got a second and began to ring around.

She phoned home, got her own voice on the answerphone, slammed off. Rang through to Bodenland Enterprises, spoke to Waldgrave. No one had heard from Joe. Rang Larry's number. No answer.
In boredom, she rang her sister Carrie in Paris, France.

'We're in bed, for God's sake. What do you want?' came Carrie's
shrill voice, a voice remembered from childhood.

Mina explained.

'Joe always was crazy,' Carrie said. 'Junk him like I told you,
Minnie. Take my advice. He's worth his weight in alimony. This
is one more suicidal episode you can do without.'

Hearing from her sister the very words she had just been formulat-
ing herself, Mina fell into a rage.

'I guess I know Joe light years better than you, Carrie, and suicidal he is not. Brave, yes, suicidal, no. He just believes he leads an
enchanted life and nothing can harm him.'

'Try divorce and see what that does.'

'He was unwanted and rejected as a small kid. He needs me and
I'm not prepared to do the dirty on him now. His whole career is
dedicated to the pursuit of power and adventure and notoriety –
well, it's an antidote to the early misery he went through. I understand that.'

The distant voice said, 'Sounds like you have been talking to his
shrink.'

Mina looked up, momentarily distracted by something fluttering at the window. It was late for a bird. The dark was closing swiftly in.

'His new shrink is real good. Joe is basically a depressive, like many famous men in history, Goethe, Luther, Tolstoy, Winston Churchill – I forget who else. He has enormous vitality, and he fends off a basic melancholia with constant activity. I have to live with it, he classifies out as a depressive.'

'Sounds like you should chuck Joe and marry the shrink. A real smart talker.'

Mina thought of Carrie's empty-headed woman-chasing husband, Adolphe. She decided to make no comment on that score.

'One thing Joe has which I have, and I like. A little fantasy-world of mixed omnipotence and powerlessness which is very hard to crack, even for a smart shrink. I have the same component, God help me.'

'For Pete's sake, Mina, Adolphe says all American woman are the same. They believe – '

'Oh, God, sorry, Carrie, I've got a bat in my room. I can't take bats.'

She put the phone down and stood up, suddenly aware of how dark it was in the room. The Moonlite sign flashed outside in puce neon. And the bat hovered inside the window.

Something unnatural in its movements transfixed her. She stood there unmoving as the pallid outline of a man formed in the dusky air. The bat was gone and, in its place, a suave-looking man with black hair brushed back from his forehead, standing immaculate in evening dress.

Fear brushed her, to be followed by a kind of puzzlement. 'Did I live this moment before? Didn't I see it in a movie? A dream . . .?'

She inhaled deeply, irrationally feeling a wave of kinship with this man, although he breathed no word.

Unconsciously, she had allowed her robe to fall open, revealing her nudity. The stranger's eyes were fixed upon her – not upon her body, her breasts, the dark bush of hair on her sexual regions, but on her throat.

Could there really be some new thrill, something unheard of and incredible, such as Joe seeks? If so . . . if so, lead me to it.

This was a different hedonism from the aerial plunge from the womb of the speeding plane.

'Hi,' she said.

He smiled, revealing good strong white teeth with emphatic canines.

'Like a drink?' she asked. 'I was just getting stewed all on my ownsome.'

'Thanks, no,' he said, advancing. 'Not alcohol. You have something more precious than alcohol.'

'I always knew it,' Mina said.

Lack of motion. Stillness. Silence.

'More goddamned trees,' Bodenland exclaimed.

At least there was no swamp this time.

He stepped over the driver, tied and cowering under his tarpaulin, and slid open the door. After a moment, he stepped down on solid earth. Somewhere a bird sang and fell silent.

These were not the trees of the Carboniferous. They were small, hazel and birch and elder, graceful, widely spaced, with the occasional oak and sycamore towering above them. Light filtered through to him almost horizontally, despite heavy green foliage on every side. He guessed it was late summer. 1896, near London, England, according to the driver and the co-ordinates. What was going on in England, 1896? Then he thought, *Oh yes, Queen Victoria* . . .

Well, the old Queen had a pretty little wood here. It seemed to represent all the normal things the time train, with its hideous freight, was not. He savoured the clear air with its scent of living things. He listened to the buzz of a bee and was pleased.

Seen from outside, the train when stationary was small, almost inconsiderable, no longer than a railroad boxcar. Its outside was studded and patterned with metal reinforcers; nothing was to be seen of the windows he knew existed inside. Somehow, the whole thing expanded in the relativism of the time quanta and contracted when stationary. He stared at it with admiration and curiosity, saying to himself, 'I'm going to get this box of tricks back to my own time and figure it all out. There's power beyond the dreams of avarice here.'

As he stood there in a reverie, it seemed to him that a shrouded female figure drifted like a leaf from the train and disappeared. Immediately, the wood seemed a less friendly place, darker too.

He shivered. Strange anxieties passed through his mind. The isolation in which, through his own reckless actions, he found himself, closed in about him. Although he had always believed himself to have a firm grip on sanity – was not the world of science sanity's loftiest bastion? – the nightmare events on the train caused him to wonder. Had that creature pinned to the torture-bench been merely a disordered phase of sadistic imagining?

He forced himself to get back into the train and to search it.

It had contracted like a concertina. In no way was it possible to enter any of the compartments, now squeezed shut like closed eyes. He listened for crying but heard nothing. The very stillness was a substance, lowering to the spirits.

'Shit,' he said, and stared out into the wood. They had come millions of years to be in this place and he strained his ears as if to listen to the sound of centuries. 'We'd better find out where the hell we are,' he said aloud. 'And I need to eat. Not one bite did I have through the whole Cretaceous . . .'

He shook himself into action.

Hoisting the driver up by his armpit, he said, 'You're coming too, buddy, I may need you.'

The smothered voice said, 'You will be damned forever for this.'

'Damned? You mean like doomed to eternal punishment? I don't believe that crap. I don't really believe in you either, so move your arse along.'

He helped the creature out of the train.

A path wound uphill, fringed with fern. Beyond, on either side, grew rhododendrons, their dark foliage hastening the approach of night. He peered ahead, alert, full of wonder and excitement. The trees were thinning. A moth fluttered by on a powdery wing and lost itself on the trunk of a birch. A brick-built house showed some way ahead. As he looked a dim light lit in one of its windows, like an eye opening.

Tugging his captive, he emerged from the copse on to the lawn. The lawn was sprinkled with daisies already closing. It led steeply up to the house, which crowned a ridge of higher ground. A row

82

of pines towered behind the roofs and chimneys of the house, which lay at ease on its eminence, overlooking a large ornamental pool, a gazebo and pleasant flowerbeds past which Bodenland now made his way.

A young gardener in waistcoat and shirtsleeves saw him coming, dropped his hoe in astonishment, and ran round the other side of the house. Bodenland halted to give his reluctant captive a pull.

On a terrace which ran the length of the house stood classical statues. The sun was setting, casting long fingers of shadow which reached towards Bodenland. As he paused, another light was lit inside the house.

Uncertain for once, he made towards the back door and took hold of the knocker.

The ginger man was watching and listening again, an opera glass in his right hand. With his left hand, he stroked his short red beard appreciatively, as if it had been a cat.

He stood in the wings of the Lyceum Theatre with the delectable Ellen Terry in costume by his side, gazing on to the lighted stage.

On the stage, before a packed auditorium, Henry Irving was playing the role of Mephistopheles in a performance of *Faust*. Dressed in black, with a black goatee beard and whitened face, the celebrated actor spread out his cloak like a giant bat's wings. Back and forth he stalked, menacing a somewhat aghast Faust, and chanting his lines:

> So great's his Christian faith, I cannot grasp
> His soul – but I'll afflict his body with
> Lament, and strew him with diverse diseases . . .

Thunderous applause from the audience, all of whom believed in one way or another that they were in some danger of damnation themselves.

When the play was finished, Irving took his bows before the curtain.

As he made his exit into the wings, he passed the ginger man with a triumphant smirk and headed for his dressing room.

Both Irving and the ginger man were smartly attired in evening dress when they finally left the theatre. The ginger man adjusted his top hat at a rakish angle, careful that some curls sizzled over the brim to the left of his head.

The stagedoor keeper fawned on them as they passed his nook.

''Night, Mr Irving. 'Night, Mr Stoker.'

The ginger man pressed a tip into his hand as they passed. Out in the night, haloed by a gas lamp, Irving's carriage awaited.

'The club?' Irving asked.

'I'll join you later,' said the ginger man, on impulse. He turned abruptly down the side alley to the main thoroughfare.

Irving swung himself up into his carriage. 'The Garrick Club,' he told his driver.

In the thoroughfare, bustle was still the order of the day, despite the lateness of the hour. Hansoms and other carriages plied back and forth in the street, while the elegant and the shabby formed a press on the pavements. And in doorways and the entrances to dim side-courts were propped those beings who had no advantages in a hard-hearted world, who had failed or been born in failure, men, women, small children. These shadowy persons, keeping their pasty faces in shadow, begged, or proffered for sale tawdry goods – matches, separate cigarettes, flowers stolen from graves – or simply lounged in their niches, awaiting a change of fortune or perhaps a nob to relieve of his wallet.

The ginger man was alert to all these lost creatures of the shadows, eyeing them with interest as he passed. A thin young woman in an old bonnet came forth from a stairway and said something to him. He tilted her head to the light to study her face. She was no more than fourteen.

'Where are you from, child?'

'Chiswick, sir. Have a feel, sir, for a penny, bless you, just a feel.'

He laughed, contemptuous of the pleasure offered. Nevertheless, he retreated with her into the shadow of the stairs with only a brief backward look. Ignoring the two children who crouched wordless on the lower steps, the girl hitched up her dress and let him get one hand firm behind her back while with the other he rifled her, feeling powerfully into her body.

'You like it, sir? Sixpence a quick knee-trembler?'

'Pah, get back to Chiswick with you, child.'

'My little brothers, sir – they're half dead of starvation.'

'And you've the pox.' He wiped his fingers on her dress, thrust a sixpenny piece into her hand, and marched off, head down in case he was recognized.

Newsboys were shouting. '*Standard*. Three Day Massacre. Read all abart it.' The ginger man pressed on, taking large strides. He shook off a transvestite who accosted him outside a penny gaff.

Only when he turned off down Glasshouse Street did he pause again, outside the Alhambra music hall, from which sounds of revelry issued. Here several better dressed whores stood, chatting together. They broke off when they saw a toff coming, to assume a businesslike pleasantness.

One of them, recognizing the ginger man, came up and took his arm familiarly. Her face was thickly painted, as if for the stage.

'Ooh, where are you off to so fast, this early? Haven't seen you for ages.' She fluttered her eyelashes and breathed cachou at him.

This was a fleshy woman in her late twenties – no frail thing like the girl Stoker had felt earlier. She was confident and brazen, with large breasts, and tall for a street walker. Her clothes, though cheap, were colourful, and bright earrings hung from the fleshy folds of her ears. She faced him head on, grinning impudently, aware with a whore's instinct that she looked common and that he liked it that way.

'What have you been up to, Violet? Behaving yourself?'

'*Course*. You know me. I'm set up better now. Got myself a billet round the corner. How about a bit? What you say? We could send out for a plate of mutton or summat.'

'Are you having your period?' His voice was low and urgent.

She looked at him and winked. 'I ain't forgotten you likes the sight of blood. Come on, you're in luck. It's a quid, mind you.'

He pressed up against her. 'You're a mercenary bitch, Violet, that you are,' he said jocularly, allowing the lilt of brogue into his speech. 'And here's me thinking you loved me.'

As she led him down the nearest back street, she said, saucily, 'I'll love what you got, guv.' She slid a hand over the front of his trousers.

He knew she would perform better for the promise of a plate of mutton. London whores were always hungry. Hungry or not, he'd have her first. The beef first, then the mutton.

'Hurry,' he said, snappishly. 'Where's this bleeding billet of yours?'

The knocker was a heavy iron affair with a fox head on it. It descended thunderously on the back door.

'Eighteen ninety-six,' said Bodenland aloud, to keep his spirits up. 'Queen Victoria on the throne . . . I'm in a dream. Well now – food and rest with any luck, and then it's back to poor Mina. Can't even phone her from here.' He laughed at the thought.

The house loomed over him, unwelcoming at close quarters to a stranger's approach.

In the sturdy door was set a panel of bull's eye glass. He became aware that someone was studying him through it. Despite the gathering dusk, he saw it was a woman. Came the sound of bolts being drawn back. A lighted candle appeared, with a hand holding the candlestick and, somewhere above it, a plump and unfriendly woman's face.

'Who are you, pray?' He was surprised to see that as she spoke she held a small crucifix in front of her. Giving her a guarded explanation, he asked for Mr Stoker and inquired if it would be possible to beg a night's lodging.

'Where are you from? Who's that you have with you?'

'Madam, I am from the United States of America. This is a criminal in my charge. I hope to return him to the USA. Perhaps we might lock him in one of your outhouses for the night.'

'You actors – all the same! You will not learn to leave poor Mr Stoker alone. He's not well. He has the doctor to him. Still, I know he would not turn you away. He has a kind heart, like all Irish people. Come in.'

They entered the rear hall, going through into a scullery which contained a large stone sink and a pump with a long curving iron handle. A maid in a mob cap was inefficiently stringing flowers up at the window. The woman, evidently Mrs Stoker, ordered her to get the key to the tool shed.

A male servant was summoned. He and the maid accompanied Bodenland out to a tool shed standing at the end of the terrace to the rear of the house. The male servant had lit a storm lantern. It was already very dark.

The driver was whimpering, and refused food and drink.

'I shall be gone from here by morning,' he said. 'And you'll have departed from human life.'

'Sleep well,' Bodenland said, and slammed the door.

When the back door was closed and the bolts drawn across, the little raw-handed maid picked up her flowers again.

'What are you doing?' Bodenland asked curiously.

'It's the garlic, sir. Against the critters of the night.'

'Is that an English custom?'

'It's Mr Stoker's custom, sir. You can ask the cook, Maria.'

Mrs Stoker returned. She was a solid middle-aged lady, impressively dressed in a gown of grey taffeta which reached to the floor. She had over it a small white frilled apron, which she now removed. Her hair was brown, streaked with grey, neatly parcelled into a bun at the back of her head. She was now smiling, all defensiveness gone from her manner.

'You'll have to excuse me, Mr Borderland.'

'It's Bodenland, ma'am. Originally of German extraction. German and English on my mother's side.'

'Mr Bodenland, pardon my hesitation in letting you in. Life is a little difficult at present. Do please come through and meet my husband. We should be happy if you would consent to stay overnight.'

As he uttered his thanks, she led him along a corridor to the front of the house. In a low voice she said, 'My poor Bram works so hard for Mr Henry Irving – he's his stage manager, you know, and much else besides. At present he's also writing a novel, which seems to depress his health. Not a happy subject. I'm not at all sure gloomy novels should be encouraged. My dear father would never allow us girls – I have four sisters, sir – to read novels, except for those of Mrs Craik. Poor Bram is quite low, and believes strange forces beseige the house.'

'How unfortunate.'

'Indeed. Happily, I inherited my father's strong nerves, bless him. He was a hero of the Crimea, don't you know.'

She showed Bodenland into a large drawing room. His first impression was of a room in a museum, greatly over-furnished with pictures – mainly of a theatrical nature – on the walls, plants

in pots on precarious stands, ornate mahogany furniture, antima-
cassars on over-stuffed chair-backs, books in rows, and heavy
drapes at windows. Numerous trophies lay about on side tables. It
seemed impossible to find a way through to a thick-set man busy
adjusting garlic flowers over the far window.

Better acquaintance with the room enabled Bodenland to appreciate its graceful proportions, its ample space, and its general air of
being a comfortable if over-loaded place in which to spend leisure
hours.

The man at the window turned, observed that it was almost
dark, and came forward smiling, plucking at his ginger beard as if
to hide a certain shyness, and put out his hand.

'Welcome, sir, welcome indeed. I'm Abraham Stoker, known to
friend and foe alike as Bram, as in bramble bush. And this is my
wife, Florence Stoker, whom you have already met, I see.'

'I've had that pleasure, thank you. My name is Joseph Bodenland,
known as Joe, as in jovial.'

'Ah, then you're a son of Jupiter – an auspicious star. Are you a
military man, Mr Bodenland?'

'No, by no means.'

'Both Florence and I are of military stock. That's why I ask. My
grandfather was Thomas Thorley of the 43rd Regiment. Fought
against Bonaparte, later took part in the conquest of Burma, 1824.
Florence's father, Lt Colonel James Balcombe, served in India and
the Crimea, with great distinction.'

'I see. Came through all right?'

Florence Stoker asked, to cover her guest's awkwardness, 'Is your
family prosperous? You Americans are so expert at business, so I
hear.'

'I know your compatriot, Mark Twain,' Stoker said, turning to
give an anxious tug at the curtains. 'Most amusing chap, I thought.
I tried to get him to write us a play.'

Genially taking Bodenland's elbow, he led him through a maze
of tables on which various keepsake albums and other mementoes
lay, towards a cheerful log fire.

Over the fireplace hung a large oil, its eroticism not entirely out
of keeping with the luxury of the rest of the room. A naked pink
woman sat fondling or being fondled by a cupid. Another figure

was offering her a honeycomb in one hand and holding a scorpion's sting in the other. The figure of Time in the background was preparing to draw a curtain over the amorous scene. Bodenland regarded it with some amazement.

'Like it? ' Stoker asked, catching his glance. 'Nice piece of classical art. Bronzino's celebrated "Venus, Cupid, Folly, and Time". An all-embracing title.' He laughed and shot a glance at his wife. 'It's a copy, of course, but a good one.'

When they had settled down in armchairs, and Mrs Stoker had rung the bell and summoned the maidservant, and the maidservant had adjusted the curtains to everyone's satisfaction – 'That girl has no feeling for the symmetry of *folds*,' said Mrs Stoker, severely – they lapsed into general conversation over a glass of sherry.

At length Bodenland said, 'Of course, I know your name best as author of *Dracula*.'

'Is that a play you would be speaking of?'

'A book, Mr Stoker, a novel. It's world-famous where I come from.' After a long pause, he added, 'All about vampires.'

'What do you know about vampires, may I ask?' Looking suspicious.

'A fair deal, I guess. I'm given to believe I have locked one in your garden shed.'

At this news, Stoker pulled again at his beard. He went further and pulled at his lip. Then he got up rapidly up from his chair, wended his way across the room, and peered through the curtains, muttering.

He came back, still muttering, frowning, his broad and rugged face all a-twitch.

'I shall have to see about that later. Anyhow, you're mistaken, allow me to say. It does so happen that I am writing a novel at present all about vampires, which I intend to entitle "*The Undead*" . . . Hm, all the same, I like the starkness of that as a title: "*Dracula*" . . . Hm.'

'He works too hard, Mr Bodenland,' said Mrs Stoker. 'He's never home till after midnight. He's back today only because tomorrow is a special day for Mr Irving.'

She rose. 'Excuse me, sir. I must confer with Maria, our cook.

89

Dinner, at which we hope you will join us, will be ready at eight o'clock prompt.'

When the two men were alone, Stoker leaned forward to poke the fire, saying as he stared into the flames, 'Tell me, do you have any theories regarding vampires?'

'I assume they are products of the imagination. As I rather assume you are too.'

Stoker then gave him a hard look, holding out a glowing poker.

'Is that some sort of joke? I don't find it funny.'

'I'm sorry, I apologize. I meant that to be sitting here with you, a famous man, seems to me like wild fantasy.'

'Wilde? Oscar Wilde? He was once engaged to my Florence. Well, he's got himself into a real pickle now, to be sure . . . Let me ask you this. Men are made to feel guilty about the sexual side of their natures. Do you believe that sex and guilt and disease and vampires are all related?'

'I never thought of it.'

'I have reason to think of it, good reason.' These words, spoken with a morbid emphasis, were accompanied by equally emphatic wags of the poker, as though the ginger man was conducting the last bars of a symphony. 'Let me ask you a riddle. What does the following refer to, if not to planets: "A night on Venus means a lifetime on Mercury"?'

Despite the obvious good nature of his host, Bodenland was beginning to wish he had looked for a simple inn for the night.

'I don't know what you're talking about.'

'Syphilis, Mr Bodenland, that's what I'm talking about. VD – the soldier's term for it. Syphilis, the vampire of our amorous natures, that's what. "Thou hast proven and visited mine heart in the night season." That's what the psalm says, and a ghastly saying it is . . . Now, perhaps you'd care to have a wash before we go in to dinner.'

This was a moment to be grasped, Bodenland saw, in which to explain how he had arrived, and how his country was more distant than even the imaginative Stoker might guess.

Stoker listened with many a tug of the beard, many a dubious shake of the head, many a 'Well, I'll be jiggered!' many a 'Saints in heaven!' At the end, he remained stubbornly unbelieving, saying he had endured many a far-fetched thing acted out on the stage,

90

but nothing like this. He knew of occupants of the wards of the nearby lunatic asylum who believed themselves to be Napoleon, but even there none imagined they came from a future when their mothers were as yet unborn.

'I come from an age where anything can be believed,' Bodenland said, half-way between amusement and irritation. 'You evidently live in an age where nothing can be. Even when you have proof.'

'What proof do you offer?'

'Tomorrow, you shall see the vehicle by which I arrived here.'

Nodding rather grimly, Stoker rose from his armchair. 'Very well then, until that time I shall be forced to play the mistrustful host, who doubts the veracity of his guest, and regards his account as merely a tall story told before dinner.'

'I hope, sir, that over the soup you may reflect that my sincerity in this matter is some token of my honesty.'

'. . . And by the cheese course I'll have swallowed your every word!' With an explosion of laughter, Stoker led his guest from the room. His good humour went some way towards smoothing Bodenland's ruffled feelings. It was only later that he came to realize how human beings came equipped with a defence mechanism which saved them accepting immediately anything which lay beyond their everyday experience; for so it was to prove in his own case.

The dining room was decorated in scarlet, and less elaborately furnished than the drawing room. They sat down to a laden table under a large chandelier, the heat from which Bodenland found uncomfortable. Round the walls of the room, mahogany dressers, sideboards and carving tables gleamed, reflecting the light muzzily.

Everything looked prosperous, safe, snug, repressive. Stoker looked through the curtains and muttered in Bodenland's ear, 'I'm worried about that hostage you put in my shed.' In other respects, he played the role of genial host.

Clutching a decanter of red wine, he ushered his doctor in to the proceedings. Dr Abraham van Helsing was a fussy little man with a sharp bright face and cold bony hands. He wore a velvet suit and smelt of cologne. He laughed and smiled rather much when introduced to Bodenland.

91

'And you should be resting, Bram, my friend,' he said, wagging a finger at Stoker. 'You should not be embarking on a heavy meal, you understand?'

Bodenland thought there might be some truth in this observation, reluctantly though it was received by his host. Before them were laid a huge cold home-cured ham, a leg of mutton, ptarmigan, and a grand brawn jelly, which trembled slightly in its eagerness to be eaten. A little tablemaid circulated with a tureen of chicken and celery soup.

'It's the full moon tonight,' announced Stoker, tucking his linen napkin under his chin. 'The lunatics will be restless.' Turning to Bodenland, he added by way of explanation, 'The lunatic asylum is next door to us – quite a way through the trees, I'm happy to say. Used to be a priory, in the days before Oliver Cromwell. It's quite a pretty place, as such places go. I thought I saw someone or something out on the terrace, by the way, but we won't go into that. Mustn't spoil our appetites.'

'You're like my father – nothing spoils your appetite,' said Florence Stoker, affectionately, smiling at her husband.

'I'm big and tough and Irish – and can't help it.'

'Nor can you ever take a holiday,' added van Helsing. 'You're too dedicated to work.'

'And to Henry Irving,' said Mrs Stoker.

Stoker winked good humouredly over his soup spoon at Bodenland.

'Well, it was Henry's Mephistopheles gave me the notion for my Count Dracula. I'm sure I shall have a hit, if I can ever get the damned book finished.'

'When do you hope to finish?'

Ignoring the question and lowering his voice, Stoker said, 'It may be because I'm writing this novel that the house is surrounded by eerie forces. Van Helsing doesn't seem to understand – in fact only the loonies next door seem to understand. Must be going loony myself, shouldn't be surprised.'

'You're sane, we live in a nice scientific world and the soup's delicious,' said van Helsing, soothingly. 'Every single problem in the world will soon be capable of a scientific resolution. Just as the savage populations of the world are being brought into the arms of civilization, so the already civilized world will soon be turned into a utopian meritocracy.'

The conversation became more general. Mrs Stoker spoke of the happily married state of each of her sisters. Servants brought in more food. More wine was poured.

As Bodenland was confronted by huge green blancmanges, plum pies with ornamental pastry crusts, bowls of cream, jellies, and trifles decorated with angelica, Stoker reverted to the subject of asylums, which seemed to prey upon his mind.

'Many of the poor fellows in the asylum suffer great pain. Dementia and its sores are treated with mercury. It's agonizing, I hear. It's a matter of wonder why such suffering should be visited on humanity, Mr Bodenland. Would you care to visit the asylum with me?'

Bodenland shook his head.

'I'm afraid all that interests me is getting home.'

Stoker leaped from his chair with a sudden impulse and went to peer through the window again.

'It's a still night,' he declared, in the voice of one announcing the worst. 'It would be ideal for cricket now, if only it was day.' He laughed.

'Come and eat your trifle, Bram,' his wife said, sharply.

Certainly, the night was still. The full moon shone across the woods that choked the valley, to glitter on the massed slate roofs of the asylum. A bell in the small clock tower crowing the institution chimed midnight, spinning out its notes as if about to run down. The cool light glittered on rows of window panes, some of them barred. It sent a dagger of light plunging down through the narrow orifice of Renfield's skylight to carve a square on the stones close by where he lay on his pallet of straw. During the day he had attacked a male nurse, and was in consequence secured in a strait-jacket, with his arms confined.

He amused himself by alternately grinding his teeth and humming like a fly trapped in a jar.

'Ummmm. Ummmm. Ummmmmmmmm.'

His eyes bulged in their sockets. He stared unblinkingly at the white square on the floor nearby. As minute by minute it slid nearer to him, it changed from rancid milk to pale pink, and then to a heartier colour until it appeared to him as a square pan of blood.

He stretched his neck to drink from it. At that moment, the whole cell was flooded with moonlight, and a great joyous humming sounded as if a thousand hornets were loose.

Crying in triumph, Renfield sprang upward, arms above his head in the attitude of a diver. He was naked as the day he was born. He burst through the skylight and landed gracefully on the icy slopes of the asylum roof, which stretched away into the distance like ski slopes.

As he danced there, a great winged thing circled overhead. He called and whistled to it with a flutelike noise, playing imagined pan pipes. Lower it came, red eyes fixed upon the naked dancer.

'I know your secrets, little lord, I know. Come down, come down. I know how human blood makes you sick – it makes you sick, yet on it you have to depend, depend, deep end. Jump in the deep end, little lord . . .'

It circled still, the beat of its wings vibrating in the air, scattering moonlight.

'Yes, you come from a time when all blood was cool and thick and slow and lizard-flavoured. That time of the great things, I know. They've gone and you have only us, little lord. So take my blood at last, slopping in its jug of flesh just for you – and I shall poison you. Ummmm. Ummmm.'

He pirouetted on the rooftree and the great winged thing swooped and took him. It enfolded him lasciviously, biting into him, into the creamy flesh like toffee-apple, as it wrapped him about with the great dry wings, biting, drinking deep with a love more terrible than fury – and then with disgust, as it flew off, vomiting back the blood into his empty face.

Renfield sniggered in his sleep. His eyes remained open and staring like glass buttons on a child's toy, but he dreamed his terrible dream.

Red curtains closed over the eye of the moon as van Helsing pulled them together after a brief scrutiny of the terrace. The Stokers were leaving the dining room as they had entered, arm-in-arm.

Bodenland was following when the doctor tugged at his sleeve and drew him back.

'Permit me to ask – is there a pretty little Mrs Bodenland back home where you come from?' He looked down at his nervous hands as he spoke, as if ashamed to pry.

'I'm married, yes, doctor. That's one good reason why I am bent on getting home just as soon as I can.'

He made to move on, but the doctor still detained him.

'You understand why I enquire. I am in charge of Mr Stoker's health. The conjugal arrangements are not good in this household. As a result – as a direct result – ' He paused, and then went on in a whisper. 'Mr Stoker has unfortunately contracted a vile disease from what the French call a *fille de joie*, a woman of the night. You understand?'

Not being fond of the doctor's fussy little ways, Bodenland made no reply, but stood solid to hear him out.

Van Helsing tapped his temple.

'His brain's affected. Or he believes it affected. Which, in the case of brains, amounts to much the same thing. He believes – well, he believes that mankind has become the host for a species of parasite beings, vampires, who come from somewhere distant. I speak scientifically, you understand. From one of the planets, let's say. He regards this as the secret of the universe, which of course he is about to reveal. You can never trust a man who thinks he knows the secret of the universe.'

'I'm not so certain about that, doctor. The secret of the universe – provided there is such a thing – is open to enquiry by anyone, by any interested party, just like the secrets of the personality.'

'What secrets of the personality?'

'Like why you rub one index finger against the other when you talk . . . No, wait, doctor, I'm sorry. That was impertinent.'

The doctor had turned on his heel in vexation, but Bodenland charmed him back, to ask what treatment he was giving Stoker for his disease.

'I treat his sores with mercury ointment. It is painful but efficacious.'

Bodenland scratched his chin.

'You won't have heard of penicillin yet awhile, but I could get a hold of some. And in a very few years Salvarsan will become available.'

'You're making no sense to me, sir.'

'You know, *Salvarsan*? Let's see, would you have heard of Dr Ehrlich's "magic bullets" at this date?'

'Oh.' The doctor gave a chuckle and nodded. 'I begin to get your drift. Bram Stoker makes his own magic bullets – to kill off his imaginary vampires, you understand.'

At that juncture, Stoker himself put his head round the dining-room door.

'There you are. I thought you must have gone into the study. Mr Bodenland, perhaps you'd care to inspect my workshop? I generally spend an hour pottering in there after dinner.'

As they went down a side-passage, Stoker put an arm round Bodenland's shoulders.

'You don't want to pay too much attention to what van Helsing says. He's a good doctor but – ' He put a finger to his temple, in unconscious imitation of van Helsing's gesture of a few minutes past. 'In some respects he has a screw loose.'

On the door before them was a notice saying, *Workshop, Keep Out.*

'My private den,' said Stoker, proudly. As they entered, he drew from an inner pocket a leather case containing large cigars, and proffered it to Bodenland. The latter shook his head vigorously.

He studied Stoker as the ginger man went through the rigmarole of lighting his cigar. The head was large and well-shaped, the ginger hair without grey in it, though a bald patch showed to the rear of the skull. The features were good, although the skin, particularly where it showed above the collar, was coarse and mottled.

Feeling the eyes of his visitor on him, Stoker looked sideways through the smoke.

'Here's my den. I must be always doing. I can't abide nothing to do.'

'I too.'

'Life's too short.'

'Agreed. I am always ambitious to make something of myself.'

'That's it – cut a dash at the least, I say. Needs courage.'

'Courage, yes, I suppose so. Do you reckon yourself courageous?'

Stoker thought, squeezing his eyes closed. 'Let's put it this way. I'm a terrible coward who's done a lot of brave things. I like cricket. You Yanks don't play cricket?'

'No. Business and invention – that's my line. And a lot of other things. There are so many possibilities in the world.'

'Do you long to be a hero?'

The question was unexpected. 'It's a strange thing to ask. My shrink certainly thinks I long to be a hero . . . One thing, I have a need for desolate places.'

Giving him a sceptical look, Stoker said, 'Mm, there's nothing more desolate than the stage of the Lyceum on a slow Monday night . . . What does your family think of you?'

The interrogation would have been irritating on other lips. But there was something in Stoker's manner, sly, teasing, yet sympathetic, to which Bodenland responded warmly, so that he answered with frankness.

'If they can't love me they have got to respect me.'

'I wish to be a hero to others, since I'll never be one to myself.' He clapped Bodenland on the shoulder. 'We have temperamental affinities. I knew it the moment I set eyes on you, even if you come from the end of next century, as you claim. Now have a butcher's hook at this, as the Cockneys say.'

The workshop was crammed with objects – a man's version of the ladies' drawing room. Curved cricket bats, old smooth-bore fowling-pieces, a mounted skeleton of a rat, stuffed animals, model steam engines, masks, theatrical prints, framed items of women's underwear, a chart of the planets, and a neat array of tools, disposed on shelves above a small lathe. These Bodenland took in slowly as Stoker, full of enthusiasm, began to talk again, lighting a gas mantle as he did so.

'My Christian belief is that there are dark forces ranged against civilization. As the story of the past unfolds, we see there were millions of years when the Earth was – shall I say unpoliced? Anything could roam at large, the most monstrous things. It's only in these last two thousand years, since Jesus Christ, that mankind has been able to take over in an active role, keeping the monsters at bay.' Foreseeing an interruption, he added, 'They may be actual monsters, or they may materialize from the human brain. Only piety can confront them. We have to war with them continuously. If Jesus were alive today, do you know what I believe he would be?'

'Er – the Pope?'

'No, no, nothing like that. A Bengal Lancer.'

After a moment's silence, Bodenland indicated the work-bench. 'What are you making here?'

'Ah, I wanted to show you this. This is part of my fight against the forces of night. Sometimes I wish I could turn the gun on myself. I know there's evil in me – I'm aware of it. I must ask you about your relationships with the fair sex, so called, some time.'

He held out for examination a cigar-box full of carefully wrought silver bullets, each decorated with a Celtic motif running about the sign of the Cross. He exhibited them with evident pride in their workmanship. An ill feeling overcame Bodenland. The sickly light of the gas mantle seemed to flare yellow and mauve as the room swayed.

'These are my own manufacture,' said Stoker and then, catching sight of Bodenland's face, 'What's the matter, old boy? Cigar smoke getting to you?'

Recovering his voice, Bodenland spoke. 'Mr Stoker, you may be right about dark forces ranged against civilization, and I may have proof of it. What do you make of this?'

He brought forth from his jacket pocket the article he had retrieved from Clift's ancient grave in the Escalante Desert. In his palm lay a silver bullet, its nose dented, but otherwise identical to the ones in Stoker's cigar-box.

'This was found,' he said, unsteadily, 'in a grave certified scientifically to be sixty-five point five million years old.'

Stoker was less impressed than Bodenland had expected. He stroked his beard and puffed at his cigar before saying, 'There's not that much time in the universe, my friend. Sixty-five point five million years? I have to say I think you're talking nonsense. Lord Kelvin's calculations have shown that, according to rigid mathematics, the entire limit of the time the sun is able to emit heat is not greater than twenty-five million years. Admittedly the computations are not exact.'

'You speak of rigid mathematics. More flexible mathematical

systems have been developed, giving us much new understanding of the universe. What once seemed certain has become less certain, more open to subjective interpretation.'

'That doesn't sound like progress to me.'

Bodenland considered deeply before speaking again. He then summoned tact to his argument. 'The remarkable progress of science in your lifetime will be built on by succeeding generations, sir. I should remind you of what you undoubtedly know, that only three generations before yours, at the end of the eighteenth century, claims that the solar system was more than a mere six thousand years old were met with scorn.

'Time has been expanding ever since. In light of later perspectives, sixty-five million years is no great length of time. We understand better than Lord Kelvin the source of the energies that power the sun.'

'Possibly you Americans might be mistaken? Do you allow that?'

With a short laugh, Bodenland said, 'Well, to some extent, certainly. This bullet, for instance, proves how little we have really been able to piece together the evolution of various forms of life in the distant past.'

Turning the bullet over in his palm, Stoker said, 'I would swear it is one of my manufacture, of course. You'd better tell me about this extraordinary grave, and I'll strive to take you at your word.'

'It's pretty astonishing – though no more so than that I should be here talking to you.'

He ran through the details of Clift's discovery, explaining how the dating of the skeleton was arrived at.

During this account, Stoker remained impassive, listening and smoking. Only when Bodenland began to describe the coffin in which the skeleton was buried did he become excited. He demanded to know what the sign on the coffin looked like, and thrust a carpenter's pencil and paper into Bodenland's hand. Bodenland drew the two fangs with the wings above them.

'That's it! That's it, sure enough – Lord Dracula's sign,' said Stoker in triumph. He seized Bodenland's hand and shook it. 'You're a man after my own heart, so you are. At last someone who believes, who has proof! Listen, this house has drawn evil to it, and you brought more evil with this feller in my tool shed, but

99

we can fight it together. We must fight it together. We'll be heroes, the heroes we dreamed of – '

'You're a great man, Mr Stoker, but this battle's not for me. I don't belong here. I have to get back home. Though I certainly invite you to see the vehicle I use, parked down in your woodlands.'

'Listen, stay another day.' He grabbed Bodenland's arm lest he escape at that very minute, and breathed smoke like an Irish dragon. 'Just one more day, because tomorrow's a special one. Come on, we'll join that old fool van Helsing and have a glass or two of port and talk filth – if the wife's not about. Tomorrow, that great actor whom I serve as manager, Henry Irving, bless his cotton socks, is to receive a knighthood from Her Majesty Queen Victoria at Windsor Palace. It's the first time any actor has been so honoured. Now what do you think of that? Come along too – it'll do your republican Yankee heart good to witness such a deed. After that you can high-tail it back to Utah or wherever you want. What do you say?'

Bodenland could not help being affected by the enthusiasm of the man.

'Very well. It's a deal.'

'Excellent, excellent. Let's go and toast ourselves in some port. And I want to hear more about your adventures.'

CHAPTER VIII

Lethargy was a deep snow drift, chill yet at the same time warm, comforting, inviting you down into even more luxurious depths of helplessness, down, to a place before birth, after death.

Mina saw her own death like the snow drift. When she opened her eyes, there were long muslin curtains billowing in the draught from the window. She was too weak to rise. She saw the curtains as her life – the gauzy life that was to be, after the consummation of death.

Dreamily, she recalled remote times, remembered the name of Joe, her Joe. But now there was another lover, the dream lover of legend. He was come again, he was in the chamber, advancing towards the bed.

She tried to rouse herself, to lift her head from the pillow. Her hair spilled about her but there was no strength in her neck. He was bending over her, elegant, powerful, distilling an aroma she drew in through her nostrils like a narcotic. When he opened his red mouth, she found strength enough to open her legs, but his attention was on the flesh of her throat. She felt the lechery of it, breathed deeper, swooned, fidgeted with desire to experience again the bite of those fangs, that sweet evacuation of life.

He in his black garb was something different. The insanity of his fantasy spilled over through their linked alleyways of blood. She saw, felt, lived the secret world of the Undead to which she would soon belong.

It was being transferred, his bridal gift to her –

The great sweltering herbivorous beast dashed from the river bank, sounding alarm to other hadrosaurs grazing nearby. It was a mottled green in coloration, yellow and white on the tender belly, with an elaborate headcomb. It balanced its ponderous body on graceful legs, and gave its melancholy call as it ran. Mina heard herself scream, saw her companions scatter, and white birds sail up in alarm from the Cretaceous marshes.

She took evasive action, running from side to side, yet still hearing the hot breath of pursuit.

'What's your name, and where's Joe gone?'

'You must forget Joe. You now have an immortal lover.'

Indeed, she heard his footsteps close. Thud thud thud. Screaming, she ran into a gingko grove, thinking to evade the heavier predator that way. Behind her, too near her tail, ·the wretched sound of branches being snapped like teeth breaking from a bottom jaw.

'Where did you come from? Tell me who you are, so I can know you.'

'Beyond your imagining lies the ancient burial site in a once-green land. It was destroyed. Remote ancestors there have been disturbed in their rest.'

'What's this to me? Why can I not breathe?'

'The Living have desecrated those graves, causing a crisis among us, the Undead. You might say a religious crisis.'

She heard the ghost of something too desiccated to call a laugh. It came again, from the sky. It brought a new alarm. For she had left the carnivore behind. She had been driven from the family. Now there was a new threat. As a shadow fell over her, she looked up, craning her neck, her throat. A pteranodon was swooping down upon her, wings closed to speed its dive.

'Why don't you take me? Why delay so long? Will I be immortal in your embrace?'

'You will be immortal in my embrace.'

'It's all I ever dream of . . .'

And as she looked up at those fangs, she fell and sprawled among ferns and it unfolded its spectacular wings –

And with the last of her strength she threw back the bedclothes to expose herself utterly –

And it closed its jaws about her neck –

And as his mouth tasted her flesh and the current flowed –

And as she fought with death –
And Mina began to writhe and moan and come at last –
Through –

'Yes, Mr Bodenland, that was when we were staying with the duke.
And later we were so proud, because the Prince of Wales came
backstage and shook Bram's hand.'

'It was during the run of *The Corsican Brothers*.'

'Edward. HRH. He's such a dear – and rather a one for the ladies,
I'm given to understand.' Florence Stoker fanned her cheeks with
her hand at the thought of it.

'HRH works hard, and so I suppose he feels entitled to play hard.
Do you work hard when you're – at home?'

'Some would say, too hard. But a man's work is one way in
which he establishes his identity.'

She sighed. 'Perhaps that is why we poor ladies have no identity
to speak of.' And she shot a glance at her husband.

Bodenland would have preferred to be alone to think over the
implications of the day's events. He listened with only half an ear
to Mrs Stoker's chatter. They were at the port and cigars stage,
sitting about the log fire, under the Bronzino painting, with van
Helsing saying little.

Stoker jumped up suddenly, to give his impression of Henry
Irving as Mephistopheles.

'Oh, this is so wicked! Bram, desist!' cried his wife.

'Please, sir – your heart,' said van Helsing. 'Resume your seat.'

But Stoker would have his way, limping about the hearthrug, at
once sinister and comical, reciting in a high chant unlike his own
voice:

> His faith is great – I cannot touch his soul –
> But what I may afflict his body with
> That will I do, and stew him in disease . . .

He interrupted himself with a fit of coughing.

'What would Henry say? – And him about to be made a knight!'
exclaimed Mrs Stoker.

'I beg you, to bed at once, sir,' said van Helsing. 'It grows late.'

'No, no, I must continue work on my novel. Must, must. More

103

chapters. Lucy Westenra is in mortal peril – ' And he dashed from the room.

A gloomy silence followed. Van Helsing sat at an escritoire, rather ostentatiously writing something, muttering to himself as he did so. Florence Stoker sat tight-lipped, stabbing at her embroidery until, with a sigh, she abandoned it and rose, to stand by the fire staring at the mantelpiece abstractedly.

'It's a fine painting, Mrs Stoker,' Bodenland said, referring to the Bronzino, to break the silence.

'It was originally called "An Allegory",' she said. 'Though an allegory of what I fail to see. Something unpleasant to do with . . . disease, we may suppose.'

The flatness of her tone did not invite response, leaving Bodenland leisure to ponder on the delights and difficulties of family life before, restlessly, she returned to her chair.

Something sought release. She looked at the ceiling to announce, 'Sometimes he's shut in his study for hours.'

'That must make you feel very lonely, Mrs Stoker,' said Bodenland.

She rose, preparing to retreat for the night, and said, grandly, 'I can survive anything, Mr Bodenland, except bad taste.'

A few minutes later, van Helsing put away his writing materials. He picked up a candle in a silver candlestick and offered to show Bodenland up to his room.

'You seem to be rather a romancer, sir,' he remarked, as he led the way upstairs. 'Your presence clearly disturbs Mr Stoker.'

'What if the man's soul is being destroyed?'

'Ha ha, I think I may claim to be a man of science. This is 1896, after all, and the "soul" has been pretty well disproved. Men get on famously without souls. We turn left at the top of the stairs.'

'Well, suppose it was possible to travel through time, to the years ahead, to obtain medicine for Stoker's condition?'

Another dry laugh. 'You are a romancer, indeed. Just along here. Most facts of science are known by this date. Winged flight may become possible in a couple of centuries, but travel through space or time -- quite impossible. Quite impossible. I'll stake my reputation on it. Here we are. I'll leave you the candle. Let's just see all's well, and the windows properly fastened.'

Bodenland entered the dark bedroom first, conscious of the fatigue brought on by the events of the last many hours.

The bedroom was warm. A small gas fire burned in the grate. He lit the gas mantle over the mantelpiece from his candle, thinking incredulously as he did so, I'm lighting a real gas mantle . . .

A woman's taste was in evidence. There were frills round the curtains and round the wash-stand. Over the bed was a pokerwork text in a wooden Oxford frame: Thou Shalt Not be Afraid for Any Terror by Night. *Psalm XCI.*

While he was taking in these details, the doctor was checking the window catches and adjusting the chain of garlic across the panes.

On the wall by the door hung a map of the world in Mercator's projection, framed by the flags of the nations, enlivened by pictures of battleships. The British Empire was coloured in red, and encompassed a quarter of the globe.

Pointing to the map, in the glass of which the gas light was reflected, Bodenland asked, 'Would you suppose there was once a time when Hudson Bay didn't exist, doctor?'

Van Helsing looked askance, as if he suspected a trick question.

'Hudson's Bay didn't exist – until it was discovered by an Englishman in the seventeenth century.'

Bidding Bodenland a good night, he left the room, and closed the door quietly behind him.

Slowly removing his jacket, Bodenland tried to take in his present situation. He found the room, large though it was, oppressive. Oil paintings of Highland cattle in ornate gilt frames occupied much of the wall space. On the bedside table stood a carafe of drinking water and a black-bound New Testament. He sat on the bed to remove his shoes, and then lay back, hands linked under his head. He began to think of Mina and of his pretty new daughter-in-law, Kylie. But would he ever be able to control the time train and get back to them?

His eyes closed.

Without any seeming discontinuity, the processes in his mind continued, leading him to leave the house he was in and descend some steps. The steps were outside, leading down a rank hillside fringed by tall cypresses; then they curved, broken and dangerous, into a crypt. The air became moist and heavy. He searched for somewhere to put down a burdensome parcel he was carrying. The underground room seemed enormous. A stained glass window let in a pattern of moonlight which hung like a curtain in the waxy atmosphere.

'No problem so far,' he or someone else said, as he seated himself in a chair.

Three maidens in diaphanous robes stood in the moonlight. They beckoned. All were beautiful. The middle one was the most beautiful. The coloured glass threw warm gules on her fair breast.

It was this middle creature who advanced on Bodenland, drawing aside her white robe as she came. Her smile was remote, her gaze unfixed.

He knew her and called her name, 'Kylie! Come to me.'

He saw – with shut eyes but acute mental vision – the pale and loving woman who had so recently become his daughter-in-law. For those beautiful features, those soft limbs, that sensuous body with its delectable secrets, lust filled Joe's body.

As he opened his arms to her, she bent eagerly towards him, letting the long dress fall away. He caught her scent, like a forgotten dream.

Now her arms were almost round his neck. He felt them intensely, was filled with rapture, when a pistol shot rang out.

Kylie was gone. The stony structure of the crypt faded.

He was back on the bed, his arms tingling with cramp behind his head. The long-horned cattle stared at him from the walls of the room.

He sat up, sick, cold. Had he heard a real shot?

Rising, he padded over to the window and drew aside a curtain a little way.

Two moons shone over the haunting nineteenth-century landscape, one in a clear night sky, the other its sister, its reflection, in the ornamental pool. The gazebo was a ghostly thing, its Chinese chimes not stirring. On the terrace, the statues stood in their dramatic attitudes, casting their shadows towards the facade of the old house.

Among the statues was a human figure. It was Stoker, his ginger coloration made snowy by the moon.

Breaking the chain of garlic flowers, Bodenland opened the window and leaned out.

'What's the matter? I thought I heard a shot.'

Stoker looked up, his features made brutal in the diffused glow.

'Keep your voice down. You aren't going to be too bucked with this, Bodenland. I've had to perform a soldierly duty. As I was turning in I heard a bit of thumping, armed myself, and came out here to see what the devil was going on.'

'The driver . . .'

'That's it – your driver. He emerged through the door. Like a ghost. One of the Undead, my boy! I put a silver bullet through him in self-defence. It's the only thing that stops his kind.'

'I'll come down.'

The window next to Bodenland's was thrown open and van Helsing thrust his head out into the night air. He was wearing a night cap.

'Now we're in trouble – real trouble, you understand? What are you going to do with the body? You'll be charged with murder.'

'I'll come down, Bram,' said Bodenland. It was the first time he had used his host's Christian name.

'Better stay where you are. There's another presence out here.'

'What?'

Stoker paused before answering, and glanced about.

'A woman's presence. I'll be in soonest, don't worry. I'll heave this damned corpse back into the shed. We'll worry about it in the morning.'

'Are you frightened?'

'Heroism, Bodenland, what we were talking about. Get to bed, and sweet dreams. And you, doctor.'

Bodenland withdrew his head and closed the window, but stood looking at the silent terrace. When Stoker disappeared, dragging the corpse, he returned to bed. But hope of sleep had been shattered.

Although he admired Stoker's courage, he still could not persuade himself to believe in vampires. His experience told him they existed, his intellect denied it. Of course, that paradox played to the advantage of vampires, if they existed. But they did exist – and somehow below the level of human intellect.

He paced about the room, trying to work it out. The human

intellect originated in the neocortex, the grey matter of the brain. Below lay deeper layers, much older on an evolutionary scale than the neocortex – layers of brain common to other mammals, the limbic brain, primed by instincts such as aggression and sub-mission and sexual response: the very instincts which propelled the processes of life on the planet.

Suppose there was a type of creature which was subject to different processes. A creature like a vampire, without intellect, and therefore almost safe from human molestation. The human species would undoubtedly kill off all vampires, as they had almost killed off wolves, if they only could believe wholeheartedly in the idea. Once you got the idea, vampires were not particularly hard to kill – to exterminate. Were they? The silver bullet. The shaft of light. The religious symbol. The stake through the heart.

He stood and stared abstractedly at the pokerwork legend: Thou Shalt Not be Afraid for Any Terror by Night . . . Nevertheless, the human race was afraid, always had been . . .

Always had been . . .

Vampires – if they existed – he could not resist adding the saving clause – were older than mankind.

How much older? Really millions and millions of years older, as Clift's discovery seemed to prove?

Why were they so feared?

They were a disease.

They brought death. Worse than death, the existence of the Undead. If legend was to be believed.

And they preyed on humankind by activating one of the strongest instincts below the neocortical level, the great archetype of sex.

As a flower attracts by its scent.

His dream . . . The incestuous dream of union with Kylie, dead or alive. Repugnant to his consciousness, evidently delightful to some more primitive layer of sensation . . .

Of a sudden, he connected the dream with the female presence which, if Stoker was to be believed, walked on the terrace below.

As he thought of it, of that shadowy thing he was wise to dread, a wave of desire came over him.

He fought it back. 'The pestilence that walketh in darkness . . .' Was that how the rest of the psalm went?

To calm himself, he measured his strides about the bedroom, trying again to think of the problem scientifically.

Why else were vampires so feared?

Because they were parasitical. Parasites were always feared.

If they long preceded humans on the scale of existence, then they had once preyed on other living things.

What had they been – he caught himself avoiding the word – what had vampires *been* before they became parasitical? Before that dreadful need for blood arose?

Many arthropod bloodsuckers existed – bed bugs, fleas, mosquitoes, ticks, all parasitical on man. As the fossil record proved, those creatures were about in the busy world long before mankind. Even before birds and mammals.

All those little plagues to human life were originally innocent suckers of fruit juice and plant juices. But the taste of blood proved addictive and they had become enslaved by parasitism.

Blood was a dangerous beverage. An addiction like any other drug.

And vampire bats . . .

So what had vampires been, many millions of years ago, before they became enslaved?

It was a short distance from gnawing on a wound to drinking its substance . . . From swooping down through the air to being called to swoop . . . From inciting the dread to inciting the lust. . . .

Almost in a fever, he thought he had glimpsed what turned an aerial predator into the pestilence that walketh in darkness. Sick with the sound and smell of the gas jet, Bodenland went to the window and flung back the curtains, letting moonlight enter the fuggy room. Brushing away the strings of white flowers, he threw open the window and took some lungfuls of air.

The moon still floated upside down in the pool.

Of Stoker there was no sign.

The woman stood there on the terrace, tall against the figure of a putti. She looked up at him, eyes agleam with a cold green fire.

His heart turned over. But his intellect remained cool.

Distantly, the clock in the asylum tower chimed one in the morning.

She lifted her arms and flew up to him.

109

She was in the bedroom, among the domestic things with her dead eyes, walking, gliding, rather. Close to him – and he staring with his hair standing on end.

'This is no dream, Joe,' she said. Her voice was deep and masculine.

She brought a chill to the room. In her whiteness, with something sparkling like frost in her hair, and the wan white robe, all shadowy yet bright – why, he thought, it's more like a fever than a person, frightening, yes, yet no more dangerous than a ghost . . . Yet he was in a prickle of lust to be touched by her, to enjoy an intimacy no one knew this side of the grave.

His intellect had no part in this encounter.

Her name was Bella, the name spoken like a bell.

'What do you want of me?'

'I know what you want of me, Joe.' Still the voice was thick, as if there was blood just below the throat. And her lips were red.

She began to talk, and he to listen, entranced.

Her people were ancient and had survived much. When oak trees die, they still stand against the storm. Her exact words never came back to him after; he only recalled – trying to recall more – that she gave an impression of the Undead as being nothing outside nature, as being of nature. Of humans as being the exiled things, cut off from the ancient world, unable to throw themselves into the streams of continuity pouring from the distant past into distant futures. She spoke, and it was in images.

For these reasons humanity was doomed. Men had to be slain for the survival of the ancient planet. Yet she, Bella, had it in her power to save him, Joe. To more than save him: to crown him with eternal life, the great stream of life from which his humanity exiled him. She spoke, and he received a picture of glaciers from which pure rivers flowed, down to teeming future oceans, unpolluted by man.

'What do I have to do?' His whisper was like the rustle of leaves.

Bella turned the full beam of her regard upon him. The eyes were red like a dog's or yellow like a cat's or green like a polar bear's – after, he could not remember. They pierced into him, confident, without conscience or consciousness.

'All Fleet Ones need to attend a great conference which our Lord has called. We are summoned, every one. We must go to the region you call Hudson Bay. There we will finally decide mankind's fate.'

'You cannot exist without us.'

'As we existed once, so we shall again. You're – but a moment.'

Again a kind of telepathic picture of the highest mountains brimming over with glaciers, slow-growing glaciers crowned with snow. And, by their striped flanks, thorn bushes growing, stiff against the wind.

Oh, it was beautiful. He longed for it. Ached.

'The great Lord Dracula will guide our decisions. All of us will have a voice. Possibly extermination, possibly total enslavement. All of you penned within . . .'

She named a place. Had she said 'green land' or 'Greenland'?

'Understand this, Joe. We are much stronger than you can imagine. As we possessed the past, so we are in possession of the far future.'

'The present? You're nothing, Bella.'

'We must have back the time train. You have to surrender it. That is what you have to do, and only that, in order that we become immortal lovers, borne on the storm of ages, like Paolo and Francesca.'

While she said these things and uttered these inhuman promises, she lightly roamed the room, as a tiger might pace.

He watched. She gave no reflection as she passed the mirror on the dressing-table or the glazed map of the British Empire, or any of the pictures which lay behind glass.

He sat on the side of the bed, unable to control his trembling.

'What does this mean – you possess the future?'

'No more talk, Joe. Talk's the human skill. Forget the future when we can together savour the present.'

The dark voice ceased. She unfolded great wings and moved towards him.

Something in her movements woke in Bodenland the promptings of a forgotten dream. All that came back to him was a picture of the thing that had rushed towards him down the corridor of the time train, covering infinite distance with infinite speed. He had time to appreciate the gloomy chamber in which, it seemed, every vertical was ashily outlined by the glare of the gas, caging him into this block of past existence, until the very scent of her, the frisson of her garments, drowned out all other impressions.

She stood by him, over him, as he remained sitting on the side of the bed, arms behind him to prop his torso as he gazed up at her face. The red lips moved and she spoke again.

'I know of your strength. Eternal life is here if you wish it. Eternal life and eternal love.'

His mouth was almost too dry to speak. He could force no derision into his voice. 'Forbidden love.'

'Forbidden by your kind, Joe, not mine.'

And with a great rustle of wings, she embraced him, pressing him into folds of the eiderdown.

Even as his body's blood flowed thick and heavy with delight, he was also living out a vision. It was antique yet imperishable, like something engraved on stone. It flowed from Bella to him.

Bella's memory was of what would one day be called Hudson Bay, and a chill part of Canada. Now the clouds rolled back like peeling skin and heat roared like breath. In the fairer climate of seventy million years past, what would be water and ice and drifting floes was all land, bush-speckled savannah or forest. The knee-deep grasses were rich to the teeth of great blundering herbivores – hadrosaurs that grazed by slow-winding rivers, brontosaurs that blundered into the marsh by the rivers.

These and other ornithischians were herded into pens and thorn-cages by the Fleet Ones, who arrived on wing and foot. They drove their captives, fat with blood and blubber, into the makeshift fields, from which they would be culled.

The savannah fills with their numbers. The beasts lumber and cry. The ground heaves.

The bed heaves. Bodenland cries aloud.

Larry was in an absolute rage. He shook with it. The mortician had said, 'I don't think you should take your mother's death like that, sir. We must show respect for the dead,' and Larry had brushed the little man aside.

He ran out of the parlour to the sidewalk, cursing and gesticulating. Kylie followed reluctantly, her pretty face pale and drawn.

In the cheerful morning sunlight, the main street of Enterprise

112

was choked with traffic, mainly rubberneckers come to see what was going on at Old John, lured by the news that mankind's history had been overturned. The cars moved so slowly that both drivers and passengers had plenty of time to watch this man performing on the sidewalk, under the mortician's sign. Many called insults, thinking they knew a drunk when they saw one.

'Stop it, Larry, will you?' Kylie seized his arm. 'Come on, I'll drive you back to the motel.'

'What have I done, Kylie? What have I done? I'm going to hang one on in the nearest bar, that's exactly what I'm going to do.'

'No, please . . . It would be better to pray. Prayer gives you more strength than whisky.'

He appeared not to have heard her.

'That was my momma lying in there, all white and withered. Stuck in that freezer . . .' Tears rolled down his face. 'Like some little pressed flower she was, her colour all faded . . .'

'Larry, darling, I know, I know. It's terrible. Poor Mina. But getting drunk won't help it one bit . . .'

Cajoling, crying herself, Kylie managed to persuade her husband back to the convertible. Wiping her tears, she managed the slow drive to the Moonlite Motel. The management had been insensitive enough to offer them Mina's old room. No other was available, owing to the unexpected influx of sightseers. They took it. In the hastily cleared room, Kylie found in the waste can a crumpled sheet of notepaper. On it her late mother-in-law had begun a letter. 'Joe you bastard – '

'What I fail to understand,' said Larry, heading straight for the mini-bar, 'is what this "Premature Ageing" bit means. I don't trust the Utah doctors – probably bribed by the motel. Hon, go down the corridor and get some ice, will you?'

She stood before him. 'I love you, Larry, and I need your support. Don't you see I'm still trembling? But you are like a greedy child. Your parents neglected you, yes, I know, I've heard it a million times. So you keep on grabbing, grabbing, just like a baby. You grabbed. Okay, so you want to keep me, so you must stop being a baby and grabbing for these other things.'

'You ever hear of a baby drinking the old Wild Turkey, hon? I'm never going to get over the death of my mom, because I should have taken better care of her. She loved me. She loved me, Kylie. Something my father never did.'

'Larry!' She screamed his name. 'Please forget about yourself! Worry about what happened to Mina. What the hell are we going to do? All human love has its failings, okay, but Joe does love you, best he knows how. But he's missing – '

'I'll go and get the ice myself, don't you worry.' He stood up. 'You always take Joe's side. I'm used to that by now, and I'm going to get a drink while you yack, if you must.'

She went over to her suitcase, which lay on the bed. She had opened it without unpacking it. They had checked in only an hour ago and gone straight from the motel to the funeral parlour.

'I'm yacking no more, husband of mine. I just can't get through to you. I've had enough. I'm off. You quit on me in Hawaii. Now I'm quitting on you in Enterprise, Utah.'

She snapped the suitcase shut. As she made for the door, Larry ran in front of her. Kylie swung the suitcase hard and hit him in the stomach.

Gasping, he made way for her.

When she had gone, Larry walked doubled up to the sofa, making what he could of the pain. After sufficient gasping, he picked up the quart bottle of Wild Turkey he had brought with him in his case. Lifting it high until it gleamed in the light from the window Kylie had opened, he saluted it.

'Only you and me now, old friend,' he said.

Later, he staggered out and got himself a hamburger from the Chock Full O' Nuts next to the Moonlite. Later still, he pulled down the blind at the window to keep out the glare of the sun. Later still, he placed the empty whisky bottle on the window sill and fell into a heavy slumber, snoring with practised ease.

Evening set in. The neon sign blinked outside, registering the minutes. Cars came and went in the parking lot. Larry slept on, uneasy in dream.

It seemed his mother visited him, to stand before him blood-lessly, with red eyes. She cried to him for comfort. She bent over him, her movements, gradual, so as not to startle.

Oh, she whispered, Larry was her dear son – so dear. Now she needed him more than ever.

The evening breeze blew the blind. It flapped inward, striking the empty whisky bottle. It tapped intermittently. The bottle fell to the floor, clattering.

Larry woke in a fright. He sat up, groaning, clutching his head, and looked round the darkened room. 'Mother?'

He was alone.

The glorious summer's day bathed the facade of Bram Stoker's residence. A row of newly planted copper beeches shielding the house from the lane gleamed in the early morning sunshine as if they were copper indeed, newly polished by the housemaid.

The carriage, with its two chestnut horses, stood in the drive before the front door. Stoker emerged, resplendent in top hat, chatting happily. He was followed by Joe Bodenland, walking slowly and saying nothing. His face was lifeless and ashen. Stoker helped him into the carriage.

Mrs Stoker was standing by the herbaceous border, talking to Spinks, the young gardener. She too was dressed in all her finery and, after a minute, came over to the carriage and was assisted aboard by James, the driver.

'Spinks is worried about the blackspot on the roses,' she said. 'And so am I.'

The wheels of the carriage crackled over the gravel as they drove off.

'The blue flowers in the border are pretty, dear. What are they?'

'Yes, they're doing better this year. *Lobelia syphilitica*. Such a funny name.'

When they turned out of the drive and headed down the hill, the spires and towers of London became visible. The great occasion made both Stoker and his wife nervous. They spent the journey primping each other, brushing away imaginary dust from one another's clothes, and adjusting their hair. They worried about what they would do while the investiture was taking place. Bodenland sat in his place, somewhat shrunken, speaking only when addressed.

The carriage took them to the splendid rail terminal of Paddington Station, built by one of the Queen's more ingenious subjects,

Isambard Kingdom Brunel. The station master came forward and installed Stoker's party in a first class carriage.

Stoker sat back, tilted his topper at a rakish angle, and lit a large cigar.

At Windsor, bunting decorated the station and a silver band played. They were met by an equerry of the Queen and escorted in style to the palace, over which the Union Jack flew lazily in the sun.

When their brougham rolled into the yard of the Castle, a clock was chiming a quarter hour after eleven. They were in good time for the investiture at twelve noon. A platoon of household guards was on parade, and a band played lively airs. Mrs Stoker clapped her gloved hands in pleasure.

'Capital chaps,' agreed Stoker, nodding towards the uniformed bandsmen. 'Pity your pater isn't here to see them, Flo.'

Crowds stared in at the gates, while children waved small paper Union Jacks.

They were assisted ceremoniously from the carriage. Their company was escorted to a reception room, where other celebrated names lounged about in nonchalant attitudes and medals, smoking if possible. Irving himself joined them in a few minutes, and Bodenland was introduced.

Henry Irving walked with a long stride, perhaps to make himself look taller than he was. He had the appearance of a great famished wolf. The hair on his magnificent head was liberally streaked with white, long, and raggedly cut, lending something bohemian to his person. He swung his famous brow towards the assembled company to make sure he was recognized, then turned all his attention to Stoker and his companions.

'I'm friendly with your compatriot, Mark Twain,' Irving said. 'I met him when we were doing our recent tour of America. Very amusing man.'

He sat down next to them and drummed his fingers on his top hat.

'No chance of a drink here, Henry,' Stoker said.

But coffee was served in porcelain cups which Mrs Stoker greatly admired. She persevered in admiring everything in sight.

In due time, they were shown into a splendid scarlet reception room. The furnishings consisted of stiff-backed chairs at one end and a plain throne on a dais at the other. Apart from this, a few lavishly framed oils of battle scenes hanging on the walls were the only decoration. In an adjoining room, light music was being played by a quartet.

Queen Victoria was escorted into the room at the far end. She seated herself on the throne without ostentation. She was a small dumpy woman, dressed in black with a blue sash running over one shoulder. She dispensed half-a-dozen knighthoods with a ceremonial sword, displaying nothing that could be interpreted as intense interest in the proceedings. As etiquette decreed, she made no conversation with her newly honoured subjects as they rose from their knees.

It was Irving's turn. He ascended the three shallow steps and knelt before his Queen. She tapped him on both shoulders with the sword.

'We were much amused, Sir Henry,' she said, and smiled.

'Ooh, she *smiled*,' Mrs Stoker whispered in her husband's ear.

He nodded vigorously.

The playing of the national anthem concluded the ceremony.

Afterwards, as they left the Castle with Irving, the talk was all of the Queen's smile. There was general agreement that it was wonderful, and that she looked extremely well for her age.

Mrs Stoker turned to Bodenland.

'You've had little to say on this truly memorable occasion, sir. What did you make of it all? A fine tale you'll have to take back to Mrs Borderland. I warrant you have nothing so impressive in America.'

'That may be so, madam. We have no royalty in our country, being a republic. All this display you see, this great castle – is it not paid for out of the pockets of the average Britisher? And your Queen – I mean no offence, but is it not the English poor who keep her in luxury?'

'That's plain silly, Joe,' said Stoker. 'The Queen's a very spartan lady. Eats almost nothing since the Prince Consort died.'

'Are you telling us America has no poor?' said Florence.

'I didn't say that, Mrs Stoker. Of course we have poor, but the poor have hope. They may – I use an old-fashioned phrase – raise

117

themselves from log cabin to White House. Whereas I doubt if any of the English poor have ever raised themselves to the throne from Whitechapel.'

'You look unwell, Mr Borderland,' said Florence, stiffly.

The ceremony was followed by a grand luncheon, held in the banqueting rooms off Whitehall, and attended by no less a figure than the Prime Minister, Lord Rosebery.

As usual, Bram Stoker had to stay close to Irving, but he came over to his new friend's side once, to introduce him to Irving's leading lady, Ellen Terry. Ellen Terry's brother Fred, also an actor, was with her, but Bodenland was able to spare no glance for him.

Ellen Terry was simply the most beautiful woman he had ever set eyes on. She wore a saffron silk dress, with hand-woven designs consisting of many-coloured threads and little jewels. The dress went with her striking colouring and eyes that – he could only feel it – looked at him and understood him. Bodenland was so overwhelmed by this sensation, entirely new to him, that he was unable to say anything sensible. He remembered afterwards only a certain manner in which she held her head, as if at once proud and modest. He remembered the way her mouth – that delightful mouth – moved, but not what it said.

Then she turned to speak to someone else. In a phrase Bram Stoker used later, Ellen Terry was like embodied sunshine.

But her amiable brother Fred stayed a moment and pointed out some notables to Bodenland as they assembled round the table.

'That feller with the green lapels to his jacket is a compatriot of yours, Edwin Abbey. Good artist but, being American, won't end up *in* the Abbey.' He laughed at his own joke, treating the whole affair like a kind of horse-race. 'See whom he's shaking hands with? That's the old war horse, Alma Tadema – he's pipped Henry at the post, he's already a knight. Wonderful painter, he entirely re-designed the Roman toga for Henry's *Coriolanus* . . . Ah, now, coming up on the straight – see that lady with the turban and the slightly too grand osprey feathers? That's none other than Mrs Perugini, daughter of the late lamented Charles Dickens, novelist. The serious-looking gent embracing Bram . . . that's one of his best friends, Hall Caine – another novelist, happily still with us.

118

'Oh, here's a treat!' Fred Terry exclaimed, as a wild-looking man with a great streaming head of hair burst into the room and flung his arms about Irving. 'It's the Polish musical genius of the age. Paderewski. They're chums, as you can tell. Quite a romantic chappie, by all accounts.' Indeed, when the guests were all seated, and before the commencement of the meal, Paderewski was prevailed upon to position himself at the grand piano and play a minuet of his own composition, attacking the keys with as much spirit as if he did so on behalf of the whole Polish people.

After wild applause, the new knight rose and made a speech, also wildly applauded, after which he gave his famous rendering of 'The Bells', the dramatic story of a man haunted by the undetected murder he had committed. Tumultuous applause. Ellen Terry sat between Irving and Lord Rosebery, and smiled like an angel.

Then the banquet began.

Enormous amounts of food were supplied by bustling waiters, bearing with aplomb the loaded dishes in and the emptied dishes out. Wine rose in such a tide in cut-glass goblets that men in their dinner jackets grew apoplectic, with cheeks as scarlet as the Bordeaux.

Slightly awed by the gargantuan consumption, Bodenland picked at his food and sipped at his claret. Florence Stoker, seated next to him, regaled him with tales of the Balcombe family.

Evidently she found him unresponsive.

'Are you one of those men who regards a woman's conversation as inconsequential?' she asked, as a towering confection resembling a Mont Blanc built of sponge, brandy, and icing sugar was set before them.

'On the contrary, ma'am. I wish it were otherwise.'

He could not stop glancing at Ellen Terry; she altered his whole feeling towards the nineteenth century.

When finally they staggered out into the light of a London day, with dim sunlight slanting through the plane trees, it was to be met by a throng of beggars, importuning for food or money.

Taking Bodenland's elbow, Stoker steered him through the outstretched hands. Bodenland looked with pity on the cadaverous faces, pale but lit with burning eyes, the rags they wore like cerements. He wondered if Stoker had drawn his picture of the Undead from this melancholy company, which swarmed in its thousands through the underworld of London.

Seeing his interest, Stoker stopped and accosted one small lad, bare of legs and feet, who held out a bony hand to them. Picking a coin from his pocket, Stoker asked the boy what he did for a living.

'I was a pure-finder, guv, following me father's trade. But times is hard, owing to competition from over the other side. Spare a copper, guv, bless you.'

He got the copper, and made off fast down a side street.

'What's a pure-finder?' Bodenland asked, as they climbed into their carriage.

'Pure's dog shit,' said Stoker, shielding the word from his wife with his topper. 'The urchin probably works for the tanners over Bermondsey way. They use the shit for tanning leather. I hear it's a profitable occupation.'

'The boy was starving.'

'You can't go by looks.'

They returned home in the evening. Lights were already on in the house as James led the horses away to the stable.

A great to-do went on in the hall with the removal of outer garments and the fussing of van Helsing, who was anxious to see that the outing had inflicted no harm on his charge. He managed to circumnavigate Stoker twice by the time the latter entered the drawing room and flung himself down in an armchair under the Bronzino.

Stoker tugged vigorously at the bellrope for wine.

'What a day, to be sure,' he said. 'It's a day of great honour to the whole of the acting profession, no less. Wouldn't you agree, Joe?'

Joe had gone over to the window to look at the daylight lingering in the garden.

'How beautiful Ellen Terry is,' he said, dreamily.

While the manservant was pouring wine, van Helsing ran over to Stoker's chair and sank down beside it on one knee, somewhat in the attitude Irving had assumed a few hours previously. He rolled up Stoker's sleeve and administered an injection from a large silver syringe.

Stoker made a face.

'It's my friend here who needs your ministry, Van,' said Stoker. Getting up, he went over to where Bodenland was standing, looking out towards the woods. As Bodenland turned, Stoker saw the two telltale marks at his throat, and understood.

'Better get some iodine, Van. Mr Bodenland cut himself shaving.' He led Bodenland over to a comfortable chair and made him sit down. After standing looking compassionately down at him, he snapped his fingers. 'I know what you need.'

In a minute, after probing in the wine cabinet, he brought forth a wine glass full of a red liquid and gave it to Joe.

'What's this? Wine?'

'Laudanum. Do you a power of good and all.'

'My god . . . Well, it is 1896 . . .' He sipped it slowly and felt some of the lassitude leave him.

'You should get out of here at once, Joe. You're a marked man. I know I've helped to delay you, but I see now you should make for home on the morrow, sure as eggs are eggs.'

Bodenland stood up, a little shakily. He took a deep breath.

'I'm okay, or near enough. Allow me to make you a small speech, since you've both been so kind and hospitable. Despite my experiences on the way to England – and I've hardly dared tell you of the full strangeness of that journey – I have fought with myself to deny the reality of . . . of vampires. To be honest, I thought they were a fiction invented for the novel you are about to finish. Even when you talked about them, I kind of reckoned you mad. Now I know you're not mad.'

'Heaven be praised! It's myself that's always thinking I'm mad, or going that way.'

'And I'm glad of your reassurance, Mr Bodenland,' said Florence, getting his name right in gratitude.

'Thanks. Let me finish my speech. Of course I still worry about my wife, Mina, and my family. I can't resist the intuition that some dreadful thing may have happened to her. But – hell, Bram, after my experience last night I know it would be cowardice to just up and quit now, and go home as if nothing had happened. I let down my old buddy Bernard Clift. Well, I'm not about to let down my new buddy as well. I'm staying, and we'll fight this foul thing together.'

To his surprise, Stoker flung his arms about him.

'You're a dear feller, sure you are.' He shook Bodenland's hand warmly. 'It's a brave decision you've made.'

Mrs Stoker ran up, casting her embroidery hoop on the carpet, and kissed him on the cheek.

'I don't want you getting my husband into trouble, now, but you spoke up like a man – like a soldier. We shall drink a sherry now, to toast you.'

'And we'll have a cigar,' said Stoker. 'At least, I will.'

This response excited Joe into a less lethargic state.

'We won't delay. I may be no Christian, but this is a kind of Christian quest.' As he spoke, he took a New Testament from a side table and waved it aloft as if in proof. 'We start tomorrow.'

'And we prepare tonight,' said Stoker, through his cigar.

When Stoker was out of the room, his wife came to Bodenland's side.

'My dear father was full of wisdom – as befitted a man who was a Lieutenant Colonel and served in the Crimea. One thing he told me was that many impossible things happen. The important thing is to decide which impossible things to believe and which not to.'

'Sound advice, ma'am.'

'My father's advice was always sound. I'm undecided as yet about your impossibilities, but I'd like to ask you, if I may – supposing it were somehow possible to venture into the future, as one ventures into London – would I be able to establish if dear Bram's latest novel will be a success?' She laughed, as if thinking it was a silly question for a colonel's daughter to ask.

'Bram will call it *Dracula*, as I advised, whatever it may be called now. It will be a great success, and translated into many languages. Maybe I could ask you a question in return, Mrs Stoker?'

'By all means.'

'What do you think your husband's novel is about?'

'He assures me he hopes to reassert the proper womanly role of Christian English decency, matronly, angelic . . .'

'Sexless?'

'Please do not be coarse. We do not speak of such things.' She lifted a hand in delicate reproach.

'I apologize, ma'am. Most readers regard *Dracula* as a horror tale, whatever Bram says. His own mother back in Ireland will write and tell him it is more frightening than Mary Shelley's marvellous *Frankenstein*. The last time I saw my new daughter-in-law Kylie . . . well, perhaps the last time bar one, she was reading Bram's novel. Everyone on the planet – in China, in the Amazon basin – probably knows the name of Dracula. Fame on an almost unprecedented scale, Mrs Stoker.'

'Well, I'm sorry about that villain Dracula's fame, though glad about all the rest. Some names, like some bodies, are best buried and forgotten.'

CHAPTER IX

It was growing dark in the woods below the house. Sunset was overcast. Spinks the gardener, assisted by the two men, was loading Stoker's home-made bullets and some rifles on the time train.

This remarkable vehicle had been inspected with many a whistle of admiration from Stoker and many a scratch of the head from Spinks. The latter was philosophical.

'If it works, then it works, sir, and you needn't worry. My stomach works, but I don't need to know the whys and wherefores of it.'

'A sensible approach,' Stoker agreed. 'The less you know about your stomach, the better it works, no doubt. Light a storm lantern, Spinks, will you? It's dark early this evening.'

As the darkness encompassed the three men, as the Earth revolving moved into its own shadow, so the ancient forces of darkness began to emerge. Not being subject to life, they were tireless. While the time train was being loaded, Bella, who had once been alive, was descending some crumbling stairs leading down to a crypt.

She was newly roused from the oblivion which overtook her in the holy hours of daylight. Her hair lay about her shoulders. About her lips was a deadly pallor. Her fragility expressed itself in the lingering way she descended the broken stair. No living man, fearing his own weakness, could have resisted the lure of the ruined madonna.

Yet she herself, the magnet for terror, was also subject to terror. She went to a rendezvous with her Lord.

Some reassurance was to be drawn from the atmosphere of the

crypt, which was dark and rank. Her keenly attuned ear caught the drip of moisture, the whisper of a spider in its web, and all the sharp-toothed harmonies of decay. It suited her, too, that the stained glass window to one side allowed in only a barest stain of light, red-tainted from the dregs of sunset.

Tombs stood all about. An open coffin lay nearby, lending its gamey flavour to the air. Bella stood by it, slightly luminous, waiting in absolute stillness.

At a sign of some kind, perhaps a change of pressure in the morbid dampness, she sank to her knees, lifting her white hands up to her breast. Her mouth opened and her pale gums made her teeth look longer and sharper than ever.

In the gloom, very distant, a mighty figure materialized. It remained for an instant at the brink of visibility. Then it began its advance towards the kneeling woman. It had infinite space to cover, but it approached at infinite speed. Suddenly it was close, robed in smouldering darkness. Its face was long, pale, powerful. It had horns, rising on bosses from its thick, coarse hair.

It had no majesty. What it had was brute presence, before which Bella cowered.

She addressed him as Lord and Count, and said that Bodenland would soon be finished as thoroughly as the other grave-defiler, Clift. She would not let him escape. She spoke submissively, in her deep growling voice.

There was no doubting the monster's power when he stood forth as now, horned and in his true guise. There was no doubting the moral ugliness of his strength – or the note of sorrow in his voice when he made his reply.

'My bride and daughter, be not too certain. Nothing is ordained. Show confidence, inwardly fear. Bear in mind that the Fleet Ones must always remain the negative side of humanity, their dark obverse. Otherwise we hold no attraction for them.'

'Our attraction, our darkness, is our strength, Great Lord.'

She might as well not have spoken. His voice ground on, with the light of hell in his mouth as well as in his eyes.

'For all our strengths, we remain forever slaves to the human imagination. You deal with a man of more than ordinary imaginative power.'

'I shall conquer, Lord, for I have learned much from you.'

'Only in the realm of Death where humans cannot go have we total supremacy. Remember that, my daughter and bride.'

'I do and I will.'

'Then come to me.' He was already aroused. With a cry, Bella moved into his arms and gave her corpselike being to him.

It grew still darker in the woods below the house. Bodenland was inside the time train, stowing away ammunition, general supplies, and Stoker's cricket bat, which he swore was his lucky mascot; he had knocked up several centuries with it, which was a good omen for travelling through long periods of time.

Examining the old rifles, Bodenland called down to the ginger man to express his doubts about them.

'But we have proof they're effective,' Stoker said, pausing and looking up at his friend. 'You're forgetting. It was a bullet from one of these that finished off the vampire in your friend's ancient grave. They'll do well. And don't forget, Joe, these ugly critters have guile but no real savvy – no human intelligence. A madman at the loony-bin told me that.'

Bodenland squatted on his haunches in the entrance to the train.

'I was trying to think over that very problem in evolutionary terms.'

'You mean Darwinism?' Stoker's broad face was lit by the uncertain light of a storm lantern.

'Exactly. Listen, Bram, we now know that vampires evolved millions of years ago from some other form of life. They adapted to parasitism. They developed sucking mouth-parts, they developed a kind of hypnotic and semi-telepathic power to attract victims. Those changes had to be at the expense of some other ability. Well, even over millions of years, as they became more or less to resemble Homo sapiens, they did not develop a neocortex.'

'But they can talk.'

'They can, but reluctantly, it seems. They have the classic one-track mind. Try them on the rules of baseball. Nix! I believe they also lost an ability. Does it make sense to you to say that their intense sexual power is generated because they are themselves sexually frustrated, having lost the power of reproduction?'

Stoker stared down at the trampled grass under his feet.

'Spinks,' he said to the young gardener, who was standing nearby with his arms akimbo, listening, 'you'd better cut on back to the house. This conversation is not for you.' When the lad did as he was told, Stoker said, 'I understand your meaning perfectly, Joe. Vampires can't get on the job, Dracula himself being an exception. All they do for sex is suck. Not F but S, you could say.'

'So how do they keep the species going?'

'That is a problem. If you can't get it up, the population goes down.'

'They recruit, don't they? It's all in your novel. They recruit humans into the ranks of the Undead. And such ex-humans also face brain-extinction.'

Stoker leaned against the train and looked up through the canopy of leaves to the darkening sky, where a flight of rooks made belated wing overhead.

'You're saying there are two strains in the vampire kind, the way it needs blacks and whites to make up humanity. So one strain is ex-humans. What is the other?'

'Overgrown vampire bats. Or their equivalent back in the Mesozoic. That is, pterodactyls and pteranodons. From devouring carrion, it was a short step to preying on the half-living.'

'No, no,' said Stoker vehemently. 'I'll not believe it. I'll not believe that such creatures – brainless – could make this amazing vehicle and travel on it through all the years of time. You can't explain that, Joe, can you?'

Bodenland laughed as he jumped to the ground.

'Nope. But I will do . . .'

'Let's get back to the house.' They trudged uphill through the copse, chatting companionably, agreeing to make a start early the following morning.

As they reached the lawn, with the house in view, van Helsing approached. Seeing that he had a speech ready on his lips, Stoker grinned and held up a hand.

'Don't tell me, Van. Joe and I are on a crusade, and nothing is going to stop us.'

'You are not fit, Mr Stoker, believe me.'

'Fit or not, I'm going. I arranged it with Irving. We believe the vampires can be stopped, and we're going to do it. Why not come with us?'

Van Helsing looked appalled.

'If you indeed are going on this dangerous errand, it is my graven duty to stay here to protect Mrs Stoker.'

Stoker patted him on the arm. 'That's right, Van. I applaud your keen sense of duty.'

He sniffed the breeze. 'I have a feeling that bad things may be abroad again later, Joe – without wishing to scare the doctor here.'

' "Thou shalt not be afraid for any terror by night . . .'''

Stoker completed the quotation for him '. . . "Nor for the arrow that flieth by day. For the pestilence that walketh in darkness: nor for the sickness that destroyeth in the noon-day." Sounds as if the old psalm-writers were regularly plagued by our friends, doesn't it?'

It was growing darker still in the extensive grounds of the lunatic asylum next door. Dim lights burned in the building, none outside it. The ruin of the old abbey behind the asylum had known no light since Cromwell's artillery had struck its ancient walls. As for the extensive and neglected grounds, so close to London, yet so near to the archaic, they retained the nature of wilderness everywhere, embracing darkness early, surrendering it late.

In his cell on the north corner of the north wing of the asylum, Renfield was on his knees, praying, counting, humming, reciting nursery rhymes, wagging his head like a pendulum, as the fit took him. Like Bram Stoker, he had scented something on the breeze, and knew ill things were abroad. In a corner of his brain he remembered the big bronze sound of the Salvation Army band playing in the gutter outside the mean room which his family rented; he banged the tune with his fists on the draughty stonework now: 'The Bells of Hell go Ting-a-ling-a-ling,' with a clash of the cymbals on the word 'Hell'; while he, almost naked and the size of a shrimp, cowered with an even tinier brother under the one bed in the room, powerless not to watch his drunken ogre of a father battering his mother to death with a chair leg; and the brass band played on triumphantly outside, drowning her last cries – 'For you but not for me-a-lee-a-lee', went his fist now on the grey stone.

On one of the walls of his cell, out of reach, was an electric light, protected from vandalism by a mesh.

A junior warden looked into the cell, saying cheerfully, 'Lights out, Renfield, old sport. Going to be all right, are we?'

The madman rolled on his back.

'Please don't switch the darkness on, Bob. Leave me the light, I beg. Something's going on in the crypt, worse than slugs and snails and puppydogs' tails. Leave me the light. Ummm-mm.'

'Sorry, old cocker, orders is orders, got to put it out. Nine o'clock.'

'Ruff, ruff, ruff.' He rolled on the floor, barking. 'Bob, Bob, there's a big dog in here, got in with me. Going to eat me. Leave me the light – my last words . . .'

'Sorry, me old cock-sparrer, I don't see no dog.'

He slammed the cell door, switching off the madman's light from outside the cell.

The wolf arrived immediately.

It appeared from wind-tossed bushes a long way distant, and made straight for Renfield at a good sharp trot. Renfield at once set up a great hullabaloo, and ran to the far corner of the cell. The wolf trotted the faster. Great was the distance, as great its speed.

The cell was awhirl with something like snow as the wolf closed on its prey. At the last minute, it changed shape. It became Count Dracula.

Renfield compressed himself into his corner, again the size of a shrimp, watching powerless, as once he had watched murder.

'Ummm-mm.'

Count Dracula was brilliantly robed. He had a cow face and horns and a powdery blue complexion. Sometimes Death comes as a clown.

'You have been talking to a neighbour, Renfield. You know more than is good for you.'

'I'll be your slave, master. You know that. Ummmm. Ummmm. I'll be your slave. Bring blood, fetch. No – '

He was lifted up, twisted, body one way, neck and head the other. Then his body was flung contemptuously against one of the whitewashed walls.

Bob found him in the morning and shed a tear.

'Poor old bugger. Wouldn't harm a fly . . .'

Total darkness and Bodenland in his bedroom with the gas fire hissing. He turned it off and listened. The brief wind had died. The stillness of the unknown British countryside came in to him.

'How silent is the nineteenth century,' he said, almost aloud. With gas and increased use of electricity, people had changed, become more active after dark, forgotten the ancient threats it masked. But in all the centuries before that, there had been no defence against sunset. Oil lamp and candle had been frail protection against the predators of night.

He sat in a chair and tried to resolve a problem. He wanted to understand why the Christian symbol of the Cross so terrified vampires – if indeed it did. That idea would have to be tested. Was every vampire similarly terrified?

He set blunt fingertip to blunt fingertip and thought.

Every vampire . . . All the facts indicated that all vampires were alike, though Dracula and a few lamia, which were possibly not true vampires, possessed greater powers. Otherwise they were as alike as . . .

As animals, as sheep or other livestock. No real individuality. And human beings had been similarly lacking in individuality when they emerged from the ape. So there had to be a period when individuality – the characteristic that set humanity apart from even the higher mammals – dawned like a light. That light would spell the end of vampiric domination. A horse cannot defend itself from a vampire bat, any more than it can open a gate; a human can.

That great moment of development, the waking of the individual spirit, must be fairly recent.

His thoughts wandered. Bodenland was not much used to considering his inner self, such were the patterns of economic life. Yet he was aware of an inner consciousness, detached from daily happening, which seemed to be regarding him.

But many ancient creeds had held ceremonies which proved men were not then individual, or regarded as individual, but merely an item in the mass. If you could sacrifice a ram or a slave to save your soul, if thousands of captives could be sacrificed to save

130

thousands of souls — as happened in the Aztec culture — then all souls were equal and interchangeable. An individual consciousness had been slow to dawn.

Signs of dawn came in the sixth century BC, with such great men as Confucius, Buddha, and the classical Greek philosophers.

The religions Christ defeated had worshipped things of wood, graven images, without living spirit. Those images could make do with burnt offerings. The solitary introspection of prayer was a new idea. No one went forty days and forty nights in the wilderness for Baal.

Christ embodied what was new and revolutionary — the value of the individual. The idea of individual salvation was consciousness-raising. It had changed the world, or most of it. It was an idea for which the time was ripe — hadn't other great religions sprung up in the same period? All with the same emphasis?

Originally the *ur*-vampires had preyed on creatures without individual consciousness. Such was their natural prey. Their dangers hugely increased when they found themselves attacking an unpredictable individual — and the Cross was the symbol of that very danger. The Cross embodied all they most dreaded.

So Bodenland hoped.

He had sat thinking, fortifying his mind, for some while — reluctant to accept completely the very idea of vampires. Yet he found himself accepting many of the tenets of Christianity — a religion he had stoutly derided all his life. It was for that reason he had refused to undergo the marriage ceremony with Mina. Maybe Kylie and Larry had something, after all.

Rising, he paced about the bedroom, preparing himself for what he anticipated would be as great a challenge as he had ever faced. After only slight hesitation, he left the bedroom and crept downstairs. As he let himself out of the back door into the chill of the waiting night, he muffled the click of the lock.

On the terrace, the statues stood frozen. The silence was unbroken, the light dim, for the moon was hidden in cloud. The line of trees bordering the bottom of the garden was as dark as an ancient sea.

As soon as he realized that an extra statue stood guard, Bodenland's senses became preternaturally alert. The figure was that of a woman, standing in an unnatural position, her head thrown right back to expose her neck and throat. Even before he identified the figure as Bella, he saw that behind it, close, something darker than the night stood there, moving, grunting quietly. He had an impression of fur, but could not tell whether it was man or beast. She – Bella – remained resistless in that embrace.

Whatever it was, it looked up with a flash of yellow slitted eyes and was immediately gone with agility over the low hedging at the edge of the terrace, to be lost to view.

With a lethargic movement, Bella pulled herself erect and her garments in order. She approached Bodenland briskly, showing her white teeth in what could have been a smile.

His body, confronted by the uncanny, went into a kind of paralysis. Here was a loss of individuality indeed! Prepared though he was for the meeting, the instinctive part of his brain took over and he fought to regain control of himself, like a man trying to swim in a deep well.

She was more beautiful than previously, seeming to glow with an inner light. She combined the innocence and waiflike quality of a small girl with the eroticism of a harlot; and these qualities of virginity and depravity seemed complementary rather than in opposition.

She came forward over the flagstones, utterly confident of her powers. Her movement released him. He made as if to give himself to her, promising to surrender the train and assist in the forthcoming attack on humanity in exchange for the bestowal of her love.

'Do you place no higher price on my love?' In contradiction to her graceful shape was that deep voice, sometimes harsh, sometimes melodious.

'With your knowledge of the future, you can say where we might find some ultimate weapon to use against humanity,' he said.

'I could discard you whenever I wished.' It was a statement of fact, said without arrogance.

'Of course. You can form no attachments. That I understand.'

'You think so? But I can tell you where an ultimate weapon will be found. The super-fusion bomb is – will be – in the Great Libyan Empire of Tripoli, known as the Silent Empire.'

132

'I have heard of the Silent Empire.'

'It will be defeated by us. Its last defence, the super-bomb, lies in the capital in AD 2599, awaiting release. After that date, human history – that brief thing – ends.'

'That's definite?'

'Even the past is indefinite. After the end of the Silent Empire, all nuclear weapons are finished with. Together with their inventors. But you could live for ever, Joe.'

She radiated a great emotional assault on him, from which even the hideous growling voice could not detract. Joe sank down on one knee, cowed by the sight of the sign emblazoned on her forehead.

In the empathy flashing between them, he caught an image of how he was seen through those alien eyes. He had shrunk to a scuttling mouse, in too-slow flight along a wainscot. About to master him was a great ox of a man – no female, but a monstrous masculine about to strike.

As its face came close, its teeth showed, gleaming clean and fascinating as cobra fangs.

Now was time for him to act. With enormous effort, he pulled the New Testament from his pocket and thrust it up before her eyes, its golden Cross outwards.

Bella hissed like a wild cat and drew back. For an instant, a massive black thing – something torn from the ground – stood there. Then it took wing and was gone, westwards towards the grounds of the asylum, howling as it went.

Bram Stoker emerged from the shadows behind the tool shed, tucking away a revolver with which he had armed himself.

'Joe, old chum!'

Joe had sunk down on the terrace and was holding his head in his hands. Stoker put a hand on his shoulder.

'Now you believe. Now you see it works.'

Joe laughed shakily. 'Thank God I didn't hold up a copy of *your* book.'

'Faith, the bitch would have stood there reading all night, till the first rays of daylight penetrated her.'

'Don't talk about penetrating her. I shudder to think what was on my mind.'

'You wouldn't get much comfort on the nest there, me lad – it's fuller of worms than a shroud.'

'I know it.' He allowed Stoker to help him up. The two men looked at each other and laughed, clapping each other on the back.

Dr van Helsing emerged from cover, pale and shivering.

'What a terrible apparition! You're certain she's gone, Mr Stoker?'

Stoker looked hastily about, pantomiming terror, and van Helsing retreated a step.

'Fear not, Van, she's gone, though I doubt very far. We're a target for their attentions. You've just encountered a lamia, Joe. That's what Bella was, a lamia, a vampire with special powers. Even the Undead have their lieutenants. And their lieutenant colonels, I suppose. It's capable of assuming the guise of either sex, male or female.'

'Which is it?' asked Bodenland.

'Neither. Neuter. That's my guess.'

'Can we kill it?'

'Oh, I think we'd better be getting to bed, Mr Bodenland,' said the doctor. 'Think of your health – it's late. The night air – '

'My health would be much better if the world were rid of such horrors.' In a sudden burst of nervous irritation, he turned on the doctor.

'How's your scientific view of the world now, Dr van Helsing? How well does Bella fit in with your beliefs?'

'I'll have to think it over . . . One is, after all, either dead or not dead – don't you think?' He looked helplessly at Bodenland.

Bodenland set his head on one side. 'There may be many degrees between dead and Undead. Doctor, in my time, I've been aqualunging below Antarctic ice two metres thick. There – twenty metres down on the sea bed, in unimaginable cold – things live. Animals. Crawling about, feeding, reproducing. In that most marginal territory, some of them – woodlice, for instance – grow much bigger than their equivalents in temperate zones. That is a continual source of astonishment to me. Maybe these creatures, vampires and lamias and the rest – maybe they live in a zone as yet unexplored, in some Antarctic ice floor of the spirit. They've fallen into a metaphysical abyss. If we knew all the facts, we'd probably feel pity for the creature that once was Bella.'

'Pity? You're talking nonsense, Joe,' said Stoker. 'The pitiless deserve no pity.'

'Is that what your father-in-law would have said?'

Stoker walked to the edge of the terrace and stared into the night. He motioned Bodenland over, and said, quietly, 'Look, Joe, we can't clear off tomorrow in quest of this Silent Empire leaving this horrible thing in the vicinity. I worry about Florence's safety. The doctor would be as much good as a sick headache in any emergency calling for more drastic action than the insertion of a suppository.'

'You've got stakes and mallets in the tool shed, I saw. I'm for finishing off the horror, count on it – but how do we track it down?'

'I had occasion to visit the asylum recently. I talked to one of the madmen. Research for the novel and that kind of thing. The asylum's built in the grounds of a ruined abbey, as I told you, and that abbey has a crypt still surviving, used by the asylum authorities on occasions. For instance, when they get outbreaks of influenza – when half the inmates meet a hasty end. I have my suspicions about that crypt.'

'Why don't we go visit it? Now?'

'Hang on to your Testament. Bella may well have a refuge there – a place to rest in daylight hours. We can cut through the woods.'

'And your doctor can guard the house while we're away.'

The decision was taken coolly enough. But first Stoker took hold of Bodenland's arm and led him back into the warmth of the house. Sitting him down, he went to his drinks cabinet, to emerge with two glasses full of a dark liquid from which fumes rolled.

'Not laudanum?' Bodenland said, raising an eyebrow and smiling rather faintly.

'This is rum,' Stoker said. 'What the British Army and Navy drink before going into action. Cheers, me boy! "What we've done before, we'll jolly well do again." '

It was strong stuff, reeking of fighting spirit.

When they had drained their glasses, they set out for the ruined abbey.

The going, in the darkness with only a storm lantern for illumination, was not easy. They made their way through extensive woods and up a ravine where a stream tumbled, before ascending a slope and coming up to the high brick walls of the asylum.

'We follow this wall round,' said Stoker, rather breathlessly. 'There used to be gates and a carriageway in the old days.'

Bodenland said nothing. For him, these were 'the old days'.

An owl was calling, as they walked by the wall. Bodenland began to like the expedition, as the rum counteracted the chilling effect of the lamia. He enjoyed the adventure of being back in Victorian England, and was pursuing a fantasy whereby, when this struggle was over, he brought Mina back on the time train to make a documentary of the period. He could also film the earlier San Francisco earthquake if he planned it right. As these dramas were running through his mind, they came upon the wooden gates of which Stoker had spoken.

They were of oak, tall and forbidding and bound with iron. The lantern light did not shine to the top of them. Some miscreant had broken in a panel on one side and they were able to squeeze through into the asylum grounds.

They plunged on through long rough grass, Stoker humming 'Lilibulero' under his breath.

Dark in outline against the night sky stood the massive structure of the asylum, refuge for the derelicts of society. Scarcely a light showed to punctuate its unwelcoming solidity. Nearer to hand, a more ragged shape presented itself. So they approached the ruin of the abbey. What was now a mere shell had once been an outpost of learning and reverence in the long abeyance of the Middle Ages. Only bats lived in what had formerly housed a thriving community. In these later days, no refuge was offered here.

Circumnavigating a bramble thicket, the two men neared the ruin. Inevitably, a mood of solemnity enveloped them, engendered by old stones, lost faiths and a sense of the ponderousness of time. Stoker fell silent. No sense of horror could be detected, rather the opposite – only an impression of the sanctity to which this ancient pile had originally been dedicated. Cromwell had gone. The gesture towards a purer life remained.

They skirted holly trees. Here stood a more modern building, itself tumbledown, built within the decaying arms of the old. This was where the founders of the asylum in the previous century – for centuries congregated here – had once accommodated the corpses of those extinguished by various epidemics. A smell of cats was pungent in the nostrils. Stoker, holding the lantern out before him, pushed through nettles to the entrance of the ancient crypt.

'Here we are. You ready?'

'Want me to go first?'

'Joe, it's my turn. "Into the valley of Death rode the six hundred." '

The original doors to the crypt had long gone. Later boardings-up had also collapsed. Now the lantern revealed only a piece of swinging board. Bodenland pushed it aside. They eyed each other, faces disembodied in the encircling gloom. Then Stoker took a deep breath and went ahead.

The dark was darker in the old building, the cold colder.

What had been stone flags were grown over by rough grass. Moving forward cautiously, they came on wide and shallow steps and started the descent, conscious that they moved into the maw of the tumbled building. The stone steps, crumbling and dangerous, led downwards, bringing Bodenland an uncomfortable shard of memory. He had been here before . . . Wasn't this the forgotten dream?

He would find Kylie at the bottom of the stairs, in the crypt.

So they entered the subterranean chamber.

The crypt was a hollow place, with echoes but without life or even the semblance of it. As Stoker came to stand close by him, Bodenland lifted the lantern above his head to survey the dismal scene. Tombs of long-dead abbots stood among thick pillars supporting the weight of buildings that once existed above. To one side on a damp wall was the stained glass window which had either escaped the ages or had been restored by some dotty early Victorian antiquarian. Nothing stirred except for almost inaudible rats.

'Nothing,' Stoker said in a whisper. 'Let's go back.'

'Wait.'

Something had moved beyond the circle of light cast by the lantern. Bodenland crossed the floor to a stone coffin lying on an ancient catafalque. Its lid was slightly out of true with the body of the coffin. Fearing what he might see, he heaved the lid to the floor.

The body of a man lay there, swollen and black, one hand clutching the dress it wore. He recognized it as Bella without a wig. Only for a moment was it a corpse. It awoke. Its eyes blazed up hatred from the place where it had taken refuge. The vampire sign on its forehead smouldered.

With a snarl, it stretched up, talons grasping at Bodenland's throat. Bodenland jumped back. He snatched up a broken fragment of the coffin lid. Engraved on it was the Holy Cross. He held it out. The creature fell back snarling and steaming, struggling to escape from its confinement.

Stoker thrust a mallet and a wooden stake into Bodenland's hand.

'It's the only way, Joe!'

He groaned. But the creature was rising again. He drove the stake down. With a savage blow of the mallet, he penetrated the thing's rib cage. It cracked like a rotten plank. The thing shrieked – more in fury than pain – and grasped Bodenland's wrist with both hands. He was pulled forward. It was bringing up its naked head to bite his upper arm, venom in its mouth.

Bodenland struck again, with his free arm, bashing the mallet against the blunt head of the stake. Black blood welled forth. He struck a third blow and the creature's shrieks kept time. It doubled back in agony, raising its clawed hands in a parody of prayer. Another lusty blow with the mallet, more blood, gouting from the wound. Sharp teeth bit pallid lips in agony. The hands fell back.

As it died, writhing, a faint treble voice shrilled – 'Thank you, sweet Jesus!' Gradually, the distorted countenance transformed itself into the lineaments of peace and was recognizable as Bella again. Momentarily, a placid child face stared up at them. But it aged as the torment left it. An old and withered thing lay there, resting in a shallow bath of blood. Bodenland stood helpless, mallet in hand, long after the disgusting transformation was complete.

He came to himself.

'Let's get out of here.'

Stoker said, 'Your train driver's in the tool shed. Now there's this old girl here. That's two bodies, and how to account for them? The police will be round questioning Flo, and I can't possibly have that.' He clutched a pillar to control his shaking.

'I see what you mean. If we put them on the train tomorrow, we could lose the bodies somewhere in the wilds of time. How do we get this horrible thing back to your place?'

'We can't carry Bella as she is. There'll be a pauper's coffin in the outbuilding. We'll use that.'

The outbuilding had a stock of pauper's coffins, awaiting eventual burial in the asylum cemetery. With trembling hands, they put the remains of the lamia in one of the coffins and screwed the lid down, before carrying the cumbersome burden back with them, beyond the ruins, through the broken gate, across the fields, through the wood, and home.

Surprisingly, Florence Stoker awaited them, bundled into a pink quilted dressing-gown and a night-cap. She asked no questions beyond inquiring if they had carried out their manoeuvre successfully. She was grim and efficient, bolting the door behind them and then, as the men warmed themselves at the kitchen range, preparing a posset. Her movements had a military precision about them.

The hot milk was flavoured with strong ale and various spices. Bodenland and Stoker lodged themselves on the edge of the table to drink the mixture, casting their vision downwards.

The kitchen table had been much scrubbed over the years. The grain of the wood stood out like the coat of a polar bear newly emerged from Arctic water. It resembled what the rough beverage tasted like.

The men did not look at each other. Although they knew well enough they had undergone an horrendous experience, the exact nature of what they had done eluded their memories. Where recollection should have been was only a barrier of oblivion. The entity calling itself Bella had gone, leaving no trace behind.

CHAPTER X

The light of dawn was as soft as Joe Bodenland had ever seen it. Stoker's elegant house sprawling on the crest of its low hill, the pleasant flower gardens, the ornamental pool stocked with fish – all were bathed in a calm that held for him a special period flavour. He was about to say goodbye to the nineteenth century. Although he knew something of the injustices it contained, he had to fight down a poignant feeling of regret. Whatever else the British had done, they had developed an intense regard for nature and its cultivation.

The gardener, Spinks, had elected to accompany Stoker and Bodenland, claiming the former needed someone to look after him. Spinks was a husky young man, brown and shiny, with an eager look in his deep-set eyes. When Stoker had hesitated, warning there might be danger ahead, Spinks had remarked that he would like a spot of adventure. And Stoker had scratched his beard and said, Oh, very well . . .

Florence accompanied them on the lawn. She had had the maids pack a wicker picnic hamper, and pressed this loaded treasure on her husband before kissing him goodbye. He embraced her warmly.

'Look after the garden, dear old girl.'

'I shall work twice as hard while you're away with Spinks.'

'I know you will that. You'll miss him more than you will me.'

'Come back soon, my darling. And remember what Daddy would have said – "Chin up!" '

On impulse she turned, put her arms round Joe's neck, and kissed his cheek.

'I have only myself to blame for Bram's everlasting restlessness,' she said in his ear. 'But some aspects of marriage are not always to a lady's liking. Look after him – he's very dear to me.'

'Of course I'll look after him, Mrs Stoker.' He kissed her powdery cheek, liking her for all her prejudices. He thought to himself, They're a couple of good people, and I'm leading him into danger. There is an element of destructiveness in me, right enough.

The two men set off down the lawn, Spinks following and van Helsing somewhere tagging along. They looked back and waved. Florence stood by the gazebo, using her handkerchief. She waved it in response, like a good soldier's daughter.

The shadows were still long as the sunlight slanted through the trees to the flanks of the time train. The two coffins, containing the driver and Bella's remains, were already loaded.

The men were about to get in when van Helsing stepped in front of them.

'Mr Stoker, may I appeal to you? Stay home. Foreign places are not for you.'

Stoker breathed deep. 'I appreciate your concern, Van. Just remember the psalmist's words, "The earth is the Lord's, and all that therein is". Look after Florence.'

Van Helsing made as if to argue, then bit his bottom lip and turned away. Bodenland stood and watched him go, unable to grasp why he was moved as the frail figure disappeared among the trees in the direction of the old house.

He thought to himself, My life makes sense to me, good sense. Yet how rarely I take the sense of other lives.

And the copse, which had seemed such a friendly place, took on a different aspect. This was the life of trees, of nature, of the great vegetable world, a world of proliferation without brain or aspiration to brain. It had a presence. Suddenly he felt it – the personality of trees: not so much indifferent as obtuse, enduring. All these pretty little trees contained within them the ambition to be forest giants, and to eclipse all the neighbouring trees. If he stood here long enough, they would rise and suffocate him. They would grow through him if he did not move.

Together with Stoker and Spinks, Bodenland climbed into the cab and slid the door closed. He turned to the controls, conscious of how inexpert he was. When he switched on the main power, the generators roared reassuringly. Somewhere, somehow, immense quantities of future solar power were being consumed.

He set the controls for 2599. Global co-ordinates would take a little more calculating. He bit his lip, still not entirely able to believe what was happening, yet eager to have his experts back home examine this miraculous piece of machinery. Behind him, Stoker spoke in his usual unruffled, genial tones.

'Faith, the dear old girl's packed us a bottle of champagne.' He raised the magnum, swathed in a linen napkin, for Bodenland's inspection. 'Let's the two of us drink to AD 2599.'

'AD 2599 – and the Silent Empire!'

Silent Empire indeed! Many hours had passed when the train emerged in real time again. They found themselves in a place of blazing heat and light, without movement or sound. No Carboniferous this time – it appeared that Bodenland had got the measure of the controls, only to make the train materialize somewhere that resembled an abstraction.

They contemplated the view without speaking for a while.

'I didn't imagine the future was going to look like this, sir,' said Spinks, with evident disappointment.

'Bit short of trees and chaps,' Stoker agreed. 'Rather a surplus of mangelwurzels, though.'

'You can't say it isn't silent . . .'

They stared out at a wide expanse of land, supine beneath a sky of cloudless blue. A haze which might have been smog stretched across row after row of a green-leafed vegetable. The vegetable grew in furrows as far as the horizon, and showed no sign of stopping there.

One by one, they climbed from the train and stood on the ground. Nothing moved in the expanse before them. No tree, no shade, could be seen. No bird flew overhead.

Their view of this monotony was obstructed by a building of spectacular dimension. The train had stopped beside it, so closely that they now stood in its shadow, although the sun was almost at its zenith. So tall was the structure they could not get a glimpse of its roof. It appeared to be without architectural feature. No window punctuated the flat grey wall with its glassy surface by which they paused, looking about alertly for signs of life. The wall, the flat land, the featureless sky: together they might have formed a simple diagram in a textbook.

'The mangelwurzels have taken over the planet,' said Stoker, as they surveyed the cheerless scene. 'Mr Darwin didn't bargain for that.'

'It's hot and no mistake,' said Spinks. He rolled up his sleeves.

Bodenland had the impression that he was searching in his mind like a blind man fumbling in a maze. Still the memory of what happened in the crypt did not return, but he managed to grasp a recollection of Bella's words to him on the terrace.

'Is there any chance that this building, whatever it is, houses the super-bomb our friendly neighbourhood lamia spoke of?'

'Here's a door or summat,' Spinks said, pointing. A few metres away was a slight indentation, grey like the wall, which the shadow of the building concealed. They went over to it.

Nothing indicated that it was a door. No handle or lock showed. Stoker put a burly shoulder to it. Nothing budged.

'There's a panel here.' The plate was certainly inconspicuous and no larger than Bodenland's hand. He placed his hand flat on it. Noiselessly, the door slid away to one side.

They entered the building.

The interior was so dark that they could see nothing until their pupils adjusted from the brilliance outside. Gradually they made out the full extent of it. The roof high above them covered acres of ground. Up there, suspended from metal beams, were gigantic bar-lights, at present switched off. The function of the lights could be to speed plant growth. But much of the ground-space where the men stood was occupied by rows of a plant needing very little light, a kind of fungus shaped like an old-fashioned coolie's hat, and at least a metre wide at the brim. It was mottled, and not particularly pleasant to their eyes. Bodenland broke a piece off one fungus and sniffed it suspiciously.

'This appears to be an agricultural factory,' he said. 'Maybe it needs no human attention. Isn't there a machine of some kind working over there?'

They watched. A large boxlike object was emerging from the

distant gloom. It drew nearer, working slowly along the ranks of the repulsive fungus. Small fingers waved on the end of a flexible arm.

'It's tickling the toadstools, sir,' said Spinks, laughing, and the sound echoed hollowly. 'Not what I'd call gardening.'

'Is this all the future boils down to? What a swindle,' said Stoker. 'Give me the good old nineteenth century anytime. I thought we'd be seeing flying automobiles and air balloons at the least.'

'Not to mention super-bombs. Come on, this is nothing. Let's have a look out of this other door.'

Much of the light entering the agricultural factory came through a door opposite the one by which they had entered. It stood open. They crossed the floor space to it.

From this second door, the view held more interest. The field of green vegetable still stretched almost endlessly in all directions, but there was also a road, running straight, away from the factory through flat countryside. And in the distance, only a mile or so away, stood a city. Smog covering the field pointed like a finger in that direction. The city itself, semi-obscured though it was by smog, looked like a number of irregularly shaped plastic containers placed on end.

The men gazed at it in some awe.

'If I fed the correct co-ordinates into the computer, that should be Tripoli, the capital of the Great Libyan – or *Silent* – Empire.'

'And this should be 2599, about teatime.'

'Well, Bram, I'll go and see, shall I?'

Just inside the door was a glass-fronted office-cum-cloakroom. It differed little from many Bodenland had had installed in his own offices. He entered, and came upon a row of lockers containing work overalls, tin hats, and photochromic face masks. He waggled a mask at Stoker.

'They have a smog problem in the twenty-sixth century. As bad as the twentieth.' He climbed into the overalls and put on the helmet, slinging the mask on top of it.

'What we lack above all is information. The city's the place. If there is a super-fusion bomb as rumoured, I'll try to find out where it is. Instead of the Undead using it on humanity, humanity had better use it on them.'

144

'Where?'

'Lots to be figured out before we tackle that one. Keep yourself amused. I'll be back.'

'Faith, don't you know the difference between heroism and insanity?' He grasped Bodenland's hand in admiration.

Bodenland gave him a grin as he left. There was nothing else to be done but visit the city.

Tripoli was farther away than he estimated, and the heat greater. It took an hour before he arrived at the low bridge crossing an almost dry canal. In that time, he had encountered no one. Now the outskirts of the city began, and soon he was in a busy thoroughfare.

And there he had to rest, propped up against a blank wall.

It was not that the walk had exhausted him. It was rather that he had fallen prey to black depression. Fighting it silently, he ascribed it to many things, to the melancholy of the scene in which they had arrived, to the forebodings he felt about his wife, to the horrifying encounter with the lamia, to his isolation from the rest of the known world. And finally to an idea that there might be a time-lag effect from travelling through millennia, equivalent to the jet-lag experienced after travel through multiple time-zones, which writers on time-travel had never bothered to mention.

Only much later did he recognize that he had been overcome by a form of depression which attacks many active, inventive, and creative people. He was now among foreigners who could never love him or recognize all he had achieved in life. He hated that hollow sensation, so empty of the power drive from which his energies derived.

He banished it by thrusting forward, dark mask in place to protect against the bitter tang of smog pervading the streets.

Tripoli appeared to be a confusing mixture of Chandigar, Houston, and old Baghdad. He realized he could recognize only the familiar aspects of an urban environment; developments since his time would take longer to sink in. This was the place where all the people had gone. He was jostled as he went forward, without hostility, without consideration. Most of the men – he saw no women – were dressed in Muslim-type clothes and wore anti-pollution helmets of ornate design, unlike his utilitarian model.

Wheeled vehicles were absent. There were those who rode on what looked like little more than a rod, travelling less than a metre above the ground. Bodenland was reminded of the old witch's broomstick.

He allowed himself to be carried along by the crowd. After crossing another bridge, the throng surged into a wide square. Here people were organizing themselves into ranks, and shouting with much fist-waving. Banners were paraded. Police were in evidence, wearing green uniforms and well-armed.

Even as Bodenland realized how conspicuous he was, standing out from the mob in his yellow overalls and basic tin helmet, an officer came up to him threateningly. Bodenland could see almost nothing of his face, shielded by his photochromic mask.

The officer demanded his papers.

Directly Bodenland tried to dive into the crowd, he was grabbed by two more police. A truncheon smashed down on the back of his neck.

The world receded. He was aware of a blur of faces, of shouts, and then the interior of somewhere, and more police. He recovered full consciousness to find himself alone in a small cell. A loud babble all around him told him that Tripoli had a booming prison population.

Staggering to the cell's one and only bench, he sat down and began gingerly to rub the top of his spine.

Florence Stoker was in her garden early, and thinking about Heaven. She stood by her ornamental pool regarding the reflection of blue sky in the water. Perhaps Earth was just a distorted reflection of somewhere better. The Earth would be a better place if Bram were with her. She prayed for his safety.

She walked calmly on her croquet lawn, surveying the long border that was her especial care, and noted that the delphiniums had suffered some damage during the night.

Van Helsing appeared from nearby bushes and greeted her. She started at his silent arrival.

'Dr van Helsing, you have a very secretive way of approaching a person. My late father, the lieutenant colonel, would have suspected something of the Pathan in you. Pathans can steal the sheets from under you while you sleep in your bed. Look what's happened to my best delphiniums. Such a shame!'

'There's the culprit.' The doctor pointed to an immense yellow slug at full stretch, about to conceal itself under a stone. 'Let me squash the beastly thing for you.'

'Indeed you will do no such thing. Let it be, doctor. The poor creature has as much right to its brief life as we have to ours. The fault is mine, that I did not get Spinks to sprinkle soot round the plants before he embarked on this adventure of Bram's.'

She looked back to where the house, with its conservatory and little spire topped by a weathervane, basked in the sun. She thought of Spinks. This afternoon, she would walk down to the village and see his mother. Probably take the old lady a ham and some raspberry preserve.

'I did my best to persuade Mr Stoker not to go, ma'am,' van Helsing said, perhaps attempting to mind-read.

She looked down at the slug withdrawing under the stone, leaving a shining trail on the earth. 'Yes, I know – you're always doing your best, doctor. I am troubled in spirit, that must be admitted.'

'Well, then. Be assured there is no "spirit" in the sense you imply, you understand, merely a response to a situation, as with animals. Mr Darwin has proved that we are simply descendants of apes.'

'As, I suppose, roast beef is a descendant of the cow.'

He coughed. 'Not precisely. Humans have the gift of intelligence.'

'As beef has the gift of mustard.'

'You do not take me seriously, ma'am.'

'I'm sorry, doctor. Perhaps if I were an ape I would. I do not mean to be impolite, but I believe I know a great deal more about my troubled spirit than does your Mr Darwin. Please leave me with my flowers and my beastly slugs.'

Van Helsing bowed and withdrew. The lady remained alone, pottering in her peaceful garden.

The creature that had been Mina Legrand was in a fury of frustration and confusion.

This is Joe's doing. It's some trouble he's brought on us. I know

147

it. It's a plague. I burn like a thing from hell, yet I'm cold. Freezing, can't eat. Where am I? It's as if – I can't understand it, as if I was dead. In some way dead. Everything's grey.

It's that man's doing. Yes, when was it? – the motel room. It's some trouble he's brought on me. I know it. It's a plague, a pox. Probably AIDS. What was I thinking about? I can't eat or drink. I long to drink. Wait . . .

That terrible . . . No, surely I did not seduce my own son . . . Who was I with on that filthy bed? Larry, Kylie? Wicked. And those lumbering monsters. Oh, why can't I think straight? I can feel my brain decay, run like coffee grounds from nose and ears.

Filth . . . something's in the bloodstream. Yes, must be AIDS, vengeance on me for sinning. No, out with it – let me die. I am dying of thirst.

The world – I never dreamed it had this dreadful curse in it.

Where's this place I'm in? Save me, Joe, save me, damn you, I'm in hell.

Drink I need, anything – blood . . .

She had emerged from her drawer and was staggering about the funeral parlour. It was dark here, lit only by the signs outside and the headlights of passing cars. The shadowy elegant creature at the Moonlite Motel had gone, his duty finished, his disease passed on.

Cursing and crying dry-eyed, the thing that had been Mina staggered against a coffin. The lid slid away, revealing the body of a woman in her sixties, made up and beautified ready for her cremation first thing in the morning. A glass lid protected her from the air.

Mina clung to the handles of the coffin. She stared through the glass at the dead woman, spoke to her cajolingly, threateningly. Spoke to her of love – love eternal. The corpse made no response: all that came back was the serene visage of death, eyes closed, face tanned by the resident beautician. Mortality had left not a tinted hair out of place. To all Mina's shrieks and whispers no answer came.

You're just like Larry. You don't respond. I'll show you love . . .

When she managed to claw away the glass lid, it slipped off the counter and shattered to pieces on the floor.

Mina climbed into the coffin. She tore away the corpse's funeral garment before easing herself down to it. Uttering endearments, she began to gnaw at the throat, just below the make-up line.

The night was a restless one for Larry, too.

At midnight, compassion overcoming instinct, Kylie returned to the motel, to find her husband weeping on the floor in a pool of vomit.

She could make no sense of his ravings at first, and was offended by the mess.

Being a practical and compassionate young lady, she went out to the Chock Full O' Nuts and bought two chilliburgers and a flask of decaff. With these, and with paracetamol, she ministered to her unhappy husband.

When he was partly restored, Larry gave a shamefaced account of how his mother had entered the room and attempted an obscene act with him. At first Kylie tried not to laugh, but the story was spun out to great length, and the narrator shed tears over his narrative.

'You know Mina is dead,' said Kylie. She located the empty Wild Turkey bottle under the sofa, to gaze sternly at him through it. 'You have to go easy on the liquor, my friend. Booze is not the best way to get yourself through a period of mourning.'

He clutched his head. 'More coffee, Kylie. You're kinder than I deserve, but I swear she was here. Oh my god, Pop's going to blame me for all this when he returns, and honest I'm not responsible . . .'

She folded her arms and walked to and fro.

'You'll have to be responsible for something some time, Larry. You know well that your mother lies in her last sleep in the mortician's. We identified her, remember? You've been suffering hallucinations.'

He stood up shakily. 'I'll have myself a shower. Honey, I will give up on the hooch. Promise. But I'll stake my life my mother . . . What am I saying? Stake? That's it – it's the curse of Clift's graves. You said there was evil and you were right. Mother has . . . become a vampire. She's become a vampire. That's it – she's become a vampire.'

149

Looking frightened, Kylie shook her head and attempted non-chalance.

'They do not permit vampires in Enterprise City – bad for tourism. Go take that shower.'

'Okay – and thanks for coming back to me, hon. I really appreciate it. My next model plane I'll name after you. We'll go to the funeral parlour in the morning and take a look . . . you know, at Mina. If there are any telltale signs – stigmata – and I tell you there will be – I am going to ACT. You'll see I'm not the wimp you think.'

'Get in that shower, you brute!' Smiling, she made as if to kick him.

They slept fitfully after that. Next morning saw them sitting in an ice-cream parlour, Trix's Licks, just off Main Street. Through the plate glass window of the parlour they could survey the mortician's shop front while gathering courage to go over. Trix herself brought their sundaes over as they sat companionably at the bar. Kylie smiled her thanks, then looked gloomy again.

As is frequently the case with young married couples, both of them had changed their minds overnight.

'I'm frightened of your drinking, Larry, dear, that's the truth. But I know you are no alcoholic. You had a bad experience. Why should I try to deny it? Maybe your mother did visit you. That note she left – "Joe you bastard" – doesn't that show she was in deep trouble of some kind? Maybe she has become a vampire.'

Larry shook his head. 'I can't believe in vampires in daylight. It's that novel you're reading getting to you.'

She laughed. 'Now you sound like your father. The Church has a proper sense of the battle of Good against Evil. It's a very ancient battle. Belief in devils and vampires goes way way back, and has to be well-founded for that reason.'

When he made no response, Kylie watched him, sitting opposite her, elbows on counter, a coloured straw at his pink lip. He was gazing calculatingly across the street at the stained glass in the mortician's window. Maybe he's planning to deliver his groceries there, she thought, then hastily retracted the treachery.

But of course the unspoken question was, was their marriage always to be like this? Could she find in herself sufficient depth

150

of character – of love – to stick with Larry Bodenland, to elicit responses that were more than perfunctory? Why was it she was always having to mop up his spew? And to tell him things? And to offer advice? Why couldn't it be vice versa?

Because when you looked at it coolly, she did not want a mother role. She liked playing the good obedient daughter. Was she not a shade fonder of Joe, bossy though he was, than his son?

'It's only your and your father's rationalism which seeks to deny the supernatural.' A verbal prod.

Larry shook his head.

'We live in a scientific age.'

So the clock was stuck at cliché time. 'Where there is no vision the people perish.' She had to stand by him, to try to induce vision into him – if not for Larry's sake, then for her own. You could not live isolated; you had to do something for others. Otherwise she'd be as dead as he was. Poor Larry. Yes, it was already 'poor Larry'.

What did vampires think about most of the time? Maybe they didn't think. But what did Larry think about, when you came down to it? Girlie magazines, screwing, Wild Turkey, and 12 x Cheesecake (Fruits of Forest Flavour) To be Stored at 0°F . . .

'I mean,' he said, turning to her with an effort, 'if you blot these bad things from your mind, they'll go away, you see, hon? The way you can persuade yourself you're not going to get a cold.'

'Okay. What if the bad things won't leave your mind? Maybe you should face them – turn and face them, not run from them. You say it's a scientific age – the age of the gas chamber. Then be scientific and face the facts. Your mother tried to suck your blood, so you told me. And worse than that. Get you in a sexual embrace.'

He wondered gloomily to himself if this was the way their marriage was going to go, with Kylie perpetually trying to get the edge on him. He could not find the strength to defy her this morning, when his head ached.

He shuddered, pressing down a blob of ice-cream in the glass so that the strawberry flavouring rushed up to the top.

'Don't remind me. To think my mother . . .'

'We have to help her, Larry. If Joe was here he would approve of that.'

'Right. It's the curse of Clift's grave,' he repeated, reaching out for her hand. 'We'll do something between us.'

In a happier mood, they stared out across the street.

A lumber yard stood next to the mortician. ENTERPRISE TIMBERS, proclaimed a large sign. 'Wood Carved to Your Requirement. Fences, Stakes.'

The bald mortician greeted them when at length they entered the funeral parlour. His hands were fluttery this morning, like doves seeking lodgement in his pale suit. When Kylie showed him a bouquet of flowers she had bought, the man merely nodded, without interest.

'Your lamented mom is in a casket now. Unhappily, we had a little accident in here last night, overnight. Hooligans, a rough element . . . The Old John site attracts a number of undesirables from other states . . . they desecrated the establishment.'

'What happened exactly?'

The mortician blinked rapidly and the doves fluttered again. 'A Lounge of Rest is not the proper place for necrophilia, sir.'

'Convenient, though . . . May we take a final farewell of mother?'

He managed to smile and nod while seeming to shake his head. 'We who as yet evade the Old Reaper . . . we gain spiritually from gazing on the countenance of those who have entered eternal peace . . .'

He led the young couple into his inner sanctum where the air was dim and sacred and a plastic sign, designed to console the bereaved, said, 'Sunlight Never Ceases'. Kylie gripped Larry's hand.

The mortician untied a mauve ribbon and removed the lid of Mina's casket with a flourish.

Mina lay in the semi-dark, hands folded on chest. Her expression was severe, her mouth red. As the lid came off, her eyelids flickered. She opened her eyes and stared up at them.

Then she spoke. Her voice was thick as if encrusted with mould.

'Larry, I need you. I'm – not what you think . . . Come to me.'

The little mortician ran for it. Larry stood fast, staring down at the distorted version of a face he had loved.

'Mother, you're dead. Don't you know that? Dead.'

'No, no – beyond death – something different. I hope for everlasting life. And for you if you come. And your daddy.' Her mouth worked, sticky and crimson. The words of promise were belied by her expression of overwhelming avidity.

As he gazed down in revulsion, her hands grasped the side of the casket, white in her endeavour to lever herself up.

'Not at that price, Mother.'

Kylie had lost her head and was running after the mortician, yelling for a priest to come and administer last rites.

Larry yelled too. 'I'll save Daddy from that fate!' He pulled out the timber stake he had been concealing under his sweat shirt.

Bearing down with his own weight, he drove it between Mina's ribs.

Her cry was unearthly. She clawed at him in her last agonies as he sank towards her, forcing the stake down into her heart.

At last she was still, and he backed away, his face bloody with lacerations.

'You see,' he said aloud. 'I can do it. I can do it.'

He tucked his mother's arms tenderly into the casket. Already her face was resuming the lineaments of the woman he had loved so desperately all his life.

Sobs wracked him. 'God bless you, Mom,' he said. His tears fell on her lined face.

Walking unsteadily, he found Kylie weeping in the outer office.

'They sell crucifixes, Larry. I'll buy one and put it in the casket. Maybe you'd put it in for me.'

'I did it. She's at peace now. I dared to do it. It was the right thing, wasn't it?'

She put her arms round him.

'You did just great. Now you'll have to explain it to Joe when he returns — if he ever does.'

CHAPTER XI

On arrival in this alien Tripoli, Joe Bodenland had fallen foul of his old enemy, depression. Once he was locked in the police cell, this mood fell away. His spirits always improved when faced with a new challenge.

The cell was basic and only doubtfully clean. He could walk four paces one way and three the other. It had no window. In the passage beyond, however, a television screen burned. He could squint at it and see what was going on, although from his oblique angle the three-dimensional effect was distorted. From it he learned something of the desperate situation in which the Silent Empire found itself in this mortal year of 2599.

He was trapped in a future blacker than he could have imagined. A large meteor, of a kind long anticipated by astronomers and others, had struck the northern hemisphere, destroying or throwing into anarchy the old civilizations of Europe and North America. Much dirt and dust had been thrown into the atmosphere, followed by smoke from extensive forest fires. The result had been a severe screening of sunlight, which brought about two years of inclement winter. In the prevailing darkness, the Fleet Ones had seen their chance. With the aid of the time train, they had come from past and future to the attack, and had prevailed over the disorganized nations of humanity.

The Silent Empire was so-called because it had no one to talk to. All other cultures in the northern hemisphere had gone under. Now it too was faced with extinction.

All this, Bodenland quickly gleaned, for the television channel broadcast nothing but political speeches – speeches made in the studio direct to camera, or speeches made in the open, addressed to crowds of thousands of people. Speeches designed to whip up defiance in the Empire's last stand.

This was certainly enough to occupy Bodenland's mind. His morale was high. He was unable to conquer the unreasonable hope that either he would be released or that the resourceful Stoker would come to his aid.

However, the hours went by. Food and drink were passed in to him. He ate a hunk of bread, a sliver of goat's cheese, and a slice of rotting pineapple.

A warder marched along the passage and switched off the television. Joe was there for the night.

By next morning, his mood was much more rebellious. He refused to look at or listen to the television. The cell was situated so that he had no contact with other prisoners. He paced as far as he was able until a warder came with a key, unlocked the door, and marched him down the passage to the check-in desk.

A tall man in grey flowing robes stood there, head enveloped in a dark visored helmet. He beckoned to Bodenland.

Bodenland looked from him to the warder.

'Out you go,' said the warder, with a brisk gesture.

'I've not been charged. What the devil was I brought in for?'

The stranger tugged his sleeve and indicated the door.

'Who the hell are you?'

'Money buys much here, even freedom. Do you come or do you wish to remain in the prison?'

'I see your point.' Without further ado, Joe followed the tall man out of the building. He did not look back.

Once they were outside, he stopped.

'Don't think I'm not glad to be out of there, but who are you?'

'Call me Ali, Mr Bodenland. I represent an official body which welcomes foreigners here – as the Libyans do not. Why should they? These are the last days of the Silent Empire. But you do not have to spend them in a stinking cell. Now, I know a quiet shop nearby where we can have a drink.' The grey-clad man made him a bow.

There has to be a trade-off, thought Bodenland. Someone's setting me up.

The quiet shop was at least shady. Entering from the hazy sunlight, Bodenland could see little, and removed his helmet and visor. Under a deep awning, the glassless coffee shop windows looked out towards a grand square. The square was full of activity. Bodenland saw little of it, for his host led the way to a table in the darkest part of the rear room.

As Ali seated himself, he clicked his fingers, and immediately two long-handled brass mugs of coffee were brought on a brass tray, together with two tots of water.

'You care for something to eat?'

'Thanks, no.'

They both sat without words. Bodenland waited for the mysterious Ali to speak, alert for danger.

'Libya is now being attacked. That is why the people are restless. Their time has come. It must have been like this in Byzantium before it finally collapsed after the long erosion. Some defiance, more resignation.'

He was not touching his coffee and continued to wear his visor.

'The human race will have had a short run for its money. The much vaunted brain, the neocortex, proved not to be a winning number.'

'You sound cheerful about it, Ali. Isn't there a super-bomb the Libyans can use on their enemies?'

'Ah, the F-bomb. Well . . . It's well known that the Fleet Ones cannot invent. Their talents are not with technology.'

'What are their talents? I've yet to learn.'

'You will learn. I'm sure of that.' Said with a smile, though it was hardly visible in their dark corner. 'As I was saying, their talents are not with technology. But when they seize on mankind's destructive weapons, the Fleet Ones can copy them in their own factories and turn the weapons back on their inventors. Their factories are invulnerable, situated as they are in the far future, where the sun grows dark.'

Bodenland played idly with the strap of his helmet, which he had placed on the table.

156

'And how can I help you in all this – this tale of defeat or triumph, depending on which side you look at it from?'

'Let's talk about the time train, Mr Bodenland.'

'Ah yes.' He brought the helmet up and over in a swing of the arm, crashing it down on the other's head. At the same moment he was up and running. He had caught a flash of canines when Ali smiled.

In the vicinity of the agricultural station, nothing moved. Nothing, that is, except young Spinks.

Spinks was a muscular fellow in his early twenties. His healthy features denoted the outdoor life he led. He walked smartly up and down between the stationary time train and the wall of the enormous building. Bram Stoker sat in the shade of the building with his back to the wall, watching idly.

'You carry yourself well, Spinks. Ever thought of joining the British Army?'

'Me, sir? No, sir.'

'A great pity that, a great pity. Now my father-in-law, James Balcombe, joined the army as a young man and made a good career of it. Would have made a full colonel but for a general who . . . Well, never mind that. He fought in the Crimean War and got a medal.'

'My grandpa fought in the Crimean War, sir. He got a wooden leg.'

Stoker was silent a moment.

'Well, it's the luck of the draw. I must say, Joe doesn't seem to be having much luck. We've been hanging about here for a month of Sundays. Maybe I'd better go and see what he thinks he's doing. On the other hand . . . Have we finished off that roast duck Mrs Stoker packed?'

'There's a wing left, sir, and a slice of cucumber.'

'Better save it, I suppose. Frugal it has to be.' He rose and stretched. 'Could be the devils have us in a trap. Always fear the Undead, who envy the living – as well they might. Ireland's a pretty place, but not if you're looking up at it from under the sod.'

Continuing with his guard duty, Spinks said, 'I don't understand one thing. If the vampires can travel through time on this here

157

train, how come they aren't aware of what's going on now? How come they don't know we're here?'

Mopping his face, Stoker said, 'It's a little hot for such problems, Spinks. But you might consider this. There's a devil of an amount of time – millions and millions of years of it, according to Mr Bodenland, wrapping the Earth around – more time than even great intellects like yours and mine can grasp, never mind the desiccated soup that vampires have for brains. They'd have an impossible job to survey any particular minute, or year even.'

'Supposing they happened to be passing in another train?'

The ginger man shook his head. 'That can't happen. Our friend who's travelling with us in his box – once no less than the driver of the train – told Joe that there was only one train, which is in our possession.' He considered. 'Though I can't understand why there should be only one.'

'I'm afraid I can't help you there, sir.'

The conversation made them nervous. They agreed, however, that they could not be in a trap, since the vampires would not strike in broad daylight, being photophobic.

The day, however, was becoming uncomfortably hot. They decided to retire into the agricultural station. It was cooler inside.

'That's better. How're the stocks of lemonade and whisky?'

'Frugal it has to be, sir. Tell you what, take your mind off things, we could play a game of French cricket between us.'

'Light's a bit poor in here for cricket, Spinks . . . Oh, yes, come on, why not? Capital idea. I bags be Hampshire. Go and get the bat and ball out of the train, there's a good feller.'

The pollution was particularly thick outside the Prime Minister's palace in Tripoli's main square. All men in the crowd wore elaborate helmets to guard against the poisons, many of them draping their *keffiyeh* over the helmets. With the cunning of a pick-pocket, Bodenland stole one of the scarves from a stall, and tied it round his own helmet, making himself less conspicuous.

He seemed to have shaken off Ali, though beyond doubt there would be other Undead agents in the crowd, awaiting the final collapse of the Silent Empire.

That time could be only days away at most.

Many of the shops were shuttered. Some carried poignant messages of farewell. Families were leaving, with a few worldly possessions piled on handcarts or donkeys, seeking to escape an inevitable doom. Bodenland searched for a lawyer, but it seemed as if the professional classes had already left Tripoli under cover of darkness. Over the many thousands of citizens who remained, an intense excitement quivered, almost as if the end were invited and – now it was so near – desired. What is most feared is secretly loved.

During the midday prayer, many prostrated themselves in the streets, facing towards a Mecca that had already been extinguished. Afterwards the Prime Minister came out of the Palace, to appear on behalf of the Emperor.

The Prime Minister was a tall solemn man. The crowds called his name and rushed forward, waving, to crush themselves at the barriers which fended common people off from the great building.

He spoke from the steps of the Palace, his amplified voice carrying round the square. Thousands listened, not all of them patiently.

From a gate in the Palace wall, a great black cube was emerging, draped in a Libyan flag. The cube was carried on a metal litter, wheeled, and supported by as many hands as could get near. It was brought out ceremoniously and placed in the square, where a flatbed truck waited.

A great cry went up at the sight of the black cube, a cry at once cheer and wail. For the Prime Minister was making it clear that the cube contained Libya's super-weapon, the F-bomb, the only one they had been able to manufacture.

Now that the hour of judgement was upon them, they knew not how to strike against the Fleet Ones. The bomb was useless as a defensive weapon. However, he, on behalf of the Emperor and his people, was not going to allow the F-bomb to fall into the hands of their enemies. Was this not correct?

A great roar from the crowd gave him an affirmative answer.

Very well, the weapon was about to be taken to the desert, and detonated a great distance away. No one would be harmed.

While the Prime Minister was speaking, a modest-sized metal suitcase painted red and green was brought out from the cube. Two men, moving with care, strapped it on the waiting truck.

And the Prime Minister said, 'My people, let us pray for wisdom and the protection of Allah in this hour of grief.'

Whereupon the whole assembly in the square fell upon their knees and touched heads to the ground. And a cry of supplication rose from them.

Of all the thousands of people there, not one was looking. Bodenland jumped into the near side of the cab of the truck and rammed a revolver at the head of the driver.

'Drive on!' Bodenland ordered, looking as desperate as he felt.

Eyes bulging, the man drove.

'Faster,' said Bodenland.

In a moment they were out of the square and heading out of town.

It looked like nowhere. No scene in the Antarctic could have been more drab. The desert here was not desert proper, the romantic desert of folds, patterns and dunes, where sand builds itself into unending hieroglyphs. This was a flat and stony place, promising none of the interest of a cryptogram. The road itself was only a dust trail through the desolation. Nothing had changed for centuries.

'We've come the wrong way,' said Bodenland.

They could not turn back into the city. He kept the revolver at the man's head as he tried to work out what to do. With set expression, the driver drove on.

Bodenland peered ahead through the dusty windscreen, trying to see if something moved through the heat haze ahead. Sticking his head out of the window, he could determine a line drawn across the desert. It wobbled in the heat as if in boiling water. As they neared, it revealed itself to be a fence, stretching across miles of desert.

It was a tall wire fence, and it bisected the landscape. He could make out no beginning or end to either side. Its one feature was a gate set in the middle of it, and to this gate the truck was heading.

A guard post with metal roof stood by the gate, resonant under the power of the sun.

'Keep going,' Bodenland yelled, pounding with a fist on the dashboard. 'Through the gate.'

'No – no use, please . . .' The driver jammed on the brake. They ground to a halt in front of the gate, skidding in a shower of gravel to end broadside on to the guard post. Before the cloud of dust had settled, four Muslim guards dashed from the hut, carbines at the ready, to stand on either side of the truck.

A loudspeaker burst into life.

'The traitor must surrender. Descend from the cab, traitor.'

The driver, whose face ran with sweat, rolled his eyes in terror. 'Don't shoot me, please. I have a family. The game's up for you.'

The four guards dragged Bodenland struggling from the cab. After all, his revolver was not loaded. He hated carrying a loaded gun.

They frog-marched him into the post to stand before the guard commander.

Inside the hut, a fan did little to disperse the heat. A rack of cots stood at one end, empty at present in the emergency. On the rear wall, behind the guard commander's desk, hung a cage containing a small captive bird, a finch. The finch was yellow and red; it sat on its perch and sang its heart out, as if it had just discovered paradise.

The commander was very pale, very young, and had grown a top-heavy black moustache to compensate for these defects.

He stood up, puffing out his chest and pointing a finger at his prisoner. 'You are a spy. You are arrested for stealing the F-bomb. I have the Prime Minister's authority to execute you. Have you anything to say in your defence?'

Bodenland out-stared him. 'I certainly have, Captain. You see your little imprisoned bird there? If it were free and had a nest full of chicks, don't you reckon it would defend its nest if attacked? Even if the attacker was an eagle, the finch would do its best. You Libyans have this super-weapon, so-called, yet you are going to detonate it in the desert! You're mad. I'm on your side in this war against the Fleet Ones, and I say drop the rotten bomb on them. Don't waste it, if it's the last thing you do. Let me go, Captain. I'll deliver it where it hurts. Don't horse around. Just give me a compass and let me go free.'

The young captain heard him out politely, nodding as the points were made.

Then he said, 'I'm afraid you do not share our philosophy. Allah

161

must have his way and we must follow. All else is an offence against God.'

'You think the Undead give a crap about Allah?'

But the captain had turned to his corporal. 'Take this man out and shoot him.'

Bodenland made a dive across the desk for the captain's gun, but the officer stepped hastily back, and two men pinned Bodenland down on the desk.

Wrenching his arms behind his back, they moved him towards the door, with Bodenland fighting every inch of the way. The bird fluttered in fright in its cage.

Another guard came running in from outside, full of excitement.

'Captain, something coming this way.'

'Our relief . . .'

'No, no, captain, from the west. Come and see.'

This event was evidently so rare that they all ran out into the desert and stared through the fence to the west.

It had come over the horizon. It was blasting in their direction. Difficult to make out what it was; its outline was blurred.

The captain tugged one end of his moustache and looked doubtfully at Bodenland.

Bodenland knew beyond a doubt, and kept his own counsel. It was the time train. Good old Stoker was coming to the rescue, just when needed. The only question was – why and how was it coming from that direction and not from the direction of the city?

The captain's intuition told him danger was on its way.

'All back inside,' he ordered. His manner was calm and commanding; Bodenland admired it. 'Be prepared to shoot when I give the order.'

Once they were inside the hot little refuge, the door was secured and the men took up positions at the window. The captain himself guarded Bodenland, covering him with a revolver.

'Give yourself up,' Bodenland advised. 'It's a buddy of mine.'

The outlines of the time train became clearer as it slowed. Losing velocity, it contracted, radiating energy as it did so, and came to a halt half-way through the wire barrier. Dust settled.

No one descended.

'I'm here, Bram,' Bodenland shouted.

In response, heavy guns swivelled from the window slits of the train. Their snouts poked towards the guard post.

A metallic amplified voice roared out over the wasteland, demanding the surrender of Bodenland.

He tried to make sense of it. His mind jumped to the obvious conclusion, that Stoker and Spinks had been captured and lost control of the train.

The metallic voice shouted its demands again.

The captain shouted back. 'I will surrender Bodenland if you guarantee that no harm will come to the rest of us.'

A pause. Outside, heavily shrouded figures climbed from the train and proceeded to unload the F-bomb from the truck.

'The Undead,' moaned one of the guards. He threw down his carbine and cowered by the desk.

'We demand only Bodenland. The rest of you are safe,' came the voice.

'It's a trick, Captain,' Bodenland said. 'Those are the Undead, the Fleet Ones. Give me a gun and come out with me. We'll do what damage we can. Take them by surprise.'

The captain gave him a wry smile. 'I must have regard for the safety of my men. I'm sorry. Out you go, and good luck.'

'Okay.' With heavy heart, he stepped into the sunlight. Four shrouded figures were stowing the F-bomb in its red and green case on to the train. The train loomed over the scene, its guns giving it a kind of pseudo-life as they swivelled to cover him. He walked forward slowly, seeking any advantage, but saw none.

A black-clad figure leaned from the first door of the train and beckoned. Bodenland did not hasten his pace. He climbed aboard, to be greeted by heavy-visored men with guns.

'Pity you gooks can't bear the daylight. It's really nice out there.'

They made no response, bundling him into the first compartment. The F-bomb was already there, lying on the seat.

He could see the guard post, with the pale face of the guard captain watching through the glass. Next second, the train's guns sounded.

The post was obliterated. The guns pounded until only a blackened crater was left. The noise died away, the smoke rolled across the Libyan desert.

'Sorry about the little bird,' Bodenland said.

A tall cadaverous Undead came into the compartment and confronted him.

'You are to meet Count Dracula immediately.'

'I'm in no hurry.'

'Follow me. Bring the bomb. It will not detonate.'

As they went into the corridor, the driver of the train was going forward to his cab. Bodenland called to him – You! Wasn't it the man he had captured and imprisoned in Stoker's tool shed, five centuries earlier? Perhaps he was mistaken.

Wait! His mind performed a somersault. The paradoxes of time confronted him. Perhaps his capture and imprisonment of the driver was *still to come*. In which case, there was certainly hope for him.

The driver gave him a glance, showed no sign of recognition, and disappeared into the shady recesses of the cab. Almost at once, the train started to move.

The corridor began to stretch. Everything became flexible and insecure. It was like being inside a tormented snake. As they progressed towards the rear of the train, it got further and further away, under the stress of relativistic velocities.

He was taken to a large compartment hung with black, and told to await the Count. A guard stood over him. The compartment expanded a little, then settled into stability as the train's speed steadied.

After a while, shadow and smoke that did not smell like smoke filled the place, and Count Dracula appeared, horned and gigantic, more devil than man. His face was like a painted skull. Bodenland stood up defiantly to face him. It was like facing a ghoul in your worst childhood dream, unreal, but more terrifying than any known reality.

Such was the impact of this creature that Bodenland found it hard to make his intellect function, especially in the first moments of confrontation. He did his best to register the features of this apparition. Later, he was to find it difficult to remember details, as if, like Bella, the unholy Count had the ability, in common with a disease of the brain, to erase engrams and deface memory.

Stoker had spoken of likening Dracula to Henry Irving. That, however, was in fiction. In reality, little resemblance existed between monster and actor. True, Dracula had a large head with streaks of white in his dark hair. The dark hair was swept back and cut long, much as Irving's had been. And there was a broad brow. But Dracula's brow was rocky and brutal, a mere base from which two short horns curled. The horns were crusted like a goat's.

Nor was the head noble. It was brachycephalic, with no curve at its rear, so that its peak fell straight down to the neck. Lower and upper jaws were remarkably pointed; even in respose, Dracula's strong sharp teeth remained on the verge of showing. Only the lips held colour. Of a mauvish red, they expressed at once luxuriance and cruelty, round which the teeth were glimpsed like fingers clutching a curtain. When the lips curled back in speech, both cheeks wrinkled up to resemble twin perineums.

To conceive of this creature as ever having been human was difficult and – when its powers were at full – near impossible.

When Dracula spoke, it was in the hoarse voice Bodenland remembered well, the voice Bella had used, a shared voice, equipment with which to talk to living human beings. As if that name had been conjured up in the roily air between them, Bella was the word on Dracula's lips.

'Bella was sent to you to lure you to the Silent Empire. As we planned, you have delivered the F-bomb to me. We have finished with you now, Joe Bodenland, but we intend you no harm. Did we not send you that beautiful vision in which your young daughter-in-law came to your bedside? You will be granted that vision again if you behave.'

'I can live without it.' He found it difficult to speak. Although the atmosphere vibrated with fear, Bodenland controlled his breathing and did not allow himself to be overcome. But this monstrous being was like death itself. To stay long in its presence would be annihilating. But there was a question he had to ask.

'Supposing you have trapped me, tell me this. You are the Father of Lies and Darkness, the antithesis of science – how is it you have invented this time train?'

'Your scientific view has blinkered you, Joe Bodenland. You should open your mind to a darkness wider than your petty light.

This is a turning point in history, when the human race become mice again, not pretentious creatures who dream of visiting other planets. In consequence, we have been observing this period for a long while, anticipating your arrival in our train. As to that train . . . a colossal amount of energy is required to alter the flow of time, and dam that great river. To power the train, the sun has had to grow dark. That suits us, as it suits us to borrow science when science can work against religion and God . . .'

His thick voice choked on the last word. A scent of decay filled Bodenland's nostrils. He dreaded to think that the train might even now be heading for that dark future, where the Fleet Ones ruled supreme, and nothing but death lived.

'You did not answer my question about the train.'

The answer rolled back like thunder. 'Joe Bodenland, you do not require an answer. This train is the instrument by which the Fleet Ones will prevail – as they would have done long since, had we not been so few – we were always so few, a handful a century – and had not Christianity once been so strong. With the time train, we are enabled to congregate across the ages and become strong.'

'So you invented it, despite your lack of science?'

'Cease this catechism.' The mighty figure gave a roar of laughter. 'We did not invent such a complex instrument. How could we? Man, you have a brain, yet you cannot feel with it how short life is, and how long death. Come, while we have a moment more of travel, I will show you the difference between the living and the Undead.'

This horrifying conversation seemed to turn and tunnel into Bodenland's mind, as if it were a living worm. Phrases kept spluttering across his synapses like the progeny of worms, robbing him of thought. Darkness wider than your petty light. We have finished with you now. How long death, how short life.

Without will, he followed the august figure into the corridor of the speeding train. All was dim and misty, well suited to the photophobic Undead. Satanic guards who crowded in the corridor lifted their visors to show their death-white faces, their razor-sharp jaws, in relaxation.

He strove to clear his mind. Memory came of Stoker's perception of the relationship between vampirism and the last stages of venereal disease. The human race become mice again. The sun has had to grow dark. Complex instrument. He could not keep the noises out. Was this not dementia? To be long in the company of this Darkness would be to fall into insanity.

Trying to induce logic back to his brain, he made to speak. All that emerged was the question he had previously asked.

'Train . . . How is it? How did you invent the train?'

The thing proceeding before him did not even turn his head. The answer came in its habitual tone of scorn.

'In your near future, where you came from, your government in Washington will forbid your toxic waste disposal scheme as being too dangerous. Your inertial invention will lapse and be forgotten in the files, Joe Bodenland. Forgotten until we revive it.

'We simply apply the principle, and for that we employ human slave scientists, millions of years ahead of Now. It's *your* principle that governs the existence of this train. That is why we owe you some forbearance. You yourself are the original inventor of time travel. You yourself are the instigator of the triumph of the Undead, Joe Bodenland – over Libya, and over the rest of the living world . . .'

He was not conscious. Paradoxically, it was the wormlike poison of Lord Dracula's previous speech which now protected him from the shock of the latest revelation. Yet he sank down into a surf of unknowing, threw up his hands, drowned.

That amazing novel of Bram Stoker's, which the modest author still regarded as unpublished, unprinted, unbound . . . It had alerted people to the dangers of vampirism. At the same time, it contained Stoker's encoded message of personal sorrow, as he fell sick of the disease that had ravaged mankind for centuries. In creating the great vampire novel, Stoker had produced the nineteenth-century masterwork on syphilis.

In so doing, he had intuitively performed a true diagnosis; the two poisons to the blood were indeed linked.

What Stoker could not have known was the extraordinary long lineage of the original vampiric strain, born of a cold-blooded winged predator in the distant greens of the Mesozoic. What nobody could have foreseen was the devious way in which those parasites had managed to infiltrate themselves into a future as distant as their origins. The way by which they had gone was the tunnel bored through the time quanta opened up by Bodenland's scientific ingenuity.

Joe's responsibility was too heavy to bear. It dragged him down like a great weight lashed to a sailor struggling in an ocean beyond the reach of aid.

Yet he was conscious.

In a manner of speaking.

A foul creature was sponging his face. The cold water steamed. A mist rose before him. So feelingless was he, he might have been embedded in glass.

The place to which he had been brought was mysteriously familiar. It was a torture cell. Gradually his sense returned.

The air was almost dark. It pressed against his face like an old cushion. Dracula was there, blacker than the dark.

Bodenland fought to regain control over himself.

Why did he recognize the iron torture instruments stowed behind glass doors? And worse . . .

For most of the space of the compartment was occupied by a heavy wooden table. The scars and cuts on it rendered it as wicked as a butcher's block.

On the table, pressed against its surface by iron bars, lay a naked man. His body colour was that of a drowned fish, its swollen greys and blues almost luminescent in the dull illumination. He was not drowned. His fanged teeth still worked, as they sought to bite through a metal rod which gagged his mouth.

Staring down at this pitiable sight, Bodenland's intellect sharpened. This was the compartment by which he and Bernard Clift had first entered the time train. He had seen this poor creature before, tortured and unable to escape his torturers through death.

The imprisoned vampire gave a stifled cry, rolling his eyes to his lord and master, presumably begging for mercy. Dracula paid no attention, beyond lifting a hand to summon an assistant to the table.

Most parts of the prisoner's body had been mutilated in some way. His head was shaven. Just above his brows a purple line had been painted round the scarred equator of his head.

The dull eyes of the prisoner now turned fearfully to see what the assistant was about to do.

'This loathsome thing always begs for mercy,' said Dracula in his cold brutish voice. A muscle worked in his ashen cheek. 'But mercy is not an available alternative.'

A consuming sickness choked Bodenland's throat. He managed to ask what crime the prisoner had committed, forseeing that the same kind of treatment might be in store for him.

From Dracula's reply it could be deduced that he enjoyed the tale he had to tell: in his words, 'a tale of what you call superstition triumphing over what you call science'.

The being pinned to the torture table was now one of the Undead. In his lifetime, he had been a scientist and savant – an intellect before which other intellects bowed. His name was then Alwyn. He had been taken from his own century to labour with others of his ilk in the far distant future, where living conditions were more congenial to the Fleet Ones than in earlier days.

'Alwyn tried to escape from servitude in a flying machine,' the Dark Lord said. 'But my powers are such I can fly at greater speeds than such machines. I recaptured Alwyn, and he has been impaled on this table through many millennia. He is without intellect now.'

'You're filth,' Bodenland exclaimed.

'We have turned him into one of us, Joe Bodenland, as you shall see immediately.'

He lifted a coarse index finger no more than an inch in order to summon an assistant forward to the table.

'You will be interested to watch this, Joe Bodenland. It will explain much you fail to understand. You will then appreciate the difficulties under which the Undead labour.' As he spoke, he signalled with another controlled gesture.

His assistant leaned towards the prisoner, who urinated with fright. He tapped with a long-nailed finger at the side of the prisoner's shaven skull. Two taps, then a third, sharper.

The top of the skull fell cleanly away, opening along the painted purple circle, to lie rocking on the table. Flies issued forth from the cranium, and the victim foamed at the mouth.

Inside the open cranium lay a small doughy brain much resembling a blob of ice cream and not divided into hemispheres.

When this creature was the scientist Alwyn, Dracula explained, his brain had been fully human. The invasion of vampiric blood, with its freights of hostile cells, had caused the neocortex to wither and fall away finally like a sere and yellow leaf.

Alwyn's identity was then lost. He had ceased to be Homo sapiens.

'So you are a disease,' Bodenland said. 'Nothing more than a disease, a contagion.'

Dracula released a fanged smile into the dark. 'The thing is human no longer. I doubt he even remembers who he once was or will be, centuries from now. He is, you might say, a diagram.'

Hie deep voice contained the mortuary echo of a chuckle.

'This is how we are, Joe Bodenland, we to whom you are so antagonistic. This brain you see here is how our brains are. The brain, you note, is similar in structure to a human brain – minus the neocortex, the higher reasoning part.'

'You mean the part with the conscience.'

'Animals have no conscience, Joe Bodenland. They nevertheless spare each other. Animals wage no wars, organize no persecutions, run no concentration camps. Nor do we, the Fleet Ones. The neocortex is a new and unwelcome adjunct to the natural world. *It* is the disease.

'Before the development of the neocortex – a random mutation only two million years before you were born – many many millions of years passed serenely. In those millions of years lived a great variety of creatures equipped with the old limbic brain only. Now that balance of nature, so much disturbed recently, will be restored.

'How? Ha, with the aid of the F-bomb. The F-bomb, Joe Bodenland, that crowning achievement of your vaunted neocortex . . .'

He was at his most terrifying when he laughed. It was a laugh brought about by throwing back the head, tossing the straggling hair, and opening wide the mouth to expose fangs and pallid gums. The sound accompanying this sudden spasm was without relish. All was over in a second, with the cold gaze fixed back on his opponent immediately, in order not to be caught off-guard for more than the briefest duration of time. A limbic laugh, thought Bodenland.

Briefly a vision came to him of those sempiternal centuries of which the brute before him spoke, centuries of fangs and foraging and mindless time, with no one alive to count the rising and setting of the sun.

In the dimness of the stifling compartment, the glazing in the doors of the torture cupboards reflected back what light there was like rows of polished teeth. Pinpoints of light glinted in Dracula's ever-watchful eyes. The poor victim on the table managed small constrained movements in a moribund *t'ai chi*. Difficult though it was to see in Dracula's presence, it was more difficult to think.

Attempting a scientific detachment, Bodenland said, 'You speak of the neocortex. It represents the highest evolutionary development so far. It achieves a complexity far above that of the old limbic brain. You are failed creatures, by nature as extinct as the massive herbivores on which you originally preyed. You're fossils, Dracula, compressed between life and death. I'll exterminate you if I can.'

He spoke more boldly than he felt. With his every fibre he had to resist Dracula's strong hypnotic spell.

The dark spectre spoke again.

'Your kind regards my kind as evil. I have been forced to observe your kind over the centuries, since you huddled in caves against the ice. Has ever a day gone by, or a night, in all those centuries, when you have not put someone to death? Women subjected to all kinds of injury, children abused, babies flung over cliffs, slaves beaten, preachers stoned, witches drowned, villages burned, wars fought over nothing . . . a litany of murder in more various forms than we of the Undead could ever command. Your sins are endless, and committed wilfully. What we do we cannot help.'

Raising his hands to his temples, Bodenland shook his head. The words burned. The worms worked in him.

'Being evil, you can see only the evil in mankind.' He choked on the uvula dry at the back of his throat, coughed, and could only say, 'Before this great victory – what of this victim of yours?'

He indicated the creature pinned to the table.

'The attendants will stick his skull on again. He'll survive. After all, he's one of the Undead. He can't die. You would call that a paradox.'

171

Thinking that he would be on this vehicle of damnation again – was it past or future? – he sighed heavily.

'What of the real paradoxes, the scientific paradoxes of travel through time?'

Dracula put mild thunder into his reply. 'For you, and even for those without neocortexes, time paradoxes are cancelled out by expenditure of energy, just as energy can cut through the thickest metal. Millions of volts drive this train of yours through time, and they iron out paradoxes flat. Power will achieve anything. As you know.'

Bodenland was silenced.

Dracula began to fade into smoke and cloud. As he disappeared, he spoke again.

'Now we are well on our way to collecting your story-writing friend.'

In the huge agricultural plant, several box-shaped robots moved among the rows of fungi, tickling and tending them almost in silence. Under the echoing acres of roof, one sound prevailed, the pleasant sound of willow striking leather.

'Pull up your socks, Spinks, my boy – Hampshire is forging ahead.'

'I think light's stopping play, sir,' gasped the gardener.

The light was certainly dim. Spinks had dropped several catches because of it. His inefficiency encouraged Hampshire, who was hitting out. Spinks's under-arm lobs proved irresistible.

The next ball came. Stoker struck out mightily. The ball sailed over Spinks's head and through the open door.

'A six!' yelled Stoker, as Spinks disappeared out of the door. 'Sure, it's a swine I am to you, my boy, and now I'll declare.'

He thought to himself as he stood alone in the vast dim building, I must keep young Spinks's spirits up as much as I can. What a reckless fool I am to have brought him on this expedition. His old mother will have it in for me when we get back. If we get back. Perhaps I should never have trusted this chap from the future. I was flattered just because he knew something about my novel . . . conned I was. Fool I am. Why didn't Flo stop me? His meditations were startlingly interrupted.

172

From the far end of the plant came a glaring light. A massive moving object appeared to hurtle through the far wall, travelling at infinite speed. The light died, somehow inertia was lost, the object slowed and stopped. It was the time train.

Stoker staggered back, flattening himself against the nearest wall, staring at this manifestation with disbelief.

As the train stopped, it ploughed through the rows of cultivated fungus, halting only a few metres from where he stood. It went through its usual sense-defying shrinkage, to end looking no larger than an ordinary railroad carriage. There it waited in the dimness, without lights or motion.

'I don't believe my eyes,' said Stoker. 'We've got you parked safe outside.' He wanted to call for Spinks, but did not dare. Spinks remained outside the building.

Stoker dropped his cricket bat in astonishment as Joe Bodenland stepped from the train, carrying the F-bomb in its red and green case. He was propelled forward by two of the Fleet Ones, the light levels obviously proving dim enough for them to tolerate. About twenty more Undead emerged – a haggard army.

Stoker picked up his bat again to defend himself.

A gun turned on him immediately.

'Even the Australians play fairer than that,' he said. 'Back to your graves, scum!' He dropped the bat.

'Sorry, Bram,' Bodenland called. 'We're caught in Bella's trap. Take it easy a moment. We have a problem.'

'So it seems.'

Stoker fell silent as Count Dracula emerged from the train, then clutched his forehead and staggered sideways with a gesture of amazed horror which would have done his master Henry Irving credit. For the first time he was confronting the character he had regarded as merely in his own imagination.

The sinister being was moving in an umbrella of shadow. His very presence seemed to lower the temperature. His cohorts were dwarfed by him. When he spoke in his deep growling voice, Dracula addressed Bodenland and Stoker.

'You two men of strong opinion shall be spared what you most fear. You shall not join in the ranks of the Undead. Instead, you shall *personally* have the honour of detonating this F-bomb. Thus you will end the Silent Empire, and have done with human resistance to me for ever.'

He turned to the guards and ordered them to secure Bodenland and Stoker to the front of the train – with the F-bomb.

The two men were roughly gathered together and could put up no effective resistance.

'Think of something,' Stoker said urgently.

'I am. I'm thinking of Mina.'

'I was thinking of finishing my novel.'

They were silenced by blows. Wire ropes were produced as they were pushed towards the front of the train. Dracula looked haughtily on.

It had taken Spinks a while to find the ball Stoker had hit so brilliantly. The ball had flown through the door, into the field, and beneath the undercarriage of the time train. When at last he discovered it, he returned to the agricultural station – and stopped short when he saw what was going on.

Then, bursting into the station, Spinks switched on the great overhead lights which controlled crop growth. The factory was flooded with their glare. Cries of agony rose from the Fleet Ones. They dropped their weapons to stagger about in disarray.

Bodenland and Bram Stoker stared with stunned amazement at the apparition of a second Bodenland and Stoker rushing in through the door on the opposite side of the factory. They were armed, and ran forward firing silver bullets, faces grim.

Vampires threw up their arms and fell to the ground under the fusillade. Some shattered and crumbled to dust beneath the brilliance pouring down on them.

Dracula, under cover of his attendant shadow, glided back into the shelter of the train.

Almost immediately, the train began to lose clarity, and to shudder into a greater length. Snakelike, it shot forward and disappeared from the building, leaving no trace. Dracula had escaped.

As the train vanished, Bodenland grasped the situation.

He gave a glad cry.

'Bram, quick! This way!'

He ran with the F-bomb, Bram following, out of the door Spinks had just entered. He slapped the gardener's shoulder as he passed.

'Great work, lad.'

The time train stood outside, immobile, now encompassed by the shadow of the immense building. There were the rows of mangelwurzels, the endless field, the endless sky – and their hope for the future.

The men climbed aboard. Stoker slammed the door shut as Bodenland started up the generator. The train began its sickening elongation as he threw the time co-ordinates into reverse – ten minutes backwards in time.

The engines, geared to millions of years, squealed in disbelief, and obeyed.

'We've got the bomb, Joe, why not head home?'

'We must save ourselves. Paradox, Bram.'

'Paradox, Joe?'

'There's just one time train, remember? The driver told me.'

'Sorry, no savvy.'

'One train. The one inside the fungus factory was this one, in another period of its existence.'

'Where's it gone?'

'It'll return, because I'll be on it. And here we are – back ten minutes in time. Get those guns and magic bullets.'

They jumped out hastily, loading the guns with Stoker's silver bullets. Everything looked as it had done ten minutes later. But, as they peered rather anxiously about, they saw the time train speeding from the horizon towards them, and flung themselves flat.

'I'm on that,' Bodenland said, through gritted teeth. 'I'd just experienced a guard post being blown up and had undergone a very nasty conversation with His Majesty himself.'

Stoker rammed a last bullet home and snapped the barrel into place. 'I'm sure you had a lot to talk about.'

'He didn't look much like Henry Irving.'

'*Sir* Henry Irving, please.'

'C'mon, let's go!' As he shouted, the speeding train contracted and vanished into the agricultural factory.

He led the way at a run, Stoker close on his heels. They ran round the rear of the building. It was longer than either had bargained for

– at least a half-mile round to the door in the far side – and there were huge agricultural implements standing in the way.

After a pause for breath, they stood by the entrance, readying the guns.

Peering round the doorpost, Bodenland waited for the moment when Spinks entered by the far door. As Spinks slammed on the overhead lights, he rushed in, with Stoker just behind him.

There was the train, there were the photophobic Undead, thrown into absolute disarray by the barrage of lights. There were they themselves, Bodenland and Stoker, by the front of the train where they had been dragged, looking very shaken.

'Fire away!'

They blazed away with the silver bullets, and had the satisfaction of seeing the vampires collapse. Dracula was not in sight, hidden by the bulk of the train. The brief gun battle was hardly over when the train gave a lurch, distended itself, blurred, and disappeared.

They stood there panting in triumph, watching themselves leave the scene, dashing through the other door to travel back ten minutes in time.

Cheering wildly, they walked over to Spinks and embraced him. Spinks looked utterly bemused. 'What a show! I never seen anything bigger than a rabbit shot.'

'Cheer up, Spinks. Thou shalt not serve two masters.'

'Oh, I enjoyed it all, sir. I must say, you really hit 'em for six!'

But Stoker rested his arm on the doorpost and his forehead on his arm. 'The next time we do this kind of thing, I'm bringing the British Army along too.'

'I'm going to celebrate our famous victory with a shower,' Bodenland said. 'I still stink of that filthy Tripoli prison. Give me five minutes.'

'I'll join you,' Stoker said. 'Spinks, keep watch, old chap.'

The agricultural factory was equipped with adequate shower facilities. The two men were soon under the hot spray, and singing the Anvil Chorus from *Il Trovatore* in enthusiastic disharmony.

'We shall now travel back into the far past and obliterate the first vampire colony at source,' said Bodenland, as they were drying off in columns of infra-red. 'We owe Bernard and the rest of humanity that much.'

'Yes, yes, I couldn't agree more,' said Stoker, and then was silent. After a while he said, 'What is it to be a vampire, Joe? I mean, when you think about it . . . It's a total perversion. In the scripture it speaks of Jesus Christ, who desireth not the death of a sinner, but rather that he may turn from his wickedness – and we may presume other people's wickedness as well – and live. Dracula offers his minions the reverse. Do they live? They die eternally, and are eternally dependent on other species for nourishment. Instead of the light of Heaven, they're stuck in the night of Earth. It's not the kind of immortality I'd find desirable at all. It's Christianity turned upside down.'

'As you describe them in your book, they are like the embodiment of some appalling ancient disease.'

Stoker scratched some of the hairier parts of his large ginger body. ' "Their throat is an open sepulchre, with their tongues they have deceived; the poison of asps is under the lips", as the psalter puts it. Which brings up the question of sex – again . . .'

He was silent as they were dressing, then burst out, 'What about the question of sex, Joe? In my eyes, the future has no flavour in it. No savour, no juice. What are the women there like? Would I enjoy 'em if I were free of this disease?'

'We're not planning a trip to the future, if that's what you have in mind.'

'Oh, I admire women so. I feel myself the equal of any woman alive – except Flo, of course. I told you she was once engaged to Oscar Wilde? I've been to bed with many crazy women. They've some – some essence . . . I can't name it. Like a forgotten dream. That's why I prefer them. Just as I prefer the lunatics among the poets, Clare, Smart, William Cowper, young Shelley, who was almost confined to a madhouse while still at Eton.'

'He was as sane as the next man. A poet but a normal man.'

'Your normal man's a dark horse.'

Bodenland laughed at that.

Stoker was still pursuing his own line of thought. 'These poor wretches of vampires don't have sex, do they? Not as we understand it. Is the future you live in very effete – Listerized, Pasteurized, in a word? I've been on the nest, as they say, in dog-fouled archways, in pure-laden courts, in a thousand louse-infested rooms, in every stinking corner of the metropolis. I suppose all that's gone by the end of the twentieth century . . .'

'Bram, as far as London is concerned – '

He was interrupted as Spinks came dashing in.

'Gents, some of these foreign blokes are approaching. Driving in armoured machines. It's not the most encouraging of sights.'

They pulled on their boots and had a look through the open door of the factory. The soldiers of the Silent Empire were advancing – on items that looked like motorized skate-boards and, more formidably, in tanks resembling boats, heavily armed.

'They want their bomb back,' Bodenland said. 'Let's go.'

Spinks was already up in the train. The others ran to it. As Stoker slammed the door of the cab, Bodenland started the engines. The first shells began to fall in the vast field of mangelwurzels, then the Libyan world faded and disappeared from view under their acceleration.

As the time train began to tunnel into the past, Bodenland sighed with relief and turned to look at Stoker. He had sunk down on a stool and was mopping his brow.

'Now then, Bram, before Dracula strikes again, my vote is that we shoot all the way back to the Mesozoic and visit the great family meeting in the Hudson Bay area which Bella mentioned.'

Stoker shook his head.

'I'm exhausted. I'm sorry. I believe I'm in need of van Helsing's ministrations – though I never expected I'd live to hear myself say so.'

Bodenland went over to him. 'I'm thoughtless, Bram. You're such an old rogue I forget you're ill. We'll make a stop in 1999 – I seem to have the controls to rights now. I'll just check that Mina and the others are fine, and we'll pick up some penicillin and get rid of that malady of yours in double quick time.'

'Excellent.' He sat with his head down, breathing heavily. Spinks came up with a bottle of brandy, part of Mrs Stoker's excellent hamper.

After taking a sip or two, Stoker perked up.

'Rid me of what ails me and I might be able to go gallivanting again. Your wedding tackle tends to atrophy if not put to regular use.'

He laughed rather miserably, and rambled on for some while along these lines. Bodenland grew impatient.

'Rest for a bit, Bram. Sup some more brandy. I have a duty to discharge.'

He worked his way back carefully through the speeding time train, now extended to its full length. He kept his revolver in his hand, vividly aware of the horror that had pursued him and Clift in this very corridor. Nothing jumped out at him. Although the corridor remained dim as ever, he observed a dull red glow suffusing the distance. It was no more than a suggestion of colour. Speculation implied it might be some kind of doppler effect generated by their progress through time; the rear of the extended train could be many centuries behind the leading carriage.

The train was empty of its previous melancholy occupants, with the exception to which Bodenland came in the torture chamber.

Here were the same glass doors fronting twisted pieces of iron, the same heavy drapes, the same table, scarred by practice of a cruel art, the same suffocating atmosphere of eternal damnation. And the same victim, pinned like a sullied Prometheus to his rock of torture.

Once more there came over Joe Bodenland the sense of having to live through some mislaid dream, a suspicion that throughout the days of his conscious life some semi-autonomous part of his mind had been undergoing dreams altogether darker, more intense, in tune with protolithic existence.

The creature on the slab still wore his skull. As on a magic Easter egg, a coloured band marked where it opened. Stirring under its confining bars, the prisoner contrived to roll its eyes almost into its head in order to survey Bodenland, hesitant on the threshold of the chamber. Its foam-fringed mouth worked against the bit confining it.

Bodenland walked round the table and levelled the gun at the creature's heart. He fired a magic silver bullet from point-blank range. The detonation filled the compartment with noise. One of the cupboard windows shattered, as if to allow exit to the soul of the prisoner. The hapless creature suffered such a convulsion that one wrist tore free of its iron bondage and gestured upwards. Then it fell. Its poor blue tendons hung like string over the side of the table.

Bodenland instinctively made the sign of the Cross.

'Amen,' he whispered. 'Farewell, Alwyn . . .'

Peace returned to the tormented features. The body, so long unnaturally imprisoned, began immediately to decay, its limbs to detumesce, to stink and liquefy.

Dracula's terrible speech in this place, in which he revealed the inevitable attitude of predator to prey, remained vivid in Bodenland's mind. Once more, he had committed an act of violence in defence of what he saw as right; but where ultimate judgement lay in such matters he did not know. Wearily, he made his way forward, to seek out Stoker's genial companionship and think of happier matters.

Spinks saluted him as he re-entered the cab. He had produced the still unopened bottle of Moet & Chandon. 'Wine, women and song, sir – without the women and song.'

'Spinks, we owe you a great deal,' Bodenland said. 'I will have a glass, and you must drink with us, of course.'

Spinks looked doubtfully at his master; but Stoker, who had revived considerably, started to sing in a rich baritone, 'Take a Pair of Sparkling Eyes'.

Relieving Spinks of the champagne, Bodenland joined in the chorus while pouring it into three glasses.

'Here's to several pairs of sparkling eyes,' said Stoker, raising his glass. 'To our wives – and others!'

'Which reminds me, Bram. Despite all the horrors we've endured, I've not forgotten the beauty of your famous Ellen Terry – lovelier than a dream. Tell me about her. You've known her long?'

'Ah, never too long. There's gaiety in the very air she breathes, like embodied sunlight.'

'Have you ever . . . I mean, you're a lusty fellow, you must have had the temptation . . .'

He let the sentence hang, seeing Stoker fall into a fury, angrier than Bodenland had known him. 'You dare suggest such a thing? Ellen's no whore, you Yankee cad. She's as pure as the mountain air, every inch of her, that's what. If I wasn't so feeble, I'd punch your head in at the very thought.'

'No offence intended.' He said no more, not understanding what to make of the violence of Stoker's denial.

Stoker's face remained red. 'Another thing. A man does not drink with his gardener. It demeans both of them. You may go, Spinks.'

Spinks moved out of the cab, looking ashamed, but taking his glass with him.

The atmosphere remained stormy. Bodenland went over to check the controls.

Leaning back and closing his eyes, Stoker said, 'I should take no offence, Joe. Ellen's a woman apart. If there were only blackness and disease and death in the world – well, who'd want to live? Thank God for women like Ellen Terry. I hope I go to meet my Maker thinking of her . . . Not that I'd ever want to shuffle off the old mortal coil while buzzing about in time in this unnatural fashion . . .'

'You'll soon be okay.'

'. . . Particularly when I can't fathom for the life of me how we do all this buzzing about from century to century. What did that hideous monster tell you about electricity wiping out all paradoxes?'

'That? Oh, it was something he must have picked up and repeated. It's meaningless. Dracula understands nothing of science. No brain, you see.'

Sighing, Stoker said, 'There I'm in the same case as Dracula. Can you explain this time business to me?'

Bodenland looked up abstractedly at the roof of the cab.

'You must understand that when the terms "time" or "space" are used scientifically, they don't mean what you mean by them. Our science uses the terms to designate an overall structure consisting of the totality of phenomena of whatever kind is under consideration. In this sense, "time" has its own phase space, consisting of all elements and polynomials within the mathematical orbit of its totality. When our laboratories were working on the theory of what became our inertial system, we isolated what's termed a strange attractor.'

'Dracula's a strange attractor.'

181

'Here the term's used in a mathematical sense. Points that are stretched far apart come close in the region of an attractor, so that in our hypothesis we were able to project "sinks" in real time, whereby periodic time simply held steady. Time stopped, if you like to put it that way.'

Emitting another sigh, Stoker held his head and said, 'I don't understand all this. Yet I've umpired cricket matches without difficulty.'

'The science of chaos is pretty complex. Anyhow, in our inertial equations we were always aware that our calculations took in only one isolated attractor. In reality, the totality of time consists of innumerable strange attractors. Improved computers in the future would no doubt be able to deal with multitudes of them.

'I can see that the fractals – oh, a fractal is simply an attractor which contains a complete structure however often you magnify it. A fractal's like eternity. It's fractals that contain the secret of time travel. Once you throw away classical mathematics, you get into multi-dimensionality, where one set of "time" elements can be switched from one strange attractor or another to another set. You could have fractal cross-over, so that actual "movement" across even millions of years could be very slight.'

He took another gulp of the champagne. 'Well, that's my guess. I'll work on it when I get home. Of course, to transform theory into physical terms is no easy matter, and it's clear that massive power expenditure would be required for the resultant prime mover across "time" quanta.'

'I'm sure it all makes sense – but not to me, Joe,' Stoker said, tugging at his beard as if to release a few brain cells. 'So what about "Time like an ever-rolling stream", as the good old hymn has it, or Time's famous Arrow? How do they fit in among your fractals?'

'To be honest, they don't fit in at all. They're metaphors for time derived from the old classical mathematics. Meaningless. As obsolete as the concept of the luminiferous aether. Time's not like that at all. It has flux but no flow – except as experienced by biological entities like you and me. It may itself prove to be a mega-fractal of some complexity.'

'Heaven preserve us all when that happens!'

CHAPTER XII

The bronzed facade of the Bodenland Corporation building reflected a rushing mechanized worm which contracted as it stopped in the ornamental garden before the administration wing. Security guards were almost immediately on the scene as alarms sounded. They stepped back respectfully when Joe Bodenland emerged from the cab.

'Stay right here,' he told them. 'Guard this precious vehicle with your lives.'

He turned to coax Bram Stoker from the cab. Stoker was reluctant to appear.

'I fear your epoch will be too much for me. The very air smells different.'

'You'll be famous here, Bram. Dallas is a great place.'

'Better than Tripoli?'

'Loads better.'

'No mangelwurzels?'

'Not a one.'

Stoker descended from the vehicle, followed by Spinks, clutching the cricket bat for protection. He gazed around, open-mouthed.

'My hat!' was all Spinks said.

Stoker walked about on the grass, looking at its neat cut suspiciously. 'Who scythes this lawn for you, Joe? Wonderful work. Better than even Spinks's old father could manage in his day . . . And this is where you live? An enormous mansion – and all built of glass? Incredible! Jolly cold in the winter, though, I'd say. All window and no wall.'

Bodenland checked his watch and began to walk briskly towards the door of the administrative wing. He said, rather absently, 'You'll soon get used to it. People themselves are just the same as in your time.'

'Not if they understand fractals they aren't, my boy!'

Bodenland took Stoker and Spinks up in the elevator to his suite. Rose Gladwin, his secretary, almost collapsed at the sight of Bodenland.

After all her cries of welcome were finished, Bodenland handed his friends over to her care, giving her strict instructions to see they were taken to the best hotel in Dallas, given a bank account, and looked after. While he was dialling his doctor regarding treatment for Stoker's illness, Rose Gladwin hurried into the adjoining office to phone Waldgrave.

'How do I tell Joe about what's happened to Mina Legrand?'

'I've known him longer than you, Rose. I'll come and break the news to him.'

'Max – it's going to bring him down hard.'

'I know it.'

Larry was out in the grounds of Gondwana with Kylie, flying one of his model planes. His father appeared in the estate Suzuki. He dropped the radio control and ran to welcome him back home.

But Joe was in a storm of fury and sorrow such as Larry had never encountered before. He fell back before the first wave of it. Why, Bodenland wanted to know, why had Larry not protected his mother? Why was she allowed to die? Kylie clung to him but he pushed her away. Why the violence in the mortician's? Why, above all, why had Mina become Dracula's victim?

Under the barrage of questions, Larry commenced his own monologue, timidly at first, then more forcefully. Mina had insisted on being alone. They hadn't been told she was going sky-diving. They had known nothing of her movements until too late. As for the stake through her heart – that needed courage – that was for her sake – that was for his father's sake. Everything he did was for his father's sake. He went into groceries so as not to compete with his father.

'You drink for my sake, too?' asked Bodenland.

'That is unfair and stupid, Joe,' Kylie said. 'Larry certainly drinks *because* of you. Maybe we were not able to protect Mina – but where were you when it came to protecting your woman? Don't try to shift your guilt.'

It was Joe's turn to be silent under her eloquence.

Her pretty face was now alight with spirit. She was just as responsible for the stake as Larry. They had to kill the evil thing in Mina to save her immortal soul – in which she at least believed. If evil survives, good perishes.

'I agree with that, Kylie,' he said. 'If evil survives, the good perishes.'

'And yet with no evil in the world, good has no reason to exist. Which is why the Lord permitted sin to enter the Garden of Eden.'

'Maybe in the end you'll convert me to the Christian faith.'

'No, Joe. I don't know whether you're cut out for the Christian faith. It might make you even more difficult than you are.'

It was not a remark he would have taken from many people, but her smile disarmed him. For a moment he thought of Bram Stoker's description of Ellen Terry as embodied sunshine. Here was another similar case.

'At least I believe that Mina had an immortal soul.' He turned to his son and held out his hand. 'I should not have bawled you out. Forgive me. It was my anguish speaking.'

Then he explained to Larry how he planned to rescue his mother from the dead.

Mina walked in her green cover-alls over to the motel room window and opened it. Dusk was falling. As she gazed out over the car park, the neon sign lit with the words MOONLITE MOTEL.

She turned away, shucked off all her clothes and stepped into the shower.

Afterwards, dressed in a towelling robe, she mixed herself a margarita and tried to write a letter. 'Joe you bastard – ' it began, and got no further. She mixed herself a second drink and started to phone around. By now, night was setting in over Enterprise. She was phoning her sister in Paris, France, when a bat flew in at the window. 'Oh, God, sorry, Carrie, I've got a bat in my room. I can't take bats.'

She put the phone down and stood up, watching the flying thing. It changed as she watched, turning into a suave man in evening dress, his hair brushed back and gleaming. Transfixed, she allowed her robe to fall open, revealing her naked body. But his avid gaze was fixed on the whiteness of her throat as he advanced.

'Hi,' she said. 'Like a drink? I was just getting stewed all on my ownsome.'

'Thanks, no,' he said. 'Not alcohol.'

As he was approaching her, the door burst open. Bodenland ran in, holding Kylie's little gold crucifix before him. He thrust this at the suave man's eyes. The man screamed with pain, instantly falling back, dwindling, smoking, turning into bat-form again. Bodenland struck at it, slammed the window shut, beat at the creature savagely as it sped trapped about the room. Snatching up a magazine, he knocked the bat into a corner. As it fell, he jumped on it, pounding it underfoot until it spurted blood and died.

Then Bodenland turned to Mina.

After they had embraced and kissed and both shed tears, he took her back in the time train to Dallas, only a few days in the future.

Here was another strange reunion, Mina with Larry and Kylie. Larry squirmed a little as he embraced the mother he had last seen gouting blood in her coffin.

Later still, they were introduced to Stoker and Spinks. Spinks was resplendent in a new bomber jacket. Stoker was under doctor's orders and receiving treatment.

Stoker's eyes gleamed when he saw Kylie. He clutched her hand longer than was necessary, and loaded her with such compliments as he deemed suitable for a seductive young lady of the future.

'It happens I'm reading your novel at present, Mr Stoker – and it terrifies me. I don't know how you think of such terrible events. Though I suppose we should pity the poor vampires, doomed to such a miserable existence. They're really one more oppressed minority, aren't they?'

'Er, well, my dear young lady, I hadn't thought of them in that regard. I simply thought of them as a bad lot – a disease, in short.'

'May I ask if you believe in Heaven and Hell?'

Stoker looked about rather helplessly and said that after all he'd been through he ought to have a ready answer to that question.

Kylie smiled and said, 'I see you believe that if a thing shouldn't exist it doesn't exist, Mr Stoker. That's why all of us have trouble in believing in the fact of Dracula or the Devil. Yet Dracula must be the invention of an Almighty God along with everything else.'

He pulled at his hairy cheek and said to Bodenland, 'This pretty daughter-in-law of yours raises questions which never entered my mind. I'll need a little time to think about the matter. My brain doesn't seem to work too well in 1999.'

'How is your hotel?' asked Mina, coming to the rescue. 'You must find everything very odd, after what you've been used to. We've all been turned upside down recently.' She laughed with some uncertainty, giving Kylie a sidelong look.

'It's a pleasant hotel, for sure,' Stoker said, in answer to Mina's question. 'The ice machine is a remarkable invention. But I miss the friendly attentions of servants such as we have at home. One thing I do enjoy is your clever cards instead of money. Abolishing money is the finest idea I ever heard of.'

'What have you bought?'

Stoker looked cautious. 'Well, I discovered magazines with pictures of pretty girls divested of every last stitch of clothes. And we took the liberty of buying a nice pair of coffins we saw in Nieman Marcus – a Him and Her – you know, for the remains of Bella and that driver of yours. And we shall have a capital Christian burial of their remains in the cemetery the day after tomorrow.'

'Fine idea, but there's no time for that,' said Bodenland, briskly. 'You can have your fun later, Bram. This very night we're leaving again in the time train. You know why, and I think you know where.'

The immensities of the Mesozoic plains. A broken line of hills and cliffs lay to the south. From their skirts the land rolled northwards, to dense forests of deciduous trees. A river had once meandered through the plain, and died, leaving a series of ox-bow lakes. Otherwise, no landmarks stood out. Tall grasses grew, interspersed here and there with clumps of small white daisies.

One particular area of this plain, between two lakes, was becoming crowded with figures. They were dwarfed by the great landscapes which contained them, and by the cumulus clouds piling up on the horizon.

These figures walked like men. They were dressed in black garb, and closely resembled men. Others circled overheard, flying on wide-spread leathery wings. And with these fliers went others who accompanied and in some ways resembled them. But these others had more distinctive reptilian faces, with long cruel mouths filled with sharp teeth.

They were watched with eager fascination by the hidden human viewers on the ground. This was the first time they had seen any prehistoric creatures – except for Joe Bodenland's untimely excursion to the Carboniferous, when he had lost Clift's body to the amphibian.

The time train was concealed under low palm trees growing in a depression on the crumbling hills which terminated the great plain. Standing outside it, and watching the gathering ahead of them, were Joe, Mina, Kylie, and Bram. Nearby, Larry was giving Spinks a hand to bury the two coffins, and grumbling at the task.

'Why don't we just junk them? There's nothing sacred about burial in the Cretaceous, even in a Nieman Marcus coffin.'

'Master Larry,' said Spinks, gravely, 'time makes little difference to a corpse. The important thing for all concerned is that they get a proper burial.'

'What, vampires? That's rubbish.'

Spinks continued stolidly to dig.

'They may be vampires, and that's why I have carved the vampire sign on both coffins, but they've paid for their crimes. They were human once, don't forget, Master Larry. There's still a right and a wrong, even in this outlandish dump.'

'Don't preach to me!'

'The intention behind preaching, Master Larry, if you excuse me saying so, is to do someone good in the spirit.'

'God!' exclaimed Larry. He hurled down his spade, threw up his hands, and walked away. In the event, the coffins were never buried, for Bodenland called everyone over to witness a strange phenomenon.

The sky was changing hue, the cloud layers were congealing. The masses of vapour curdled and writhed as if in pain.

It was evident this peculiarity had been observed by the population on the plain.

Until now, the Undead had been busily driving herds of hadrosaurs and other related genera across the wastes and into pens of thorn. The duck-billed monsters went docilely enough, though their melancholy hoots filtered up even to the distant viewers. The reason for this docility could be discerned; one or two of the lead dinosaurs had been saddled and domesticated and were being used as bellwethers which the rest of the great reptiles followed.

Some of the Undead were already in the pens, feasting on their captives.

Now the feasting was over and the herding ceased. Every being on the plain became immobile, gazing upwards. Stoker crossed himself. 'Faith, it's like the Second Coming and all,' he exclaimed.

'Don't forget He hasn't come the first time yet,' said Mina, dryly. 'The Mesozoic wasn't exactly Jesus territory.'

All six crouched in their place of concealment and peered at the clouds on the distant horizon. They were moving rapidly together, growing darker as they went, while lightning curdled their stomachs. The sky itself grew dim with an ochre light as the cloud mass rose to obscure the sun.

A great pillar of shadow fell across the plain. And the pillar became a ramp, on which was seen the figure of Count Dracula, descending.

Dracula alighted on the plain, took on almost human form, and raised his arms. The hordes on the plain began to converge slowly towards him, obedient to his sign.

'Okay,' Bodenland said. 'Their conference is going to start. I want us to hold a quick conference, too.'

His face was lined and drawn as he looked from one to the other.

'You're all very dear to me. I know I've been autocratic in the past. The family has its troubles – which I hope to remedy. Now here's a momentous issue and I want us all to be in on it together – '

Stoker snorted with disgust. 'Come on, Joe. The Duke of Wellington didn't write his wife a sonnet on the battlefield at Waterloo.'

'Just a minute, Bram. There's more responsibility here than I can shoulder alone. You all have to be a part of this. We hold here an F-bomb, the greatest destructive force we know of, and the possibility

189

exists to drop it on Dracula and his cohorts. We think that will finish him off once and for all. I need your agreement. Do we drop the bomb?'

'That's what we've come to do,' said Stoker at once. 'Let's get on with it, Joe. This destruction is foretold in the scriptures.'

'But by so doing, we also become mass killers. We become no better than the other side. I have found before now that if you kill someone you are destined to take their place. What do the rest of you think?'

The two women spoke together. Kylie smiled at her mother-in-law, nodding to her to go ahead. 'I say you should not drop it, Joe, since you are asking,' Mina said. 'For a simple practical reason. The vampires are not going to be destroyed. You told me that they faded out as a reproductive species long before mankind came on the scene – Bernard's two graves are their only memorial we've found – '

'Well?' he said, impatiently.

'Well, suppose the F-bomb won't work. It's untested. You drop it, then Dracula knows we are here, and we all get killed.'

'No, Mina, the F-bomb will work.'

'You don't know that, Joe.'

'I do. We have the proof. Every map of Canada in the modern world depicts that proof. The great circle of Hudson Bay – filled with sea in our time, that's the ancient F-bomb crater. It'll work just fine. Kylie, your objection?'

The girl looked levelly at him. 'Mine is a religious objection, as you might expect. Yet it goes with your hesitation. An evil weapon like your F-bomb cannot destroy evil. It can only propagate it.'

'Kylie, dear, despite all I've been through I still can hardly credit the existence of these malign supernatural beings. My intellect rebels against accepting them! I'd much rather regard them as a disease. But there they are, down there in their thousands, from all times and climes. We would destroy two evils at once – them and the F-bomb. Think again. Larry, how do you feel on this issue?'

Larry gestured dismissively.

'I'm with you, Joe, all the way.'

Taking a step forward, Spinks said, 'If I might also have a say in this, Mr Bodenland . . .'

'Of course. Make it fast.'

Spinks glanced at his employer, then went ahead. 'All right. Suppose you don't drop this bomb. Do we just all go home to our proper centuries? That's no way to win a war. There's a time comes to all of us when we are forced to do something we'd rather not, in the hope and prayer that it will bring about a greater good. There's good wars and bad wars, good causes and bad causes. I say this is a good war in a good cause. Drop the bloody thing and let's get home.'

He blushed crimson to see that everyone was looking at him.

'Four against two, ladies,' said Joe. 'Want to change your minds?'

'No,' said Kylie.

'Yes,' said Mina. 'If the bomb will work, drop it, I say. I wouldn't want what happened to me to happen to another soul. I don't – I can't figure out all the moral niceties, but those things are evil right enough, so, yes, let's drop it on them right now.'

Without speaking, Bodenland looked at Kylie. She looked back, then looked down.

'Joe, dear, I know I'm the new member of the family, but I just *can't* say yes to this. I was brought up to believe that human beings shouldn't have power of life and death over others. I stick with that. Besides . . . Well, look, if I said okay, wouldn't it be kind of sick for a family to all agree, yes, fine, let's kill off thousands? A family! Isn't that sick?'

A growl came from Stoker.

'What family could ever agree among itself? Little lady, it's my belief that all of us understand your scruples. But it's five against one. You'll go to Heaven, the rest of us will depart for elsewhere. Come on, Joe, Larry – the bomb.'

With a sigh, Bodenland said, 'You are outvoted, Kylie, my dear. Five to one.'

'That's democratic,' Larry said, going to embrace her, but she turned away.

'You didn't support me,' she said. 'Don't you see there's evil within us?'

'And also right out there, Kylie,' he said, pointing to the rolling plain.

*   *   *

191

They got rapidly down to work.

Pteranodons were still passing overhead on their featherless wings, so everything had to be done under cover of the palms. Mina and Stoker kept watch at either end of the train while Kylie wept inside it. Bodenland and his son squatted on the ground and secured the F-bomb to the underside of his new radio-controlled plane.

'It's a replica of a nineteen-forties Flying Fortress, Joe,' Larry said, enthusiastically. 'It goes like a bomb.'

'The F-bomb does not detonate on impact. When you're ready, I shall turn this red dial.' He indicated the casing. 'A contained fission process then begins, and only when the temperature is raised to many thousand degrees is the essential fusion process triggered. The detonation will be several score times the power of any bomb the US can command in the twentieth century, despite its small size.'

'What I can't understand,' said Spinks, who was looking on, 'is how these vampire creatures all appear as bold as brass in broad daylight. Remember how they all crumbled when I switched on the lights in that there plant factory, and – '

'No time for these minor puzzles now, Spinks,' said Bodenland, standing up. Larry lifted the plane, with the red and green bomb wired on underneath it. He shook his head, raised an eyebrow, and looked at his father. Both were thinking the same thing: though the plane had a fifteen-foot wingspan, the bomb was almost too heavy for it.

Then began the next phase of the nightmare. All their psychic energies were focused on the launching of the plane – and Larry had misgivings. He said he would go forward to the very brink of the cliffs, to gain the advantage of the updraught. His father protested it was too dangerous. Nevertheless, he went, running forward, doubled over his plane.

'Directly it gets airborne, come back, right?'

Larry did not answer.

'Want me to go with him?' asked Spinks.

'No. Get everyone else in the train, Spinks, will you? We have to be away before the strike, or we're all dead ducks.'

It seemed that everyone was milling about. The great leather

192

lizards still winged grandly overhead like angels from hell, to circle about the distant figure of Count Dracula.

Stoker climbed out of the train toting a bulky pistol.

'It's an Edward Very light,' he said, excitedly. 'Lights up the whole sky.'

'We don't need it. The bomb will light up the whole world. Get inside. Be ready to go as soon as Larry gets back.'

But Stoker was carried away by the excitement of the moment. He began to recite in ringing tones.

' "For behold, the day cometh that shall burn as an oven. And all the proud, yea, and all that do wickedly, shall be stubble" . . . !'

Kylie came up behind him and said, 'And what else will the bomb kill beside the vampires? How about the animals, who are innocent, the trees, the land itself? Perhaps you aren't so ecologically conscious as we are in 1999.'

'That's what the Bible says, my dear. "Ye shall tread down the wicked, for they shall be ashes under the soles of your feet." '

'Perhaps you'd like to come inside and sit quietly with me, Mr Stoker. I don't think it is up to us to use punishments which are devastating enough to belong to a higher power.'

He looked into her normally sunny face, and scratched his beard.

'You're a very attractive young lady, for a liberal,' he said, 'but I'm not going to miss this bang for anything or anyone.'

Bodenland had gone forward, leaving the shelter of the palms. He was anxious for his son. Larry had disappeared behind low hills. The pteranodons overhead were capable of attacking and killing a man, in Bodenland's consideration.

Larry had reached a bluff where the ground was crumbling and sandy. He dropped to his knees, out of breath. Just ahead, the cliffs in a flurry of broken rock sloped down to the wide plain. This was as far as he could go, although the concourse of the Undead was still a distance away. He could only hope that his model would fly that far.

He started the engines of the model Flying Fortress. They gave no trouble and caught at once. Just for a moment he paused, unable to bring himself to let go of the plane. Then he launched it. It dropped steadily, caught the updraught from the cliffs, and began slowly to climb, heading straight for the unhallowed congregation.

Larry stood looking, marvelling at the Boeing's beauty and strength. The bomb glinted below its fuselage. The fission process was already in progress.

The plane was still climbing gradually as it flew. The entire sky was clear of cloud now. He had no trouble following its path, and little need to guide it. Sounds of its engines became faint. Then he saw a flight of three pteranodons moving in towards it, like fighter planes to the attack.

The danger was at once apparent. Dropping the control box, Larry turned and began running back to the time train. The going was rough. He stumbled once, and fell full length. He looked back. One of the flying lizards had caught hold of the plane's wing. It was about to fall out of the sky.

And at that moment, brightness filled the air above the plain.

Picking himself up, he ran on. His father had come to meet him, and was beckoning him on.

He fell into his father's arms.

'Bravely done,' Joe said. 'Quick – we've only got a minute. We must get away.'

Bram Stoker, who had insisted on firing his Very pistol, jumped into the train before them. The others were already standing there. Still red-eyed, Kylie clung fiercely to Larry as he entered.

Bodenland triggered the door shut behind them and turned to the controls.

The detonation of the F-bomb was an event on an immense scale. It was as if a great door slammed in the depths of Hell. The first fronts of heat and sound to belly out obliterated the plain and all life on it. They were followed by wave after wave of radioactive emission.

The pillar of fire that rose into the stratosphere resembled a solid thing – a massive tree that would forever remain. From its topmost branches wastes grew, spreading layer after layer of dirt round among the new winds born into the upper atmosphere. The sky became dark – and so it would stay for many days, like a filthy lung ceasing to breathe, eclipsing the sun.

The ensuing cold, the devastation of the climate of the northern hemisphere, would have a lasting effect, the death of the Cretaceous dinosaurs, and would be forever graven in Earth's rocks, to be discovered by scientists millions of centuries later, and christened the K/T boundary.

Of all this havoc, its instigators saw nothing. The time train had elongated itself and disappeared into the recurrent pattern of years.

CHAPTER XIII

It was, in a sense, a family reunion – and spiced, like all such reunions, with memories of what had happened in the past. But this was a family reunion with its own allotted time and place. They were safely back in the Gondwana estate in AD 1999 and the time train was standing, with all the appearance of an ancient monument, where once children, Joe's grandchildren, had played. The family gathered by the poolside, where Mina was pouring them celebratory drinks.

The train stood in an area they called the Beach. A grey stone wall had isolated the play area from the pool. There, long ago – but how long is long? – Molly and Dick's orphaned children had played, and had buried a machine, and bees had buzzed in the jasmine.

Joe Bodenland carried these memories in his brain, along with many less pleasant things. Now Molly and Dick's dear kids were at school. They'd be back. And what governing fantasies would they have in their minds, to help them play out their brief span on the stage of life?

Never travel in time. It was too stern a reminder of the brevity of individual life. It was like swimming out into a dark Pacific ocean, leaving the coast behind, leaving the day, the continental shelf, everything . . .

He realized that he was getting a little drunk on his – well, how many of Mina's tall margaritas had gone round as they sat about the swimming pool? And he was content – or as content as he ever could be.

Let Kylie chatter. Any girl who looked that good in a bikini did not have to make too much sense. Let Bram Stoker ramble on, making them laugh with his theatre gossip a century old. Let his darling Mina talk about her next sky-diving festival in the Rockies. Let Larry brag about the way he had bought up a Softways chain, whatever that was, so that he had control of distribution as far as Denver. Let it all go by.

Washington could wait till Monday. This weekend would be passed in a haze. A pretty triumphant haze, by god.

Lazily, he picked up the silver bullet lying on the table by his right hand, where the near-empty glass stood.

'It's all over,' he said. 'Just return old Bram – and you, young Spinks – to Victorian England, and the whole damned thing's over and done with.'

Spinks, clad in a pair of trunks bestowed by Larry, was the only one listening to him.

'Sir, apart from my old mother in the village, I have no attachments, as you might say. No young lady I'm walking out with. I would like to stay and serve you. I could do your gardens. Or I could join the police force, if they use guns.'

'You're young. Why not? America's a land of opportunity.'

'I didn't find life all that interesting in 1896, just being a gardener, much though I respect Mr and Mrs Stoker.' He kept his voice low. 'I think that the United States in 1999 looks – well, sir, a bit more fun. You see – '

'Go on, Spinks. Have another drink. Help yourself.'

'I would like to watch your amazing television and see other inventions. Also – well, Mr Bodenland, I really liked the way we dropped the bomb on those bloody vampires. That was fun, wasn't it?'

'Not for them.'

Spinks laughed. 'I mean for me it was. Remember I asked you how those vampires appeared happy in daylight, whereas in later ages they couldn't stand it? You didn't answer, so I worked it out for myself. They were all looking up, weren't they, when the F-bomb went off what done 'em in? Looking up at the Very light. So that horror of light and disintegration was – inherited. A folk memory. Isn't that so, don't you reckon?'

Bodenland sat up in alarm.

'Jesus, Spinks, you may be right . . . If so, some of them survived, or no one would inherit anything. You'd better keep quiet about this. Don't tell the family.'

''Course they survived, sir. They came calling soon as you and Mr Clift dug up them two coffins.'

This last remark was overheard by Bram Stoker, who strolled over, a towel draped round his hairy ginger shoulders.

'Yes, Joe, I meant to ask you. Do your fractals account for the way those two coffins managed to get from Canada to Utah – given they were the same two?'

The family, Mina, Larry, and Kylie, were laughing at something Larry had said. Bodenland glanced approvingly at them, and stood up.

'Look, guys, it's all over. I don't know the answers. Despite science, much remains a mystery. Don't ask me. Ask some genius from the fiftieth century. I just want to hold my family together on an even keel.'

Stoker patted his shoulder and held it firmly.

'Joe, you are the best of fellows. But you are never going to rest quiet while you still have proof that Dracula still exists and goes about his rotten business.'

'Meaning?'

Stoker indicated the time train, standing silent in the Texas sun.

'Unlike the F-bomb, that train is not an evil weapon. You are yourself its part-inventor, and I regard you as a force for good. But what you need to do, when you have delivered me back to my wife and Irving, is to destroy the train. Eradicate it. Sever that one link between the remote past and the present and future which gave Dracula his chance.'

'Bram, I can't do that. I need to get people working on the train, to see if we can duplicate the technology. I can't destroy it. It's too precious.'

Stoker shook his head vigorously. 'You must destroy it. Do not allow your people to work on it. Don't you understand – forgive my brutal nineteenth-century mind – don't you understand that if they worked on it, you would then solve all this fractal business I don't understand, and you would be entirely responsible for travel through time? You'd be another Frankenstein. And you would know that at some point the train would pass into Dracula's hands. That's what must never happen.'

Once he was persuaded, Bodenland acted swiftly. He took Bram Stoker safely back into the arms of Florence, and bade them both an affectionate farewell. Aided by Larry and Spinks – who now became part of the Bodenland entourage – he prepared the time train for its final journey through the Escalante Desert.

So it was that, going forward in time, the train met itself travelling in the opposite direction.

Two strange attractors intersected.

All the windows in Enterprise were shattered by this spectacular collision. The plate glass in the mortician's was shattered and lay scattered over the coffins inside. The train was entirely destroyed and pieces of metal no bigger than confetti were later discovered spread over the Old John site.

'It was pretty simple to arrange,' Joe told Mina.

'No, it was genius,' Larry said, as his father embarked on a technical explanation. Smiling, Kylie switched on the television as she went over to the other side of the room to unpack her baggage; technical explanation was not for her.

'And,' Bodenland concluded, 'as I learnt from Larry, much can be done by remote control. We soon rigged that up.'

Mina squeezed his hand. 'The less remote we all are in future, the better.'

'Right,' said Larry, laughing, as he broke away to see what Kylie was doing.

Passing the television set, he saw that cable was running an old movie. Bela Lugosi was descending the stairs of that evil castle in the Carpathians, in old Transylvania. Larry switched it off before the others could see what was running.

But as he reached his wife's side, to put an arm round her waist, she unzipped a side pocket of her baggage, and out tumbled her well-thumbed copy of Stoker's famous novel, published and bound, and now signed by its author.